WAVES OF SORCERY

THE CURSED SOUL

K.C. SMITH

Published by K.C. Smith

Cover Illustrated by Hillary Bardin

Map by K.C. Smith

Editing by Alexis Aumagamanaia

ISBN (Paperback) 9798986459059
ISBN (Hardcover) 9798986459066

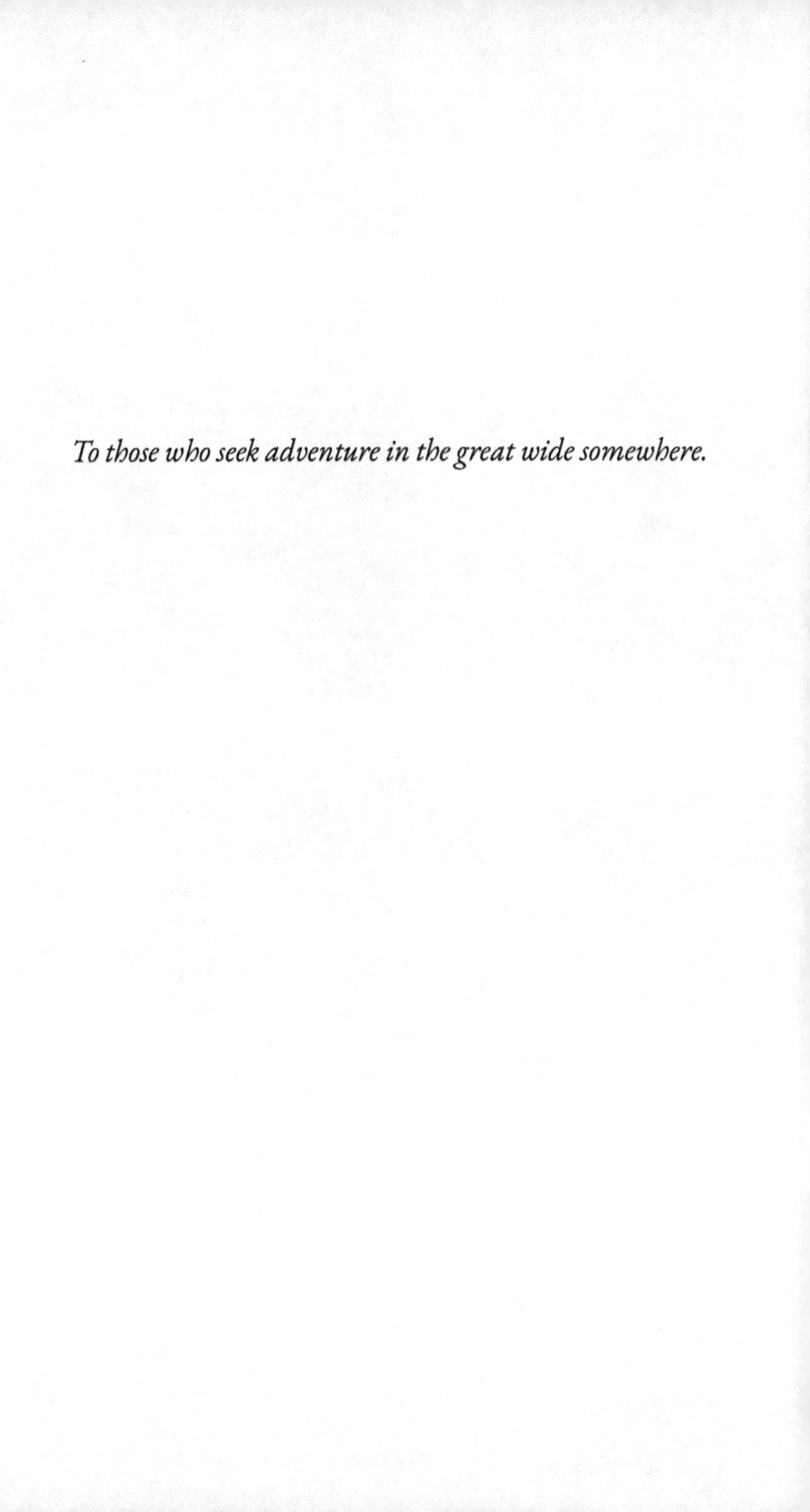

To those who seek adventure in the great wide somewhere.

Uskdar Sea
Emmoria
N
W E
S
Sumaaria
The Emerald
Peaks
Torheim
Cha
Ostdar Sea

Floating Temple
of Gorria
Neilmaar
Spring of
Zjanoak
Estdar Sea
Ruins of Marta
ferra
Kyriim
Tower of
Fajar
Jaaria
Aksahri
Awndar Sea
Crescent
Rock

Pronunciation Guide

CHARACTERS

Doraan – door-en

Kamira – kah-meer-uh

Cormac – core-mac

Forcina – for-see-na

Adonis – a-don-ess

Jaario – y-are-io

Tarkiin – tar-kin

PLACES

Emmoria – ee-more-ia

Aksahri – awe-k-sorry

Sumaaria – sue-mar-ia

Torheim – tore-high-m

Neilmaar – kneel-mar

Gorria – gore-ia

OCEANS

Awndar – on-dar
Ostdar – o-st-dar
Uskdar – us-k-dar
Estdar – est-dar

OTHER
Zjarnok – z-are-knock
Koruum – core-um

THE CURSED SOUL

1

DORAAN

Doraan gazed at the lights sparkling along the shoreline, illuminating his home city in a glow of amber and gold. He longed to be there, to bathe in its desert warmth beneath the setting sun. To breathe in the scent of cinnamon and lily that hung in the air, wrapping its way through the town like the vines of a massive dragon-flower, encasing the city of Aksahri in a comforting hug. He inhaled deeply and swore he could smell a faint hint of that soothing scent even this far out at sea.

It had been nearly ten years since he last set foot upon any expanse of land. He ached to feel the soft white sand of the Aksahri beaches glide between his toes, to climb the rough, slender trunk of a palm looking out over the sprawling city streets, and to swim through the crystal-clear waters of the Awndar Sea on a scorching day.

He missed home.

He missed the mouth-watering aroma of baking pastries that would waft up through his bedroom window every morning. He missed the bustling sounds of the market as merchants haggled with the townspeople selling their wares. He missed the sound of children playing in the cobbled streets, giggling as they chased one another through the maze of vendor carts and people. He even missed those early mornings when his mother would make him go with her in secret to pray to the old gods. But, most of all, he missed his parents.

Doraan often wondered what had happened in their lives since the day their only child was ripped from their home. Did they think of him often? Were they trying to get him back? Did they have another child?

That last question always brought with it a sadness that hovered over him relentlessly, like a dark cloud, setting him on edge. It only caused far darker thoughts to form in his mind. Had they forgotten him completely? Were they happy to live their lives without him? Did they even care about him anymore?

His chest constricted, yearning to feel his mother's warm embrace and longing for her lilac and lemon perfume to fill his nose, like it had as a child. He even wished to hear his father's bellowing, jovial laugh again.

"We're all ready to go, Cap'n," Doraan's quartermaster, Cormac, said in his usual gruff baritone.

After ten years of living on a ship full of pirates, Doraan had realized that what you see or hear on the outside wasn't always what it seemed. A pirate wasn't always a treasure-seeking, bloodthirsty marauder—a pirate was just a person like any other trying to survive the only way they could. Cormac was more of a father to Doraan than his own self-absorbed, power-hungry father ever was. His quartermaster had come to be someone that Doraan didn't think he could ever live without. Pirate or not, he was certainly a better man than his father. A better man than himself, even.

Not that Doraan didn't care for his biological father. It was hard not to have some feeling of adoration for one's own family, but the man had never truly treated Doraan as a son. He had always been more of a legacy to his father, just a way to further the family line.

"Who's staying aboard the *Cursed Soul*?" Doraan asked.

Tonight he and his crew would step foot onto his home soil for the first time in ten long years. One of the crew members, forfeiting the chance to see his loved ones, had volunteered to stay on board the ship in case any unsuspecting souls came lurking. Not that anyone could or ever had, but that wasn't a risk Doraan was willing to take.

"Jorne will stay on board, Cap." Cormac came up beside him and leaned his thick forearms on the starboard railing of the *Cursed Soul*. "It has been a long time."

Doraan didn't miss the sorrow that laced Cormac's words and the hard line of his bushy, graying brows.

"Yes, it has been," was all he could think to say in response.

"A lot will have changed, no doubt. Prepare yourself, lad." When they were alone, Cormac tended to move back into the casual conversation they shared when Doraan was still only a boy of fourteen, thrust into this life of piracy.

His shoulders rose, tension stiffening his neck. "I know. I'm prepared for it."

Cormac's mouth formed a thin line, his brows furrowing in concern. Doraan turned away, not wanting the look on his quartermaster's face to further twist the cords of stress tightening along his shoulders.

"It's time we head to Crescent Rock to weigh anchor and ready the boats." Doraan huffed, pushing away from the railing with a wince as he shifted his full weight onto his left leg. Shooting pain radiated up his spine and all the way down to the toes that were no longer there. Cormac missed nothing as he gripped Doraan's arm to steady him.

"You need more rest. You're not used to walking on it yet. You're only going to cause further injury to other areas of your body if you don't take the time to learn how to walk properly."

"It's been months." Doraan yanked his arm from Cormac's grasp and limped his way toward the steps leading to the ship's helm.

He knew that the spasms and pain that scorched through his back at random moments throughout the day were caused by his new odd way of walking, but he didn't care. He needed to move around on his own. He needed to feel normal again.

"Your leg is still healing, Doraan." Cormac only used his name when he was serious or cross with him.

"I said I'm fine," Doraan repeated, a hint of a growl in his tone.

Seven months ago, he had been cocky and sailed his crew head long into a snare they barely escaped from. Doraan had severely overestimated their ability to overtake a larger ship. Cormac told him it wasn't his fault, that there was no way of knowing what was waiting for them, but he had seen the doubt in the eyes of his crew even before they went after the vessel. They had followed him, their captain, and he had failed them all.

It was greed that encouraged him that day. The idea of scoring a loot large enough to last them several months and effectively restore their depleted food stores and other necessities had been too great. But it was a grave mistake, one that he would live with for the rest of his life, because not only had it cost him his left leg, but also the lives of two crew members.

The ironic thing was that he remembered thinking in the moment how lucky they were to have stumbled upon a large Sumaarian cargo ship.

Besides Neilmaar, which was on the eastern coast of Emmoria, Sumaaria was one of the richest cities in the Empire. They were completely landlocked, surrounded by the treacherous line of mountains known as the Emerald Peaks. They encircled the city like a coiled snake creating a protective shield. The peaks were filled with the only mineral deposits in all of Emmoria, making the Sumaarian's a monopoly in the production of ore and all precious metals. It was said that you could catch glimpses of the city's golden towers and silver spires from between the peaks, glittering in the sun. They often boasted about their streets of gold, their expansive mansions, and their intricate, silver-threaded clothing. You could always spot a Sumaarian from their clothing alone.

However, due to the fact they didn't have an easily accessible port, it wasn't often one of their large, expensive vessels was found roaming the open seas. It was always easy to catch sight of their ships from a far distance because of their sheer size and the pure gold figurehead of a serpent at the front.

Doraan had assumed the vessel was heading to Aksahri with a shipment of goods, and he wanted that loot for him and his men.

Night had long fallen when the *Cursed Soul* began its assault on the Sumaarian ship. For such a massive vessel, they needed the element of surprise to ensure their success, and with sails as black as the evening sky, nightfall would provide them with just that. What the darkened sky also hid were the three decks of gun ports with cannons pointed directly at them and the full battalion of soldiers on the main deck, pistols cocked and loaded.

The entire encounter was still a blur in Doraan's muddled mind. He remembered very little after the first cannon fired. It had been a mess of smoke and debris. The *Cursed Soul* was exceedingly lighter, making them much faster than the hulking Sumaarian warship, which was the only reason they had made it out alive without too much damage to the ship. The only thing Doraan could remember with absolute certainty from that day was the excruciating pain that had raked through his body, coursing through him like a bolt of lightning.

As soon as they had gotten out of range of the gun and cannon fire of the Sumaarians, Cormac's booming voice had barked out orders across the deck, and his face emerged blurrily above him. *"Stay still! Don't get up!"* Cormac kept yelling at him, and that was when Doraan knew something was very wrong. He needed to see. Pushing against Cormac's hold, he forced the old man off his shoulders. As soon as he sat up fully and caught a glimpse of his mangled limb, he vomited and lost consciousness.

Pain burned through him like wildfire, all emanating from a piece of him that was no longer there. His left leg from just below the knee was gone.

"We had no choice," Cormac's words echoed in his mind, his eyes glistening with unshed tears. *"The bones were shattered beyond repair. It was the only option."*

Even though Doraan knew it was the only possible outcome, a small part of him resented Cormac for cutting off his leg, for not finding an impossible solution that could have saved it.

They never did find out what that Sumaarian ship was or where it went. Doraan was convinced it was heading for Aksahri, but it wasn't there when they sailed after it. It was as if it disappeared into thin air. They should have been able to catch up to a large ship like that. The soldiers hadn't been members of the emperor's army. They were definitely something else—a mystery Doraan hoped to solve. The idea of an unknown army sailing around Emmoria disguised as a Sumaarian cargo vessel was unsettling.

Life since that day had been hard. Doraan was forced to relearn how to walk and somehow function without a piece of himself. The crew built him a set of crutches to use, but that required the use of his arms and leg, otherwise leaving him bitterly useless.

That was when Cormac created a false wooden limb Doraan could strap around his thigh. The old man even carved out a foot that he could fit into his boot for a small sense of normalcy. Although nothing would ever feel normal about having a wooden limb.

Bruises lined his palms, elbows, hips and backside from attempting to relearn how to walk with a stiff, awkward piece of wood strapped to his leg. It was almost impossible to bend his knee. The muscles had grown weak from disuse, and the fake appendage was heavy. A soreness had settled into his hip, traveling all the way up his side from using the new apparatus. But he knew the more he used it, the stronger he would become, and eventually, he might not look like a toddler learning how to walk.

Doraan sighed, closing his eyes and swearing under his breath as the phantom pain of his missing appendage throbbed relentlessly, momentarily taking his mind off the fact that he could no longer walk as he used to, false limb or not. One awkward step and Doraan was tumbling to the splintered floorboards of the ship's helm.

The men knew not to help him. He didn't want their help, and he especially did not want their pity. He needed to be able to do things on his own and be treated as if nothing about him had ever been abnormal at all.

He glanced around at his men scattered across the ship, none of them paying him even a small fleeting glance. *Good.*

Doraan grabbed onto the ship's wheel, hoisting himself back up to a standing position. Cormac stood next to him, staring off at Crescent Rock as if nothing happened.

"Make ready for anchor!" Doraan bellowed down to his men, pulling down the pant leg that had ridden up to reveal the smooth wood beneath.

He held the wheel steady as his men went to work, preparing for their journey. Including Doraan and Cormac, only eighteen men remained of their already ghostly crew. Both men who lost their lives the day of the attack were given the customary water burial of warriors lost in battle, sending them off with honor into the sea.

Doraan wished he had been there to pay them tribute and thank them for all they had unwillingly sacrificed over the years. Never once had they complained about the awful situation they were forced into because of him and his family.

In fact, none of the crew ever complained about their circumstance. Doraan didn't understand it, but he was thankful to them.

"Furl the sails!" Doraan's voice rang out, pulled by the wind to each member of the crew.

As the ship slowed, his heart raced in his chest. In just a few short minutes, they would get into the tender and row their way home. Doraan looked up at the moon. It was just a small silvery crescent tonight, the surrounding stars twinkling brighter than he had ever seen them on this clear night. They only had one hour to spend. One single hour to see their families before being forced to return to this prison of a ship. He rubbed sweaty palms against his vest before clenching them at his sides.

He had no idea what to expect once they reached Aksahri. Once per year they were given this opportunity, but over the past ten years, Doraan had never had the courage to go. But tonight was his twenty-fifth birthday, and when the clock struck midnight, it would mark eleven years on the sea. Doraan had decided it was time—time to stop running from fate and return home to see what had become of Aksahri. And he couldn't deprive his crew of the opportunity any longer, either.

"Drop anchor!" Cormac ordered the men. The *Cursed Soul* bobbed up and down as the gentle waves of the Awndar Sea kissed the ship's port side as if wishing him luck on his voyage back home.

Doraan watched as his crew lowered the tender down into the whispering sea, calling him onward. "Are you ready?" A quiet voice came from behind him.

"I'm ready, Cormac," Doraan said with a heavy breath that caused his chest to rise and fall in one drawn out motion of acceptance. "Let's go home."

2

KAMIRA

Kamira's arms burned as she rowed herself out to sea, a salty mist spraying across her face with each pull through the inky waves. She shivered against the night air, wishing she had thought to bring a shawl or blanket before fleeing in the dead of night with no destination or plan in mind apart from getting far, far away.

Fear had taken over her wits, spurring her limbs into motion before she could even form a coherent thought. She had bolted like a spooked hare from Asharr Manor, dressed only in her silken evening gown and slippers, running straight for the dock.

Her heart thudded loudly in her ears, the strong smell of salt and fish filling her nose with each stride. She swallowed the bile rising in her throat from the overwhelming stench. Her stomach lurched as the faintest feeling of being followed sent chills racing down her spine. Kamira glanced over her shoulder, looking to the top of the hill she had just barreled down, and gasped. She blinked, confident her eyes were playing tricks on her because she could have sworn the silhouette of a man had just been there. His image still lingered in her mind, a ghostly streak of moonlight revealing a flash of white hair. Kamira shook her head, convinced the adrenaline of fleeing was causing her eyes to play tricks on her.

She pushed herself faster, stumbling once her feet thudded on the uneven wood of the dock, almost toppling off into the waves. She dove into the small boat tied at the end of the dock and sat on the bench, her feet splashing into the small puddle of water at the base of the craft from the previous night's rain. She grabbed the oars and rowed as quickly as her arms could carry her out to sea, watching the shoreline until the glowing lights of the manor house were no more than specks along the horizon.

She knew very well that she couldn't row herself all the way to another town in this tiny craft and, even if she was able, the probability of being found by the Aksahrian Guard was too high to risk. They'd tear the neighboring cities apart first, stopping at nothing until they found her. She would be as good as dead if she went back ashore, but if she stayed out here, alone and without any food or water, she would be dead all the same.

Kamira groaned loudly, dropping the paddles beside her, and sank wearily into the bottom of the boat. It had been maybe an hour, probably more, since she'd set off from the docks and her arms felt like they might fall off if she rowed one more stroke.

It was in this moment that Kamira found herself immeasurably grateful for her brother, Adonis. If he hadn't taught her the ways of the world, what was beyond a life locked away in a manor as someone's wife, and how to survive, she didn't know what would have happened tonight. She probably wouldn't have fled, because she wouldn't have been coherent enough to devise an actual plan of escape, even if she had no idea what to do with herself now.

The stars winked in and out above her, almost as if they were performing a ballet of lights for her and her alone. She wrapped her arms around herself in a feeble attempt to warm her shivering body, but it was useless. The sea air was too cool without the warmth of the sun shining down upon her and the chill of the night settled around her like a blanket of ice, cutting straight to the bone.

If only she had mastered the use of her elemental gifts, she might have been able to use them to warm herself. But even if she had, she couldn't spark a flame to life without a source nearby.

There were two types of people in Emmoria: Sorcerers who could channel and manipulate the elements, and the Ungifted, who could not. She was a Sorcerer, one of only a few left in the realm.

Her mind wandered to a memory of her brother, Adonis, telling her about the history of Emmoria and what it had been like all those years ago. Back when the Empire was full of Elementalists. It was hard for Kamira to imagine what the world could have been like then. All she had ever known was a time where having elemental gifts would mean her death. In this Emmoria, Sorcerers were hunted, and even the small use of one's gift would put them on the gallows.

It was quiet this far out in the ocean, only the calming sound of her oars cutting through the dark water. She pushed herself back onto the bench, kicking off her soaked slippers and crossing her legs beneath her before grabbing the oars once again as she continued to row.

The chilly evening air brought her back to that winter night, home with her brother, sitting by a roaring fire, watching the snowfall out of the sitting room window as he spoke to her of Elementalists.

"Hundreds of years ago, in the time before the Ungifted, we were free. We ruled Emmoria." Adonis' eyes sparkled in the dim light of the popping fire. *"The Ungifted came to our shores in search of rescue, their own world being destroyed.*

We gave them refuge and provided them with all they needed to survive in exchange for servitude."

When a tree branch tapped the window, Kamira startled and moved closer to Adonis, snuggling up beside him as he wrapped an arm around her.

"The Ungifted accepted and served the Elementalists willingly, thankful for their new found asylum. However, as the years passed, the Ungifted grew resentful of their masters, and unhappy with their station. They became restless and the Elementalists, seeing this, tried to gain back control by closing them off in the back alley corners of the cities with heavy guard, reminding them that their asylum in Emmoria was a kindness granted to them, but they were still outsiders."

The memory felt as if it were yesterday. Kamira remembered how Adonis stroked her hair, resting his head upon hers. She missed those small moments of affection from him. He was her elder by several years and she had always looked up to him. It was thanks to him that she knew how to control her gifts at all. He had always been the overprotective older brother wanting to make sure she was safe and knew how to take care of herself. He was her best friend.

She closed her eyes, letting her mind settle back into the memory.

"Many years of unrest led to the Ungifted Revolution changing everything for us." He said, his eyes growing dis-

tant as he rubbed soothing circles along her back. "One day the Sorcerers were living their lives as they always had and the next they were fighting for them. In a single night, the entire ruling family, high council, and generals of the guard were murdered in their sleep. By morning, a new Ungifted Emperor sat on the throne, and the former Sorcerer guard was replaced by a larger Ungifted army of men and women who combed the city streets, killing any and everyone who showed the slightest hint of elemental gifts." Adonis' eyes cleared, and he looked down at her. "That Emperor still sits on the throne today. For forty years he has been hunting us."

"But father keeps us safe from him, right? Because the Emperor trusts him." Kamira said, looking up into his face as he smiled down at her.

"Yes, he keeps us safe." He soothed, winding a lock of her hair around his finger. "We are all that's left in this world. Any of the surviving Sorcerers fled long ago. The numbers of the Ungifted were just too great and their attack too swift. The Sorcerers never had the chance to fight back."

"That's why mother says we can't use our gifts, because the Emperor will find us and kill us."

Adonis stared into the dancing flames and wound his finger tighter around her lock of hair until it pulled painfully at her scalp. "Ouch!" she yelled out, reaching for his hand and trying to push it away, but he was lost in a daze, so lost that the stone floor beneath them cracked and Kamira squealed. "Adonis! Stop, you're not supposed to!"

He shook his head, coming out of the stupor, and instantly released her hair, looking at the crack that spider webbed out beneath them. "I—I'm sorry, Kamira. Are you okay?"

She rubbed the aching spot on her scalp. "I'm okay. You have to fix it before mother sees." She said, pointing to the shattered stone.

Adonis grabbed her shoulders, spinning her to face him. There was a frantic gleam in his eyes. "Listen to me Kamira. Mother is a liar. You cannot suppress your gifts in the hopes that they will disappear. Sorcery is as much a part of you as the color of your eyes. You must learn to use and control it. That is what will keep you safe."

She stared at him wide eyed, "But father keeps us safe. If we use our powers, they will know."

"The world is full of lies and treachery, Kamira." His tone was forceful and his grip tightened on her shoulders with each word. "You must rely on no one but yourself. You are your only means of survival. We are hunted, captured, and killed for our power, which is why you must learn to control it. Even the smallest amount of emotion from an untrained Sorcerer can be your doom. Your only way to stay safe is not Father, it is to use and control your gifts."

Kamira opened her eyes, the memory fading into the star filled night. It had been five years since she had last seen Adonis, but he had taught her everything she knew about Sorcery. If it weren't for him and their stolen moments practicing together in the early hours of the morning, she would have never known how to control her abilities.

Their mother would have punished them for even thinking of using their Sorcery, but Kamira had always treasured those sleepless nights with Adonis. It had brought them closer and formed a bond that ran deeper than shared blood. They were two of the only Sorcerers left in the Empire, and they only had each other to share that with. She hoped one day they would see each other again.

Even with his help, she still didn't know the full extent of what she could do. Her affinity was for water, but she could only accomplish rudimentary tasks such as moving wisps of water through the air and pulling moisture from the earth to form into a floating liquid orb.

It was enough for her to understand it and recognize the feeling as it moved through her so that she could squelch it before it made itself known in public. But she could feel something much deeper within her. A power, resting, waiting to be provoked.

Kamira sighed sleepily and closed her eyes. She could feel the water's movements in her core. It sang to her, making her feel more alive than she had in years. It caressed her bones, lulling her to sleep like a mother would her child. It felt like home.

It had been almost a year since she last used her power, and she suddenly let out a loud barking laugh, only now realizing that she could have saved her arms the trouble if she had only thought to use sorcery to move the boat through the waves. Not that sorcery didn't have its own draining effects on a person, but she would have been much less exhausted right now.

She had never used enough power to even make her muscles ache, much less to get close to a drained state. Adonis explained to her that using too much power in too short a time was dangerous—something that would both physically and mentally drain a Sorcerer, with extreme cases ending in a comatose state or worse, death.

Kamira's teeth clicked together as she hugged her arms tighter around herself, shivering helplessly. Her veins held a power in them that not many left in the realm had, and yet she could not keep herself from freezing to death.

She looked back toward the shore, now so far away that she could only see the small twinkles of lights like fireflies along the shoreline, and wondered when they would come looking for her. But then a far more devastating thought came to mind. What would happen to her parents? Would they face the consequences of her rash actions?

"Blazing stars," she breathed. "What have I done?"

Kamira brought her knees to her chest and wrapped her arms around them as she turned to lay on her side across the bench, the full weight of the evening crashing into her like a massive wave, suffocating her.

A tear slid down her cheek, dripping into the puddle of seawater at the bottom of the craft, rippling outward in a ring of sorrow. Her family would be fine, she reassured herself. They knew how to take care of themselves. They would be fine.

She let out a shaky breath, trying to ease the stress of the night, but it did nothing to relax her body. Her shoulders rose with tension, her feet flexing as she continued to hug herself tighter, cutting off her own air supply.

Suddenly, she noticed that the night around her had grown darker, as if a cloud traveled through the sky and positioned itself just over top of her, blocking out the bright glow of the stars and moon.

She looked up only to find that, instead of a cloud, a ship was blocking her view of the sky above. Kamira quickly pushed herself back up to a sitting position, peering up at the looming mass of wood before her.

The ship's figurehead was a ghostly form, hooded and mysterious, with skeletal hands reaching out as if attempting to draw lost souls aboard. Her entire body shook involuntarily at the eerie sight. Normally, she would have taken that as a sign to flee as fast as she could in the opposite direction, but desperation drew her forward.

This might be the only chance she had. She could stow away on this ship and sail far away from Asharr Manor, disembark at a distant port, and make a new life for herself.

Decision made, Kamira spotted the anchor rode and didn't even bother picking up the paddles for such a small distance. Instead, she let her power roam free, pulling against the water's flow and using it to push the boat until it floated just next to the large rope tethering the strange black ship to the ocean's floor.

Luckily, the rode was at the perfect angle for her to wrap her arms and legs around, hanging like a sloth with her back to the sea, as she climbed her way up to the top, making sure to take slow and precise movements. The last thing she needed was to freefall into the dark waves.

Climbing this rope was nothing compared to scaling the stone walls of her childhood home—Adonis would make her plan escape routes during their nightly sorcery lessons for no reason other than *"just in case."* The twisted threads of the rope created grooves large enough to act as footholds, and she was able to hook her heels onto them the entire way up, relieving much of the stress from her already tired arms.

Once at the top, Kamira perched herself in the hawsepipe where the anchor would be pulled through and let out a deep sigh of relief. This had to work. She had no other ideas.

She looked back down at the small craft that had brought her all this way and moved the water around it, pushing it back toward the shore. She had left her soaked slippers behind, hoping that they would find the craft and assume she had drowned at sea.

Kamira poked her head through the hawsehole inside the ship, peering through the darkness. It was quiet, and that same shiver from before threatened to travel down her spine, but she shook it off, not allowing her fear to creep in. To her relieved surprise, the deck was completely empty.

She climbed aboard, staying hidden in the shadows to observe her surroundings. It wasn't a particularly large ship, but big enough to assume a full crew would be aboard. It definitely wasn't abandoned. Several lanterns swayed in the light breeze, casting long shadows across the wooden floors of the deck. She raised a brow at the unfamiliar fading emblem of a horned human skull encased with strange marks painted in the center of the wood. Unease resurfaced, and she shivered involuntarily.

The wood and sails of the vessel were so dark, they blended into the night. The entire ship looked to be in immaculate shape. Nothing aged with wear or rotting with disuse. There were no signs of mold or fungus growing through the cracks of the floorboards—everything was well organized and cared for as if a worthy crew worked aboard it. *So where were they?*

Jaw clenched and heart pounding, Kamira lifted the long fabric of her dress and edged her way closer to the steps that led into the belly of the ship. She had almost reached them when a loud thump had her stopping short and diving behind a large barrel to her left. The sound of footfalls echoed, growing louder with each frantic beat of her heart. Cautiously peeking around the wooden barrel, Kamira watched as a rather stocky man with hair as red as a cooked lobster, and a thin set of pink lips set in a frown stepped onto the main deck. She didn't miss the set of pistols strapped to either side of his hips or the hilt of a dagger poking out of his boot.

Kamira held her breath as the heavy-set man ascended the flight of stairs leading up to the helm. Fearing he would turn and spot her instantly, she crouched lower behind her hiding place, but instead, he disappeared into the shadows.

"Blazing biscuits!" she cursed. Without clear sight of the man, she couldn't risk sprinting to the steps that lead into the ship's hull.

Her heart hammered in her chest like the beat of a drum as she kept an eye locked on the dark spot where the man had disappeared. She remained hidden and waited, gritting her teeth when her legs cramped from the awkward position, but she didn't dare move. Finally, he came back into view and she waited with bated breath until his back was finally turned toward her.

Kamira darted to the steps on light, almost silent feet, a gift granted by her petite frame and a childhood of sneaking through an old creaking house. At the bottom of the shallow oaken steps, Kamira found herself in a hallway lined with two doors on either side and another set of steps leading down even further at the far end.

Muffled foot falls sounded above, letting her know she didn't have time to figure out if any of the rooms were unoccupied, so she took a chance and entered the door furthest to her right. She gently closed the thick wooden door behind her and placed an ear against it, listening for footsteps nearing.

When no sound of movement was heard, she let out the breath she had been holding and spun to examine the chamber she had entered. It was pitch dark, almost impossible to see anything but the window on the wall opposite her. The moon offered barely enough light to see with as it glowed through the small, circular pane of glass. Squinting her eyes, she walked toward the window, spotting a desk scattered with papers, the ink smeared across them in a tightly looped script. An oil lamp sat just next to them.

"Thank the sea," she whispered, fumbling blindly in the dark until her fingers finally wrapped around a small box of matches. She grabbed it, shaking it lightly for the telltale sound of the firesticks jumbling up and down inside. "Yes!" she exclaimed, pulling one out and quickly striking it against the side of the box. When it flared to life, she lit the lamp in one swift motion. Light spread through the room, illuminating every crevice and dark corner of the cramped space. She could now clearly see that this was someone's quarters. A pallet lay just to the right of the desk, feathers poking through the seams of the linen bedding. On the other side of the desk, pushed up against the left wall, was a trunk. Kamira opened it to inspect the contents and found a few books, a worn brown cloak, a sword, and a handful of small daggers. Sensing a dagger could prove useful, she grabbed one for herself before closing the lid.

Turning back toward the door, she noticed a tall dresser with five drawers beside it. Just as she took a step in its direction, voices sounded overhead. There were maybe two, no three, probably more.

"Bleeding stars," she muttered.

She wasn't daft enough to think she could actually hide away on this ship until it made it to the next port. Plus, she had no idea where this ship was even headed. It could just be going to another port along Aksahri. And when they inevitably found her, they definitely wouldn't keep a woman on board. Since most men, especially pirates, believed a woman aboard to be a bad omen, they would either assume she was someone's lost property and take her home, or they'd toss her overboard. She needed some kind of disguise. Her heart raced, eyes darting around the room looking for something, anything she could use.

Kamira sprinted to the dresser as an idea began to form in her mind. She couldn't disguise herself as a man. The first thing they would do if they found a strange man aboard their ship was shoot, and besides that, she was much too tiny to pass for a man—but a boy, that might be believed. She could probably pass for a boy of maybe thirteen or fourteen years of age. She thought of her cousin Zev. He was fourteen and already a few inches taller than she was.

It was crazy, but it might just work.

If they found a lad hiding aboard their ship, they would be more likely to let him stay as an extra hand on board, at least she hoped. Not that Kamira knew a lot about sailing or what was required to run a vessel, but neither would a boy of fourteen. She could learn; it would be hard, she knew, but she would suck it up and do anything and everything they needed if it meant getting as far away from Aksahri as possible. Kamira looked out the window, once again staring off at those distant lights scattered along the shoreline. They looked more like the glowing eyes of a sand lion scaring her away. She shivered at the sight. No, she couldn't go back there. Not ever.

The voices overhead grew louder and she hurriedly rummaged through the drawers, finding one linen shirt among the rest that was just a bit smaller. In the next drawer, she grabbed a pair of pants, and the smallest belt she could find so that all these men's clothes would actually stay put on her small frame.

Pulling her gown and chemise overhead, she tore a few long strips from the fabric; she needed them to strap her breasts down tight against her chest if she was to pull this off. Her breasts had never been considered a sizable blessing, but they would have been evident to any man if she let them hang free beneath the thin shirt. Most of her curves resided in the lower half of her body. Her hips swelled slightly outward, and her round backside was large for her slight frame. A pair of baggy brown pants would hopefully be enough to hide her feminine curves.

She donned the cream linen shirt and oversized pants, securing them around her hips with a worn black leather belt she had found. A mirror hung securely just above the dresser and she backed up to see her entire body, spinning before it, observing the costume she had constructed. She blew out a breath and glanced down, panicking slightly from the way her backside filled the baggy pants. "Shit," she whispered. It wasn't perfect, but it would have to do. It was the only option she had. Her eyes traveled back up to her hair and her heart picked up speed once again, realizing what she had to do to complete her disguise.

Kamira's hair was a thick mane of auburn waves that cascaded down her back, reaching almost to her bottom. It was an instant giveaway to her womanhood, and if she was to follow through with this plan, it had to go. She looked at herself in the mirror one last time before she gripped the hilt of the blade she had swiped earlier.

The knife felt cold in her grasp as she pulled a clump of hair away from her head and brought the sharp blade up with shaking hands to meet it. The first cut brought tears along with it as she watched a large clump of her shining hair fall to the floor, replaced by a tight curl sticking up atop her head. With each slice of the blade through her silken locks, the tears fell unbidden down her face until there was nothing left but a shaggy mess of short curls atop her head, longer on the top and shorter on the sides. She had shorn it as close to her scalp as she could without skinning herself.

She observed her new look in the mirror once more, her normally bright sapphire eyes now rimmed with red from all the tears she had shed.

"It's just hair," she whispered to herself. She loved her hair; it had always felt like a piece of her identity, and now, looking at her reflection, she no longer recognized herself. But she supposed that was the point. It didn't make it any less hard to see and she turned away from the mirror with a sorrowful sigh. At least she looked as close to a young boy as she ever would.

Kamira moved to pick up her heap of auburn tresses but froze mid step to the unmistakable sound of a gun firing overhead. Her eyes widened and the dagger tumbled from her hand to land silently atop the pile of hair. This was definitely not a friendly ship. She had either made a grave mistake and boarded an Aksahrian military ship or this really was a pirate ship.

"Bloody seas," she breathed. She wouldn't survive a day with a crew of pirates. This might end up being a very, very bad idea after all. But, it was too late, she was here now. She would rather take her chances on this ship—and hopefully survive another day—than go back to Aksahri and face the gallows. Her palms grew clammy at the thought, her heart picking up speed.

Muffled voices sounded overhead, spurring Kamira into action. She scooped up her discarded gown and chemise along with the heaping pile of her hair and pushed it all through the small circular window. Quickly, she grabbed for the lamp, extinguishing the flame before setting it back on the desk and grabbing the dagger tightly, tucking it behind her back just before the door swung open.

A man stumbled his way into the room, slamming the door behind him with the force of a great wind, making Kamira jump. He held a lantern in hand, but had yet to see her cowering in the corner of the room, his scowl set pointedly on the bed in front of him.

Kamira couldn't help but notice the limp he had as he walked toward the bed. She brought a hand up to her mouth, biting her lip to hold back a gasp as gooseflesh climbed up her arms. Had he just been shot above deck? Her eyes darted to the floor beneath him, but she didn't spot any blood trailing behind him. She was certain she had heard a gunshot. Did that mean if she were to make her way up to the main deck, she would find a body lying there? The thought made her shiver as flashes of memory came to her mind—of a body lying on a cold marble floor, blood pooling beneath it. Kamira gulped, biting her lip harder, the pain sending those memories scattering away. If this was a pirate ship, she wouldn't put it past them to shoot one another over a simple disagreement, and she would have to prepare herself for the worst. Living with this crew wouldn't be easy, but she was determined to ensure her survival.

Kamira cocked her head, studying the man. She had never actually seen a pirate before, but this man was definitely not what she expected one to look like. She always imagined large, rough, ugly men with great bushy beards, soot and dirt smeared across their faces, and mouths full of rotting teeth. This man was not any of those things. He was young; he didn't look much older than Kamira herself, maybe in his mid twenties. He was extraordinarily handsome with a tall, thinly muscled frame and brown skin. His hair was shaved almost completely down to his scalp, with just a short layer of black hair on top that faded into the shaved sides. He actually looked quite well-groomed and put together, more like a young naval officer than a pirate.

She watched as he sat heavily onto the bed, setting his lantern on the floor and rubbing at his left thigh, grunting and wincing as he kneaded further down toward his knee. A shadow of black hair stubbled his jawline, giving him a strikingly rugged look that kept her gaze pinned to him. She watched as his face contorted into a look of torture, making her want to call out to him and help ease his pain.

As if those very thoughts called his attention, the man swung his head in her direction, the look of surprise spreading across his features quickly turning into one of pure rage. "Who the bloody blazes are you and how did you get into my chamber?"

3

DORAAN

Doraan's anger boiled like a volcano ready to erupt. His men said nothing as they rowed the tender through the calm waters of the Awndar Sea, keeping a smooth and even pace with one another. His visit back home had been eye opening—and not in a good way.

By the time they finally made it back to the *Cursed Soul*, Doraan was ready to commit murder. His eyes were glazed over with the red haze of his rage, and to make things even worse, his leg felt as if it had just been freshly severed from his body. Pain radiated throughout his hips and back, all leading to his knee, where he could have sworn an open lesion had torn, dripping blood down his false leg. He knew it hadn't, and he would find only scarred flesh crudely stitched together with new skin if he lifted his pant leg to check.

As soon as he boarded the ship, he shuffled straight for the steps leading down into the hull. He needed to be alone before he did anything rash. Before he could disappear into the belly of the ship, a soft lilting voice had his skin crawling, every nerve-ending on high alert as it wrapped around him, echoing unnaturally in his ears. He turned, drawing both pistols and turning to face the culprit.

Standing at the bow of the ship with a devilish smile spread across her ruby lips and dark red hair flowing behind her like the wings of a phoenix, was Forcina.

"Well, well, was your visit home not all you hoped for?" Her words were always laced with a stinging poison, both sweet and pungent.

"What are you doing here, Forcina?" Doraan spat, pistols held out in front of him.

"I was curious to see how your birthday had gone."

He glared at her, nostrils flaring. "How do you think it went?"

"Honestly, I'm surprised it took you this long."

"You bitch! You couldn't even give us one hour. One *single* hour to visit our families."

"What's the matter, Doraan? Have you finally realized the implications of your curse?"

Doraan said nothing, his thumbs cocking both pistols.

Her smirk turned venomous, like a cobra ready to strike. "At least they are still alive," she hissed. "At least you got to see them again. I will never have that chance."

Doraan barked a humorless laugh. "It's nothing you don't deserve, witch."

Forcina growled, the air around them swirling with her anger, causing the rigging to creak and strain, the sails flapping with the sudden whirlwind. "You know nothing, child."

"I know enough," Doraan pulled the triggers of his pistols one after the other. Smoke billowed and sparks flew as the bullets sailed through the crisp midnight air, but just before they met their mark, they fell upon the hard wood of the ship and rolled like discarded marbles, stopping just in front of his foot.

Her cackle pierced through the night air like daggers. "This is all you will ever be, Doraan. A boy cursed to live a life of piracy. A man left with nothing but this rotten old ship."

He kept his face devoid of emotion, refusing to let her see how deeply her words had cut, and stared at the two round metal balls at his foot. He knew the bullets wouldn't meet their mark. Forcina wasn't invincible, but she could not be wounded so easily either. She was a powerful Sorceress with an affinity for air.

Doraan hadn't thought tonight could get any worse, but Forcina's arrival had caused any semblance of patience he had to evaporate. When he looked up from the bullets, the witch had vanished into the night.

"I'll be in my quarters. Do not bother me, not even if one of you sorry fools is at death's door," he barked at his men before grabbing the hanging lantern at the top of the steps, stomping down to his quarters, and slamming his door with as much force as he could muster.

He wanted nothing more than to lay down and forget this night had ever happened. Why had he gone back to Aksahri? Wouldn't it have been better to live in blissful ignorance, living out the rest of his days as a captive of the sea?

He hadn't known what to expect upon returning home—it had been ten years after all. He had expected many changes, of course, but not the hard reality that he had stumbled into. He felt as if someone had shoved him into a barrel full of ice water, forcing him to wake from a bad dream only to step into a nightmare.

Doraan closed his eyes and tried to breathe in slow, steady breaths. *The bastards,* he thought. They had written him off, forgotten him as if he were no more than mud under the soles of their shoes. They were the reason he was even in this situation. The reason Forcina cursed him.

Doraan grunted, sitting heavily on the edge of his bed, setting the lantern on his bedside table as he rubbed his throbbing thigh.

Tonight had been eye opening to say the least. It was a rude awakening to realize that ten years of his life had been completely wasted on the dream that his family cared for him, that they were working tirelessly to get him back, when all this time they had simply cast him off as dead. Well, if they weren't going to find a way to break the wretched curse Forcina had cast upon him, then he would have to do it himself. He would show them that he was worthy, that they shouldn't have given up on him without even trying. That they should not have stopped caring. It was high time he took his fate into his own hands.

He closed his eyes once again, blowing out a long, heated breath, and bringing a hand up to rub at the pressure building along his forehead. Doraan was contemplating laying down to try and sleep when the hairs stood at the nape of his neck, unease roiling through his gut as the feeling of being watched washed over him. He jerked his head, expecting to see Forcina standing there but was surprised instead to see a small, rather frail looking creature shaking in the corner of his room. His surprise quickly turned into the rage he had been trying to suppress. "Who the bloody blazes are you and how did you get into my chamber?"

The boy opened his mouth, but no words came out. Doraan pushed himself up a little too quickly, not allowing himself the time he needed to adjust his footing and stumbled, careening into the child, unable to stop himself. To his surprise, the boy released his grip of something he had hidden behind his back and rushed forward, placing delicate hands against Doraan's chest, giving him just enough leverage for Doraan to balance and stand up straight.

"Are you alright?" the boy asked.

He narrowed his eyes at the youth, suddenly wondering if he had been wrong and he wasn't a child at all. He was small, but there was something about his face—the boldness in his blue eyes, and the firm set of his mouth that made Doraan second guess his assumption. He honestly couldn't tell if the boy was fourteen or twenty. But before he could really get a good look at the lad, he noticed the item the boy had dropped. One of Doraan's own daggers lay discarded on the floor. His anger rushed forward like a tidal wave once again.

"You dare come into my quarters and try to kill me with one of my own blades!" he yelled, grabbing the lad by the front of his shirt.

"I wasn't trying to kill you!" the boy squealed. Doraan could smell the panic leaking from his pores.

"Why are you here? Who sent you?" Doraan roared. Had Forcina dropped this boy off to spy on him? Was it possible that his family wanted to make sure he never returned, so they had sent someone to murder him? As soon as the thought came to mind, he pushed it away. It didn't make any sense. Even if they had sent someone after him, they wouldn't have been able to come aboard. No one could.

"No one!" the boy screamed. "No one sent me!"

It was then that Doraan realized what his immediate anger had overshadowed. This *boy* had gotten onto the ship. How had he gotten onto the ship? That shouldn't have even been possible.

At least, he didn't *think* it was possible.

"Who are you and how did you board this vessel?" Doraan held firm to the boy's shirt, his eyes boring into the lad, brows drawn tight together. The only person who ever came aboard the *Cursed Soul* was Forcina.

"I-I, my name is Zev," the boy stuttered. "I've come for work."

"Work?" Doraan scoffed. "You're telling me you couldn't find work in the city, so you paddled miles out to sea and boarded the first vessel you saw, in the dead of night, hoping for work?"

"Y-yes," the boy said, his voice stilted and unconvincing.

Doraan narrowed his eyes at the lad for a long moment, nostrils flaring, watching the child try not to squirm beneath his scrutiny. "Do you work for Forcina? Did she send you here to watch my movements after tonight?"

"I don't know who that is!" he squeaked.

"Sure you don't," he snorted. "How about a quick walk to the main deck? These waters are swarming with sharks. I'm sure you'll have a lot to say once we chum the sea and get them ready for the main course."

The boy's eyes went wide. "I swear! No one sent me. I came on my own! I'm telling the truth! Please, I just want to get away from Aksahri. I want to work!"

"Come, boy." Doraan released the lad's shirt only to grab onto one of his boney, meatless arms, and forced the child out of his cabin.

He would be lying to himself if he said he hadn't used the boy for stability as they trekked their way up to the main deck. Doraan's leg still throbbed in a steady rhythm, quickly turning into sharp stabbing pains with each step. And, salt and sea help him, Doraan could have sworn the lad was actually pushing upward against his grip in an attempt to help Doraan walk easier.

"Please, don't throw me in. I just want to get away," the lad whispered.

Doraan chanced a quick glance down at the boy. There was something about the lad's tone, a hint of defeated desperation, that stopped him short. That and the sad, exhausted look in his eyes that had Doraan believing what he told him. He was probably just searching for a way out of a bad situation.

Doraan grumbled as he stared down at the boy. How in the sea's name had this lad come onto the ship?

Over the years, he'd watched men attempt to come aboard during their raids and attacks against merchant ships, but they were always pushed back by an unseeable force—sometimes even catapulted through the air and thrown into the sea.

Doraan had always assumed that only those locked in the curse's grasp were able to board, yet here was a lad who was *definitely* not part of their curse, walking beside him and trembling beneath his grip. *Who was this kid?*

As they ascended the last step, Doraan let his voice boom across the deck, "Jorne! Care to tell me how you allowed this child to get aboard the *Cursed Soul*?"

Jorne's usually lifeless eyes went wide, alight with surprise. "I've kept watch all night on the main deck, Cap'n. Not a soul was spotted all night. H—how is it even possible that...I—I don't understand."

Doraan narrowed his eyes. Those were his thoughts exactly. He looked down at the boy. "How exactly *did* you get on board?"

When the boy showed no indication of answering, Doraan shook him hard, "You best answer lad, lest you wish to be stranded on Crescent Rock for the rest of your days."

"I climbed up the anchor rode," the boy finally said in an almost inaudible whisper.

"The anchor rode?" Doraan said, turning his lethal gaze back upon Jorne. "Then you must have been on the main deck, is that right?"

The boy only nodded once in reply.

"Care to state your case again, Jorne?" Doraan prodded.

"Cap'n, I don't know how the lad got aboard. Like I said, I stood watch all night, just here, searching the seas." The stocky pirate pointed to the bridge, which provided the best vantage point for watching the ship and its surroundings.

Doraan glanced once again at the boy shivering beside him and sighed. Maybe this boy boarding the ship was just sheer luck. They'd recently lost two men and could use someone to do the more menial tasks aboard the *Cursed Soul*. Doraan was not someone who believed everything happened for a reason. He believed very much the opposite: that everything was just random chance and people making up their own rules. His entire life had been a series of cruel human intentions and dire circumstances, but maybe this kid was some sort of sign that there were no absolutes—that circumstances could change.

"Have you ever worked aboard a vessel before, lad?" Doraan released his grip and the boy's hand instantly shot up to rub the spot that Doraan had been gripping.

"No," he said, eyes cast upon the wooden boards of the ship. It seemed that being the only child on board a ship full of rough edged pirates was making the boy nervous.

"We don't bite," he said, nudging the child with an elbow before adding, "Too much."

The glare that the lad turned on Doraan was full of fire. *There might be some spark in the kid after all*, Doraan thought.

"Well men, looks like we have a new cabin boy! Give him a dressing down," Doraan said, turning his back on the crew. He paused at the top of the steps leading down into the hull, looking once more at the young man. The wind shifted around him, bringing with it the familiar scent of lily mixed with something sweet, like vanilla. Something strange was churning in the atmosphere; something, he feared, was changing.

He narrowed his eyes, giving the boy a final nod. "Welcome aboard the *Cursed Soul*."

4

KAMIRA

Kamira's eyes widened at the young Captain's words. All she could think was that these men were about to disrobe her.

"Nothing to worry about, lad." She jumped as an older man, who she would have originally thought to be the Captain, stepped up beside her. His eyes held a softness that eased her fear.

"Don't worry, son. Dressing down has to do with treating the sails. Come, I'll show you." He smiled, beckoning Kamira forward. "It's a messy task, but it needs to be done."

Kamira let her eyes travel, observing each member of the crew on the main deck. Each man she looked at was staring at her with a look that seemed both curious and cautious, as if saying, *one wrong move and we'll throw you overboard.* It sent an uneasiness through her causing her limbs to shake of their own volition. She tried to hide it by focusing on the man in front of her.

"The name's Cormac by the way."

"Zev," she offered. "What is your role on the ship?" If she was going to stay on board and work as a member of the crew, she needed to know the proper chain of command. If this man wasn't the Captain, she assumed he was someone important. .

"Quartermaster. I'm the Captain's right hand."

Kamira hesitantly followed the older man, noticing the gray peppered evenly through his full head of auburn hair and thick beard. Wrinkles were etched on either side of his cerulean eyes like a creased sheet of paper, a clear indication that this man spent a good deal of time laughing. The observation brought her father to mind. He had the same lines carved into his features. She doubted she would ever be able to see him again. If she were going to kill off who she'd been, she would need to ensure her past stayed buried. She could never go back home again.

"Alright." Cormac pulled her from her harsh thoughts. "See how this sail is worn and thin?"

She nodded numbly.

"We use the wax and oil to treat them so that they can still be of use to us. Like this." She watched as he gently rubbed the wax over the sail, careful not to tear any of the thinner spots of the fabric. He held out the wax brush to her. "Here, you try now."

She took it from him with trembling fingers. The faded brown sail still showed patches of black along one edge, untouched from the sun's hot, bleaching rays. The fabric was thicker than she expected it to be, stiff and rough to the touch, but still light in her hands. She took the jar of wax from him and dipped the coarse brush inside before painting the mixture across the fabric, mirroring his demonstration.

"Good, good. Do that until you have completed the entire sail," the Quartermaster said before leaving her alone at the bow of the ship.

Was this to be her life now? Could she really do this? Kamira thought to herself. It had seemed a genius plan, a sure way of survival, but now that she was here and these men had kept her on board, could she live this life?

A stinging began behind her eyes and a thickness clogged her throat as tears welled, threatening to spill free. One single moment, one decision, and her entire life was flipped on its axis. She refused to cry about it. She needed to accept it, to adapt and survive just like her brother had taught her. She swallowed the lump in her throat, forcing the tears back down and continued working along the sail.

Kamira watched as the other crew members moved about the main deck, each with a job, preparing for departure. She couldn't help but notice the age of the men in comparison to the Captain. Most of them looked as if they could be his father, and the one the Captain had called Jorne could have been his grandfather, if she was being honest. It made her wonder how someone so young came to command an entire crew, no matter how small the crew was. As far as she could tell, they were missing a number of members, but it didn't seem to slow them down. They had readied the ship and set sail almost as fast as a fully manned vessel.

"How did you get by me?"

Kamira froze, heart racing as a large shadow stretched across the sail. She turned to find Jorne towering over her. His thick forearms were blanketed with orange hair as he folded them over his broad chest. She gulped down the fear that threatened to crawl up her throat, resisting the urge to cry out. He was definitely the largest man on the ship and he didn't seem like someone who took things lightly.

She clenched her trembling hands around the jar of wax and wooden brush handle, willing them to stop. She blew out a shaking breath before saying, "I hid behind that barrel there and ran down the steps into the hull when your back was turned."

There was no use lying.

Jorne cocked his head to the side, small eyes narrowed as he pursed his lips. Kamira looked back down to the sail in her hands, unsure if his anger would bring forth any retaliation. She closed her eyes, waiting for whatever was about to come.

"Well done, lad."

What? She looked back up to see a wide grin spread across his red face and almost choked on relief as a laugh bubbled up her throat, which only made Jorne's smile grow wider. He was exactly what Kamira expected a pirate to look like. His smile revealed two missing teeth, and a scraggly orange beard matched the thinning hair on his head perfectly. A jagged pink scar traveled from the left corner of his mouth all the way across his nose and along his right cheek, giving him an almost menacing look. His eyes seemed far too small and close together for his round face — their color so dark they appeared black in the firelight. He was rough and unkept, and not an attractive man in the slightest.

He was the very picture of a storybook pirate.

"Well done?" She gaped at him. "Are you mad?"

That only brought forth a hearty, low-bellied laugh from him. "We are all a bit mad here," he said with a wink. "Anyone who can get by me without making a sound is worthy to join our crew, if you ask me. I've got the ears of a bat. Can hear the smallest of sounds well before the others. It's why they left me in charge of the *Cursed Soul* while they were gone." He hooked his thumbs through the straps of his gun holster and rocked himself up onto his toes before settling back down on his heels.

"Well, I have been told that I have light feet, and it makes it easier when you don't have any shoes." She pointed down to her bare feet caked in grime. She could barely feel them any longer from how cold they were.

"You ain't got no shoes, lad! That's a good way to get yourself sick. Best ask Cap'n for a pair of his old ones. He was only a lad like yourself when he first came upon this vessel. Probably still has his old boots thrown somewhere." Jorne threw out the words casually, but she drank them in like she had been dying of thirst.

So the Captain had only been a boy when he joined this crew. How had he become Captain then? Had he staged some kind of mutiny with the previous Captain and these men had stayed by his side? That would explain the lack of a full crew.

"How long have you been a part of the Captain's crew?" she found herself asking, curiosity getting the better of her.

"Ten years we've been together," Jorne said, looking over his shoulder toward the Quartermaster at the helm.

"Who do you sail for?"

Jorne frowned, but then huffed out a short laugh, "We sail for ourselves, lad. We're pirates."

Kamira hadn't expected another answer, but she had tried anyway, wondering if, just maybe, this crew was more than what it seemed. So, she tried another tactic. "How did the Captain and well, all of you, form your pirate crew?"

He cast his gaze out toward the shrinking shoreline of Aksahri. "We were forced into it. Most of us were officers of the Aksahrian Navy. A few were merchant ship sailors. I was a fisherman. Cormac was once a Navy Admiral and the Captain, well, he was something else entirely." Jorne looked behind him again and Kamira followed his gaze to see the Quartermaster watching their conversation intently.

Kamira looked away as she continued working the wax into the sail. She had learned a lot during their short conversation, but it also left her with so many more questions. Mainly, what had happened to force them into a life of piracy? And what did Jorne mean by the Captain being something else entirely? What sort of strange ship had she wormed herself onto?

"Best get a few hours of sleep once you're done treating the sail. It's well past midnight and we've an early start in the morning," Jorne huffed. "There are a few extra hammocks down in the crew's quarters that you can choose from, but you should go to the Captain for a pair of boots before then." Jorne nodded and turned away, heading down into the ship's hull.

Kamira watched him go, a look of horror frozen on her face at his words. She hadn't thought about where she would sleep on the ship.

"Blazing biscuits," she muttered into the night.

Kamira stood outside the Captain's quarters, staring at the wooden door as if it might reach out and bite her.

It was late. She had just finished the sails and, as the night had gotten colder, so too had her feet. Pins and needles traveled through them with each step and she was desperate for a pair of wool socks and some boots.

She breathed in deeply, holding the breath in her core as she knocked once on the door.

"What do you want!" the Captain yelled through the door. "I said I didn't want to be bothered!"

Kamira blew out her breath, "It's Zev. I was wondering—" The door swung open before she even had the chance to finish her thought. She was greeted by a shirtless Captain, still in his pants and boots. His umber skin gleamed in the dim light, muscles shifting as he leaned against the door.

She tried her best not to stare at his torso, but she couldn't seem to tear her eyes away from the chiseled flesh. There was not one soft part, and a thin coating of dark hair covered the top of his chest and traveled down his center, creating a 'T' shape as if pointing to... Her breath quickened at the sight.

"If you need something you can ask the crew, but not me, understand?" He was about to slam the door, but she put her hand on it before he had the chance, remembering what she had bothered him for in the first place.

"I was told you might have a pair of boots I could use." She glanced down at her toes, wiggling them in an attempt to accentuate her point.

He grunted and rolled his eyes in annoyance. "Wait there."

She nodded, but stepped inside anyway, noticing the crumpled blankets and the pillow propped against the wall on his bed. He rummaged through a drawer hidden under it, grunting when he didn't find what he was looking for.

"I thought I told you to wait outside," he grumbled, limping past her toward a small bench next to his dresser. "I don't want you in here stealing one of my daggers again."

It was her turn to roll her eyes at him.

She decided to use this opportunity to try and coax some information from him. "Did you hurt your leg?" she asked, hands clasped behind her back as she glanced around the room, hoping it looked as if she was just trying to make small talk.

She was unsurprised when he didn't provide her with an answer. Kamira watched as he lifted the cushioned top of the bench, revealing a compartment beneath from which he pulled a pair of leather boots and tossed them at her.

She caught them before they could fall and crush her frigid toes. "So, you didn't hurt your leg then?" she tried again.

"That is none of your business." He pointed toward the door, glaring at her. "You've got your boots, now leave."

"Um, I don't have any socks either." She graced him with a wide, awkward smile. Her entire wardrobe had come from this man and he didn't even know it.

"Bloody sails, boy! Why did you not have socks and boots on when you snuck aboard?" He growled, but went to his chest of drawers and pulled out a pair of old, holey socks.

She wasn't about to complain that they would do little to keep her feet warm with large gaping holes in them. She would just have to make due, or maybe she could mend them.

Ripping the scraps of fabric from his grasp, she thanked him as he pushed her out the door and slammed it shut behind her.

5

DORAAN

Doraan paced the length of his chamber. His head pounded incessantly, growing more and more persistent with each shooting stab of pain through his skull. A throbbing pressure was building behind his eyes and blurring his vision.

Everything that happened tonight was grating at his skull, scraping against it like the talons of a falcon. His trip home, Forcina, the boy. It was all too much and he didn't know how to handle it.

He brought a fist down onto his desk, sending papers scattering to the floor.

This had quite possibly been the worst birthday of his entire life, even worse than the one when Forcina had cast the curse upon him.

He closed his eyes, replaying the evening of going ashore in his mind.

The boat ride to Aksahri felt as if it had taken an eternity. Each stroke of the oars through the water sent a tingle of unease down his spine until he was wound so tight that he nearly sprung out of the tender to swim his way back to the *Cursed Soul*.

Doraan held his breath to the point of nearly fainting as they passed through the threshold that would normally propel them away from the shore. The curse only allowed them access to land for a single hour, once a year, on the evening of his birthday. From eleven to midnight, they could actually experience walking on the solid earth. Any other time, it was as if an invisible barrier blocked them from sailing any closer. They were left to simply gaze at their home city from miles away.

The anticipation of walking on land again set a hush over the entire crew. No one spoke as they rowed to shore, and he wasn't sure anyone was even breathing as the tender struck land. It took them a full minute before they timidly rose to step out onto the beach, waiting for Doraan to take the first step.

He recalled looking down at the sand and watching the small waves wash ashore, bubbling as the current pulled them back into the shallow swells. How long he stood there staring at the ground, he couldn't say. With a shuddering breath, he stepped off onto the beach, but he did not feel solid earth beneath his foot. In fact, he felt nothing at all.

Doraan looked down at his hands and balked as he looked straight through them to the sand below. He yelled as he fell backward, but felt no impact from landing on the unshifting sand, as if the weight of him made no difference.

The witch had made him a ghost.

A small part of him had always believed that Forcina's offer had been too good to be true. It wasn't in her character to allow him to have an ounce of interaction with his family, and as it turned out, his suspicions were correct.

The anger that settled in him since that realization hadn't yet left and he didn't think it ever would. The entire evening had rolled like a boulder downhill, picking up speed with each passing minute, and barreling through any hope Doraan had ever had.

For the last ten years, he had held onto the belief his family was looking for a way to help him, looking for something to set him free. But what he found while walking through Aksahri as a ghost was a city that thought him dead and a family who was living their life as if he actually *were* dead, even though they knew he wasn't. They had even gone so far as to create a gravesite for him. Any semblance of hope that remained in him had been replaced with a fire that burned bright and hot, searing his inside like resting embers.

His fist soared through the air and collided with the oaken wall of his quarters. His knuckles came away bloody from the impact, but his steaming rage masked any sting from his physical wounds.

He didn't understand it. He was their only son, their flesh and blood. How could they just pretend he was dead? *Especially* his mother. They had always shared a special bond, a deep connection that only a mother and son knew. His mind wandered back to early morning walks with his mother in the garden. What he wouldn't give to see the exquisite array of purple and yellow flowers spread throughout the city gardens, to touch their velvet petals and watch the bees as they gathered pollen, flying from one bloom to another. The fragrant perfume of those flowers was now just a distant, cherished memory, slowly fading the longer he was gone from home.

He closed his eyes, picturing his mothers' crooked, comforting smile, her kind, deep-set eyes, and braided black hair that fell to her waist. She always dressed in bright, sunny colors of orange and yellow—*happy colors,* she would call them. He would have thought she would move sky and sea to get him back to her.

Apparently not.

Doraan's nostrils flared, and he spat on the ground beside him, setting those memories he cherished so much ablaze in his mind, turning them to ash and letting them float away with his dreams.

He expected as much from his father. Doraan knew his father didn't love him, but he thought he at least cared for him in some capacity. If not as a son, then as a pawn to further the family line.

The few memories he shared with his father were short and sometimes harsh. There was one in particular that made him think his father might care for him more than he let on—one late evening Doraan had found his father still awake and bent over his desk looking over heaps of papers. He recalled how the light of the fire gleamed against his fair skin, his hazel eyes flashing as he looked up at Doraan. Surprisingly, his father motioned him into his rooms and spent the night showing Doraan what he was working on. It had been one of the best days of his life. His heart and soul soared with each small smile his father bestowed upon him. He had even let Doraan sit on his lap. Doraan couldn't even remember what his father said to him at that moment; he was simply content to be close to him, to feel as if his father truly cared for him. It was the first time he had ever felt like a son to his father. The first and the last time, because it had all been lies. Why had he even missed his father at all?

His parents didn't care for him at all. They were the very reason he was in his current predicament, and they had the audacity to simply brush him from their lives as if he were no more than a speck of dust upon their shoulders. Doraan punched the wall again, his hand eliciting a loud crack as pain pulsed through his knuckles, spreading through his hand and into his wrist. He bit back a curse, almost welcoming the throbbing ache that proved he was still very much alive.

The thought lit a new fire beneath him. It was time to stop dwelling on dreams and take life into his own hands. Hope had gotten him nowhere. It had only wasted ten long years of his life. Ten years of fighting to survive, of pirating and pillaging just to live. Ten years of nothing.

It was high time he did something to change that.

He would spend every waking minute searching for a way to break the curse Forcina had cast upon him. And then he would go home and show his parents that they should never have forgotten him, that he is worthy of their love, worthy of *life*.

The only problem was, where did he begin?

6

KAMIRA

Kamira felt as if she had barely fallen asleep before she was torn from her slumber by the loud clanging of a bell ringing out through the entire ship.

She bolted upright and rubbed the sleep from her eyes, trying to focus on her surroundings. Light streamed in through the cabin windows. How could it be morning already? She didn't remember much after falling into one of the empty hammocks in the crew's cabin. Exhaustion had won out and sleep had claimed her the moment her head hit the pillow.

The hammock was surprisingly comfortable for a bed suspended in the air. The swaying of the ship rocked it back and forth, lulling her to sleep. It was morbid, but she thought they looked a little like floating coffins—minus the promise of eternal rest.

"Get up, lad," Jorne said, passing by her hammock. "Cap'n's orders."

Kamira groaned, pressing the heels of her palms against sleep-crusted eyes and feeling the puffiness of too little sleep. "What time is it?"

"Sun up. Rise and shine, we've work to do," Jorne yelled back before heading out the door.

Pushing herself lazily from the hammock, she pulled on the borrowed socks and boots. Luckily, she was the last one to awaken, so she missed seeing any bits of exposed flesh from the crew around her. She could have sworn one of the men was completely nude in a hammock near hers when she had finally come down to sleep, but she hadn't looked long enough to confirm.

She stumbled up to the main deck of the ship where the entire crew was assembled in a horizontal line. Kamira followed suit, standing beside one of the lankier crew members. The Captain and Quartermaster stood facing them, both their arms crossed in front of them.

"Good of you to join us, cabin boy." The Captain glared down at her with enough contempt to make her combust on the spot. If he were a Sorcerer, she probably would have been nothing but a pile of bone and ash right now.

"We are heading North. Let's sail, men." He said before turning to Cormac, engaging with him in hushed tones.

Kamira noticed a few of the crew exchange confused glances at one another as they dispersed, heading to whatever jobs they held upon the ship. *What was that about?* she wondered.

From what Jorne had told her last night, almost all of these men were from Aksahri, so she imagined they might not go North very often, rather staying close to home. Could that be why they seemed a bit stunned by the Captain's words?

She could understand staying close to home. It had been a shock when she moved from her northern home in Torheim to the hot sands of Aksahri. The vast deserts and dry climate were so different from the lush forests of her home that she never truly felt comfortable there. She missed the thick woods and vibrant greenery of her home. She even missed the chill of the air in the winter months and the humidity that would cling like a frog's sticky feet to everything it could in the summertime. It had been a beautiful place to live and she was immensely grateful to have lived most of her life there among friends and family, versus the capital city of Aksahri, where Sorcerers were sniffed out and executed daily. She couldn't imagine the stress of that kind of life, especially for an innocent child.

The North had always been a little more forgiving, turning a blind eye to those who let their abilities slip. It was a more peaceful and accepting place, where many did not agree with the Emperor's rule.

In her home city of Torheim, much of that was because her father was the General of the Aksahrian military stationed there. Though not a Sorcerer himself, he was accepting of the abilities his children and wife possessed.

When the rebellion tore through the realm, her father's family was one of the few Ungifted households that did not agree with the new emperor's laws and views, taking in Kamira's mother, which led to her parents falling in love. As a result, her father spent many years working tirelessly to get into the position of power he now held to aid the Sorcerers and, ultimately, his own family.

But even so, he was still the General of the Aksahrian-Torheim military branch and he could only turn a blind eye so often. There were still executions displayed in the city center and soldiers patrolling the streets daily, their sights set on snuffing out any rogue Sorcerers hiding out.

All that remained in Torheim were Kamira, her mother, and four others hidden in the city. Even her brother, Adonis, had left long ago, fleeing across the realm to Neilmaar where he could stay more easily hidden.

The amount of Sorcerers remaining throughout the realm continued to dwindle. The Emperor would never stop. He would send his troops out until they'd been completely wiped from the face of the Empire.

Kamira had lived a much different life than many other Sorcerers. Being a part of a noble house came with perks and had taken a major target off her back. Instead of hiding and living a life with one eye always open, she had lived a privileged life, spending much of her time reading, drawing, playing the piano, going to parties and balls, and learning everything possible about being the mistress of a house for her future life as a nobleman's wife.

She was immeasurably grateful for the life of luxury she had been given, never worrying or wanting for anything, but at the same time, it had always felt like a slow, agonizing walk with a noose around her neck that grew tighter each day. The best she had to look forward to in life was being the wife of a Lord without the opportunity to ever reveal who she *truly* was. Her sorcery was as much a part of herself as her mind, and if she couldn't live without that, then how was she to live a life without her gifts?

"Cabin boy!" The Captain yelled down to her from his spot at the helm, ripping her from her thoughts. His hazel eyes bore into her like shards of ice. "You're with me."

"Wonderful..." she sighed and rolled her eyes before venturing to join him at the helm. She didn't know why, but she found it hard to take the Captain seriously. Maybe it was his youth and the fact that he was many years younger than anyone else on the ship, or maybe it was because she could tell how hard he was trying to rattle her. It was almost as if he was constantly wearing a rugged mask of indifference.

When she had observed him alone in his room before he had noticed her, there seemed to be a great weight sagging his shoulders—a sadness and vulnerability that she hadn't seen since. On the outside, he might look hardened, but he was struggling internally.

It made her think about her own struggles and the reason she was on this vessel. Had it really only been last night? It hadn't sunken in yet—it all felt like some sort of far off dream. She'd expected to feel sad or remorseful, but she couldn't really say she felt much of anything. Her entire body was just numb, the events of the previous evening locked away in a deep dark corner of her mind. Her heart was riddled with frost, and she didn't know when she would feel warm again.

"How good is your eyesight?" the Captain asked, bringing her back to the present.

"Good. Why?"

"We need a lookout to watch for oncoming ships. Here, take this."

She grabbed the bronze spyglass from him and held it to her eye, extending it toward the Captain's face. "You should really stop frowning, Captain, you're starting to get wrinkles."

His frown deepened as he snatched the spyglass from her. "Use it up there, not down here." He pointed to the small perch at the top of the main mast. "Got that, smart ass?"

Smirking, Kamira crossed her arms.

His nostrils flared as he grunted, "Your only job is to call out as soon as you spot another ship, understand?"

Before she could make a comment about her understanding of the simplistic task, she stopped short. To him, she was only a child, and naive obedience would be her best defense. "Yes, Captain," she said, nodding.

"Good, now go."

Kamira's eyes wandered to the lookout point high above. It was definitely only big enough for one person. A thread of nervousness snaked down her spine as her stomach flipped at the thought of being so high above the ship. She had never been afraid of heights, but she had never been put in a position to develop that fear either.

"Go ahead," the Captain said again, gently pushing her toward the netting that led up to the lookout. If she could successfully climb the wobbling web of ropes, her prize would be the wooden railing at the top that would prevent her from tumbling back down.

Kamira stretched out her arms, grabbed onto the coarse netting, and took a deep breath. Her grip was firm as she began to climb. Contrary to when she'd climbed the anchor rode to stowaway on the ship, the rope ladder was surprisingly easy. But as she scaled higher, the wind swept harder, twisting the netting and she held on tighter.

She kept her gaze fixed on her destination, refusing to look down until she reached the perch. When she finally made it and her feet were firmly planted on the sturdy platform, she peered over the railing, gasping in awe at the stunning view all around her.

The sparkling ocean spread out farther than she could see in a mixture of bright turquoise and the darkest blues. "Extraordinary," she breathed.

"Alright up there?" called the Captain from far below.

"This is amazing!" she hollered down to him. "It's the most beautiful sight I've ever seen!"

She looked down at him grinning from ear to ear. Her eyes must have been playing tricks on her because it looked like the handsome young Captain was smiling back at her. It was the first time she had seen anything other than a scowl or a hard glare on his face, and it gifted him with a youthful glow. She averted her gaze back to the rolling blues and greens of the sea, hiding her smirk at the small crack in his hard demeanor.

"Keep your eyes open for any oncoming ships or shallow waters. I know it's hard to not *just* focus on its beauty, but we don't want to be surprised."

"Aye, Aye, Cap'n," she yelled back, bringing her hand up in a mocking salute. *Ah, there is that glare again*, she thought as her mouth spread into a satisfied grin.

There was no land in sight—Aksahri was long gone, and they were surrounded by nothing but water. It was a heady feeling, but it was also freeing to be so far out to sea, away from everyone and everything. Adventure was not something she realized her soul had craved until this moment. She was untethered from a life shackled to a husband. She was free from a life of hiding her gifts, never able to use them—well, to an extent. She didn't know how this crew felt about Sorcerers. Did they agree or disagree with the Emperor? What would they do if they found out? Would they shoot her on the spot?

She would worry about that later. Right now, she was surrounded by the element that made her heart sing: water.

She took a cautious look at the crew below. None of them were paying her any attention. The waves were calling her name, begging her to play with them. She *could* use her gifts, practice a bit of sorcery this far out in the ocean, and no one would even know it.

Kamira closed her eyes and focused on the sprawling sea. She could *feel* the currents, *see* through the depths of the deep-blue water. She tugged against it lightly, feeling the water move at her command, eliciting laughter. Yanking harder, Kamira directed the ocean to spin, reveling in the tickle of her sorcery as it coursed through every inch of her body.

It had been cooped up for so long, aching to break free and invoke its power on the world. It was exhilarating and refreshing to taste that freedom. She drank it in, every last drop. As the power continued to flow through her, Kamira pushed against it harder, using more of the thrilling force that belonged to her.

"Captain!" someone yelled far below. "There's a whirlpool! Hard-a-port!"

Kamira's eyes shot open at the pirate's words, looking out at the ocean for the first time since she began using her power. She took in a sharp breath at the sight. She had caused the opposing tidal currents to collide in a swirling fury, creating a gaping hole of dark water.

She glanced to the helm to see the Captain spinning the wheel hard to the right. The ship lurched and she squealed, holding on tightly to the railing of her lookout. The Captain pressed himself against the ship's wheel with all his might as he fought the spinning current that had begun pulling them toward the whirlpool she had unintentionally created.

"Bleeding skies!" Kamira cursed. She had to stop it before they were all pulled under.

Closing her eyes, she brushed against her power, easing its ferocity, calming it as she pushed the currents away from one another. She could feel the water as it heeded her call, conceding to her will.

"Zev! You one-eyed donkey! Did you not see the swirling current of death coming our way?" the Captain yelled up to her.

"S—sorry, Captain! I was looking the other way." She called back. "It came up out of nowhere!"

"You'll be shark bait if it happens again, understand?"

Kamira swallowed the lump that had formed in her throat. She could have killed them all. If she were to practice her sorcery further, it would have to be on a smaller scale. It was apparent that she had much to learn about the limits to her gifts.

7

DORAAN

"Were you ever going to tell me about our change of course?" Doraan stiffened as Cormac's deep voice drifted over his shoulder from behind him.

"Yes," he said, not turning to look at him. "I was planning to tell you along with the rest of the crew today, which I did."

Cormac grunted, "Why north? What are you planning?"

"I don't know," Doraan whispered honestly. He didn't know where they were headed. He didn't really have an actual plan or destination in mind. All he knew was that they needed to go North, somewhere that they tended to stay away from due to the cold and rough seas. But it was rumored that any surviving Sorcerers after the rebellion had fled from the South, seeking refuge in the hidden crevices of the Emerald Peaks, and back alleys of the smaller northern cities. Doraan thought that if a surviving Sorcerer was tucked away somewhere, they could help break the bloody curse that had been cast over them, and finally go home for good. It was a shot in the dark, but it was the only idea he had.

"Doraan, there is only one way to break the curse," Cormac said as if reading his thoughts.

"I gave up on that option a long time ago. There has to be another way."

Ten years ago, when Forcina had cursed Doraan, along with every person on this ship, she had woven a way out of it through her twisted words, but it was so astronomically absurd that he had never given it a second thought. It couldn't be done. She had created the most impractical act possible to assure he could never break free.

Doraan finally spun on Cormac, ready to offer a few terse words of annoyance, when he caught his Quartermaster squinting up to the crow's nest. Doraan followed his gaze to where Zev still sat, staring out at the expanse of sea around them.

"Have you found anything out about the boy?" Cormac questioned.

"No, I haven't really had another chance. Have you?"

Cormac shook his head. "I thought about it last night, but I didn't want to scare him off."

"I think we should give him another day or two before we start grilling him, but he is definitely hiding something. I don't like it."

"He's here for a reason. It could be that the sea blessed us after our loss, or it could be something more sinister."

Doraan raised a single brow and glared at Cormac, "What the bloody sails is that supposed to mean?"

"Everything happens for a reason, Doraan."

Doraan only glared at him harder, crossing his arms over his chest. " Sometimes you are completely unbearable to be around. It's your turn to man the helm. I'm going to rest before my shift tonight."

Cormac only nodded in his casual, stoic way. Doraan smirked, shaking his head at the old man.

He proceeded to the main deck, turning to head down into the hull, but risked a quick glance at Zev once more before descending. The boy was sitting on the edge of the platform, his legs dangling through the railing slats, swinging as he made strange movements with his hands.

Doraan's brows drew together as he watched. What in all the realm was he doing? This boy was not an ordinary one, and tomorrow he would question the strange kid until he gave him a straight answer. Zev continued flicking his hands as if no one could see him. Doraan snorted and sighed before heading down to his room.

Doraan brought a hand up, rubbing at the back of his neck. He really needed to solidify a plan. Sailing North wasn't enough. Finding a Sorcerer in Emmoria was comparable to finding a diamond in the desert sands of the South—highly unlikely. And the more he thought about it, the more he wondered if he even wanted to find another Sorcerer. He hadn't had much luck with the first one he'd met.

When he was in school in Aksahri, he learned about the Ungifted Rebellion, the Sorcerer's massacre, and the aftermath. By the time Doraan was born, it had been fourteen years since the Sorcerers were overthrown and nearly annihilated. There were almost none left, and any that were discovered throughout the realm were either shot or hung up in the city centers alongside any Ungifted who had aided them. It was a power play, a fear tactic to keep all of Emmoria in line and help the Emperor eradicate every last Sorcerer left.

Doraan was sixteen the first time he'd met a Sorcerer. For all of his life, he had been told of their evil, malicious ways—how they enslaved the Ungifted for hundreds of years, forced them to do their bidding, and whipped and maimed them for sport. His father had been the slave of the Sorcerer Emperor who was overthrown and had ultimately taken his place as Emperor of the realm.

But his mother had told him a completely different story. She told him of the Sorcerers' compassion, how they used their power to help. There were even some who were able to heal the sick and wounded. They weren't all dishonorable, she would say, there were many who treated the Ungifted as equals rather than as servants or slaves. Many had given the Ungifted true and honest work, working alongside Sorcerers rather than beneath them. It was only in Aksahri and the larger cities where the Ungifted had truly been miserable.

He didn't know what to believe. On one hand, his mother was the one person he trusted more than anyone in the realm, but on the other, every school text and person he knew in Aksahri thought they were terrible creatures of power whose only goal in life was to harm and enslave the Ungifted.

So, on his sixteenth birthday when a Sorcerer showed up out of thin air, he hadn't known what to expect, but he should have known they weren't there for pleasantries. No, Forcina had come for revenge. He witnessed firsthand the true power of a Sorcerer and it was fearsome indeed.

He only caught bits and pieces of what she said to his father, but the next thing he knew, he was in the west docks of Aksahri on a strange black ship with seventeen men as clueless as he was. And when one of them tried to disembark only to be thrown back onto the ship by an invisible force, and then another, and a third, Doraan realized what the words Forcina had spoken meant. Her lyrical idiom had solidified his fate and the fates of the seventeen men, weaving them together. They had been cursed by a powerful Sorcerer, and that was the moment that Doraan made his mind up about them all. They *were* evil and they deserved to perish, just like his father said.

He would find a Sorcerer, force them to break the curse, and then kill them before heading home to continue his father's work of eradicating the realm of every Sorcerer left alive.

8

KAMIRA

I t had been a long day.

Kamira spent hours keeping watch in the crow's nest and baking under the relentless, blazing rays of the sun. After being called down, she was given food and water before being tasked with the exhausting job of swabbing the deck.

By the time evening struck, she went straight to the galley to eat her fill of supper and then dove into her gloriously cushioned hammock, muscles and back spasming from overuse. There was only one problem; Kamira couldn't sleep.

All she could do was lay there, wide awake, the pungent scent of body odor thick in the air. Her hammock rocked with the ocean's waves, the heavy breathing and

loud snores of the crew echoing throughout the cabin —
all sound asleep, used to a life on the sea.

She stared into the darkness, willing herself to sleep.
The exhaustion of the day weighed heavily on her limbs,
but still, sleep never came. A weary sigh escaped her
wind-chapped lips. *What was she doing here?*

It wasn't the first time in the past two days Kamira
wondered why she remained aboard a ship full of pirates.
She had barely found the time to think about her new life.
Her night of fleeing and full day of hard work had left
her little time to think about all that happened, and now
that she was far away from Aksahri, she felt some relief.
Although, now she couldn't seem to stop revisiting the
events of that night over and over again.

Kamira rolled over, groaning at her perpetually running mind. She needed rest, especially for another full day
of hard work tomorrow. The dark circles under her eyes
were becoming a permanent fixture on her features. She
could feel the bags growing under her eyes with every hour
that sleep eluded her. Maybe she needed some fresh air.

Pushing herself out of the hammock, Kamira quietly
tip-toed around the snoring crew, slipped out of the cabin
door, and headed up to the main deck.

The cool sea breeze was a welcomed embrace—a magnificent breath of fresh air from the dank, musty cabin.
The sea was mesmerizing at night. Nothing but the sounds
of the ship cutting through the waves. The crescent moon

and twinkling stars looked down upon her, bathing the ship in a milky glow. A swift breeze caressed her face, tousling her hair, and Kamira closed her eyes, feasting in the delight of the vast ocean around her.

She sensed each swell and current that swirled beneath the surface. Kamira opened her eyes and pulled against it. The sea obeyed, coming up to meet her palm, where she willed it to dance within her hand and wind between her fingers. This playful sorcery had always come easily to her. She had never pushed herself much further. Her life and circumstances had not allowed for it. But now that she was free, she could try something new; a sorcery much greater than anything she had attempted before. The whirlpool from this morning was proof that she had barely scratched the surface of her power.

Kamira closed her eyes once more and brought her hands straight out in front of her, palms facing the horizon. She stilled her mind and released a slow rhythm of calming breaths. Her shoulders sagged as her entire body relaxed.

It was just her and the sea.

"You should be asleep," a smooth, baritone voice came from behind her. She jumped and dropped her hands instantly, wincing at the sound of her water splashing into the sea.

Turning, she was greeted with the now familiar scowl on the young Captain's face, and the ever-present arms crossed over his chest.

She almost laughed at the look he was giving her. She couldn't tell if he was trying to frighten her or if he lived his entire life with that eternal frown. If it was the former, it might have worked on a young boy, but it would certainly not work on her. "I couldn't sleep."

"There is no *'sleeping in'* aboard a ship. When the sun begins to wake, so will you, and I have many tasks for you to do tomorrow." He stepped closer and she raised a brow at his blatant attempt to scare her.

Kamira was getting tired of his brutish performance. "Yes, I am aware." A smirk ghosted over her lips as he held her stare with the same stoney expression, as if he'd rather throw her overboard for the bottomless ocean to swallow her whole than stand here with her. She couldn't keep her mouth shut about it any longer. "You know if you keep scowling at me, your face will freeze that way."

His mouth fell open in surprise, his brows rising and his arms falling slack at his sides. There was a long moment of silence between them until his features finally settled back to their normal stoic state and he said, "You are unlike any boy I've ever met. I can't quite place it, but there is something off about you."

The shimmering light of the moon illuminated his face, causing his amber colored eyes to glow like pools of gold in the darkness. "You are unlike any Captain I've ever met," she countered, crossing her arms over her chest to mirror him.

"And how many ship Captains have you met in your short life?" A black brow rose in question.

"A few." She wasn't about to tell him how many times she had actually traveled by ship. At least once a year during her twenty-one years of life she had traveled from Torheim to Aksahri for a forced interaction with her intended. She had been on many ships and had never encountered a Captain like him.

"And what exactly makes me so different from all these other Captains you have met?" He narrowed his eyes on her.

"They were all old. You don't seem much older than twenty." She said, holding her ground.

"My age doesn't dictate my ability to Captain a crew."

"I never said it did."

The Captain bent his head closer to her, narrowing his eyes as he searched her face and…was he examining her body?

She felt tremendously exposed, "What are you doing?"

"How old did you say you were, again?" he asked, not stopping his perusal of her.

"I didn't." Kamira said, anxiety pricking her nerves, sending her heart racing as his eyes lingered on her chest.

"Where are you from?" he asked, stopping for a moment as their gazes locked. His eyes still gleamed eerily in the moonlight, and she rubbed at her arms as gooseflesh prickled her skin.

Kamira tried not to hold her breath, "Jaaria," she said quickly.

"Jaaria? You don't look like a Jaarian," he said and stepped closer, lingering less than a hand's width from her.

"I-I was an orphan, never knew my parents," she continued, spreading her lie like a tangled spider's web. It was becoming harder to fabricate these stories. She didn't normally stutter, but coming up with a new life on the spot had her grasping for words. It was like trying to catch fire in her hands.

"Why did you board this vessel, Zev?" He continued to assess her with his gaze, intensely studying every inch.

Kamira took an instinctive step backward, only to realize she was at the ship's portside railing.

"Who are you?" He gripped her shirt the same way he had when he found her in his quarters.

Kamira threw her hands out and pushed his chest as hard as she could, desperate to stop him from looking at her so closely and from asking more questions.

The Captain twisted awkwardly from her shove and released her shirt as he toppled to the ground. He landed on the floorboards with a grunt as he held his left wrist in his hand.

She knelt before him. "Oh stars! Are you alright? I'm so sorry. I didn't think I would be able to push you that hard."

"Why the bloody seas did you push me at all?" he growled, gingerly moving his wrist in circles and wincing in pain.

"Are you truly asking me that question? Here, let me see your wrist." She reached for it, but he pulled away.

"I think you have done enough, cabin boy. Go back to your quarters and get some rest before tomorrow." He returned to glaring at her.

"My mother is a healer. I might be able to help if you hurt your wrist badly," she urged.

He went very still, staring at her in a way that sent a shiver dancing down her spine. "I thought you were an orphan."

She froze, instantly realizing her mistake. "My adoptive mother." She was awful at lying. She knew she would slip up eventually. Her web of lies was quickly becoming impossible to navigate.

The Captain just glowered at her. She knew he didn't believe her. He knew she was hiding something, but her unease melted away when she noticed that his left pant leg had ridden up during his fall, exposing smooth, carved wood.

She gasped, her fingers pushing up the fabric before considering the consequences. "What happened?"

With a sudden smack, he pushed her hand away and roughly tugged the clothing back down to cover his wooden limb. His eyes flashed with anger as he snarled, "How dare you?! That is none of your business."

She recalled the way he had rubbed his thigh when she had first seen him and the significant limp he sported at all times. "Does it give you a lot of pain?"

"Enough!" he snapped. "Go back to your chamber and go to bed."

"I can..." she began, but he cut her off instantly.

"That is an order, boy," he spat.

Beneath the fury on his face was great sorrow. To lose a limb so young had to be a heavy burden to bear, and with the slight shame in the downturn of his eyes, she wondered if it was demoralizing, too.

She almost protested further, but Cormac's voice traveled from the stairwell. "Go and get some sleep, Zev. I can help the Captain."

Kamira looked up at the older man and then back to the Captain, whose nostrils were flaring like an angry bull.

She finally conceded, nodding with a solemn, "Goodnight."

As she headed back for the room full of snoring pirates, she glanced back to see Cormac kneeling before the Captain in a fatherly way, speaking in hushed tones. The Captain's eyes were closed, but she could have sworn that something wet twinkled in the moonlight as it rolled down his cheek.

9

DORAAN

"Doraan." Cormac held out a hand. He grasped it, wiping away the irritating tear that had slipped free from embarrassment. Zev's sympathetic expression upon seeing his leg wasn't as humiliating as being pitied. He wasn't a charity case that needed coddling and mending. What he needed was to be left alone. What he needed was to be strong. He wasn't helpless and he wasn't about to take any help from a child—a lying child, no less.

Cormac pulled him up and he balanced himself on his foot, steadying himself before letting go, nodding his thanks to his second. "Are you alright?" Cormac inquired.

"Yes," he huffed. "I'm fine…. The cabin boy, he—he is hiding something."

Cormac grunted in acknowledgement.

"I mean to find out what it is." Doraan narrowed his eyes at the steps Zev had descended.

"The men have been talking," Cormac cut in. "They aren't happy with our course. What do you think you will find in the North?"

Doraan turned from him and limped toward the railing to lean heavily against it, looking out over the calm sea. "Answers."

"Answers to what?"

He spun, fury rising to the surface. "To this curse! To sorcery!" He stopped, chest rising and falling with one final angry breath before he turned, leaning once again over the railing and whispering, "To why my parents don't care."

Cormac said nothing for a long time before stepping beside him. "How do you hope to find these answers?"

"I don't know, Cormac!" he yelled, throwing his hands up into the air before slamming them back onto the wooden beam. "I don't know. But I'm done sitting back and letting my life pass me by. I want to go back. I want to live the life I once had again." Cormac remained silent, so Doraan continued, "There has to be a way, something that will break it. I've been a ghost for ten years. I want to be seen again." He sighed, sinking further against the railing. "I am taking us to the channel. It's the only place I know of that is directly connected to sorcery."

According to legend, the Channel of Efferra was created during the Ungifted Revolution when the Sorcerers were fleeing. In their attempt to find safety, the most powerful of the Sorcerers combined their gifts to create the Temple of Gorria and, in so doing, broke the world, leaving a raging river of rapids and whirlpools no ship could sail through. He knew it was foolish to go there, but he was desperate and it was the only idea he had. The Channel of Effera was the only place he knew that was directly linked to Sorcery.

Cormac's nostrils flared. "There is nothing in the channel but death, Doraan."

"I've been thinking a lot about this, and studying through some of the histories. It could lead us to the Temple," Doraan said. "It's the only thing that makes sense."

Cormac sighed, "It's just a tale, Doraan. There is no Temple of Gorria. It's nothing more than a myth."

Doraan knew there was truth to Cormac's words but he didn't want to listen. The Temple *was* a legend. No one had *actually* seen it before. It was a story told in pubs and sung about in sonnets, but it was Doraan's only hope, because the Temple of Gorria had not been built on land. The irony was not lost on him, that the Temple—an entirely Sorcerer built structure—was the only place he could actually step upon and possibly the only place that could help him break free from the chains of his curse.

It was said to be floating out on the sea. Per the legend, it housed the most powerful Sorcerers left in the realm, hidden on the water as a sanctuary for any Gifted fleeing the Empire.

His desperation would cause him to do just about anything, even if it meant coming face-to-face with Sorcerers. He might hate them, *might* want them all eradicated from the realm just like his father, but it was a necessary evil. He needed them to get rid of the curse, but once it was broken and he returned home, he would ensure the entire Temple was destroyed with them in it.

"It's a fool's errand." Cormac's voice thundered through Doraan's thoughts.

"It's the only hope I have left, Cormac."

"There's no use in chasing fairytales, Doraan. They will only let you down time and again."

Doraan didn't respond, only stared at the swells crashing against the ship's hull. The tension was so thick in the air between them that even the cool sea breeze couldn't cut through it, ricocheting overhead, rattling the ropes and rigging high above them.

He knew it was petty and immature, but the words spilled free from his lips before he could stop them, "Well, it's a good thing I'm the Captain then."

Cormac's shoulders tensed at his words and he turned away from Doraan, leaving him with a clipped, "Aye, aye, Captain."

Doraan sighed as he watched his quartermaster leave. There was an incessant ache in his chest. He rubbed at it, massaging the flesh over his heart. It had been there since he visited home. He hadn't known what to expect when he visited, having put it off for so many years, but what he had walked into, the conversations he overheard, were not at all what he expected.

Doraan grabbed onto the railing of the steps leading to the helm, and slowly pulled his way up them, one step at a time until he was at the top. The sea was quiet tonight, the wind a faint breeze that kissed across his face as the ship cut through the calm waters. He closed his eyes against it, feeling the ocean's presence. He loved early mornings like these. Alone at the helm, the tranquil night offered him a small ounce of peace.

Doraan looked out over the beauty of the horizon, watching as the sun's rays began to lighten the sky, revealing the solid line between it and the dark blue of the ocean. He surveyed the bubbling white between the water's ripples, the swells moving fluidly along the surface of the sea, rocking the ship as it sailed over them. As much as he loved the ocean, this wasn't the way he wanted to live. It wasn't what he had spent his life preparing for. It was a hard life, so unlike how he had lived before. A life of solitude and anger. A life he didn't want.

Much of their time was spent floating in the Awndar Sea. Its warmth and depth, a constant companion, provided calm waters and an endless supply of fish. Not many sailed that far south, because no one knew what lay beyond it. Some thought it was just endless seas and certain death, others argued it ended at a cliff, a bottomless pit at the edge of the world.

Doraan often found himself wondering if he sailed far enough away from his home, far enough out into the Awndar Sea, would the curse be broken? Would the distance somehow set him free? Might he find another piece of land, a distant world where he could step foot and make a new life for himself? But deep down he knew that was only a dream—a fruitless wish. A curse didn't work that way. No distance, however great, could break it. There was only one way to break it and he had given up on it a long time ago, accepting his fate as a pirate stuck upon the sea. He had never really given it much thought, because to break the curse, he had to sacrifice his own life. Even being a pirate left to sail the endless ocean seemed a better fate than death.

His hand began to tingle and he looked down, only now noticing how hard he was gripping the ship's wheel. He released it, hand throbbing as the blood rushed back into it.

With a heavy sigh, Doraan pressed his palms into his eyes, rubbing as pressure built behind them.

"The Temple isn't in the channel," a lilting voice came from the shadows, only adding to the tension that had yet to leave Doraan's neck and shoulders.

He looked up at Forcina as she sauntered out from her hiding place. "Two visits in two days. Must be my lucky week."

Forcina narrowed her eyes at him, placing a hand on her amply curved hip.

"Haven't you better things to do than eavesdrop on my conversations, Forcina?"

"Oh I have many things I could be doing, but watching your pitiful life is just far too entertaining." She wound a lock of her ruby hair around a perfectly manicured finger. "Your scheme is useless. The Sorcerers of this world are long gone, forced out by your pig of a father." She spat upon the ground at the mention of his father.

"At least I'm not sitting around doing nothing. At least I'm trying to claim my life back."

"And for what?" She crossed her arms over her chest, slowly circling him. "To go back to a family who doesn't care about you? They have all but forgotten you. Do you know they are planning to crown a new heir? It's no use, Doraan. You can't win." Her smile was filled with mischief; it made his skin tingle as if it were on fire.

His eyes frosted over, sending shards of ice her way. These mind games she constantly played were exhausting. "I have not lost yet."

Her smirk morphed into something far more sinister as the wind picked up, howling like an angry ghost. Her voice rose over the raging storm as she laughed, "It's only a matter of time."

Doraan gritted his teeth, holding his ground as the wind threatened to sweep him up into the air. He leaned into it, pressing his foot hard into the ship's surface, until with one final gust she was gone and the final sound of her echoing cackle faded into the night with her.

10

KAMIRA

Kamira didn't return to the crew's quarters. Instead, she wandered to the stern of the ship. On any normal vessel, it would be the location of the Captain's quarters, but if she had learned anything over the past few days on the *Cursed Soul*, it was that this ship was *not* normal. So instead of the stern housing the Captain's quarters, it housed the galley.

She grabbed a piece of bread from one of the long dining tables before crawling through one of the four large windows that provided a spectacular view of the trailing ocean. Perching along the small ledge, she allowed her feet to dangle and took a deep, calming breath of the fresh sea air before blowing it out with a sigh and biting into the chunk of bread.

"Blazing biscuits!" she cursed. The bread was so stale, she brought a hand up to touch her mouth, certain she had broken one of her teeth. "How can anyone even eat this?" she grunted, tossing it into the bubbling sea below.

Kamira rubbed her tired eyes. She supposed this new life was what she deserved—one full of long days, hard work, and stale bread.

Looking up at the night sky, she watched as the stars winked in and out and wondered if her life would ever be normal again. Something had obviously happened to these men, something to make them turn their backs from whatever life they once had to live this life of piracy.

Maybe like called to like. Maybe the sea had brought her to this ship for a reason. But in all honesty, did anyone ever choose to be a pirate? An outlaw? Or did it choose them?

Her mind wandered to the young Captain's wooden leg. No one would have chosen a harsh life on the sea — one that could only be survived by thieving and constantly putting your life on the line. That didn't seem like any way to live at all. She wished the Captain would have let her examine his leg. That wooden contraption couldn't be comfortable and her gifts could help him tremendously.

Kamira's mother, even though she forbade Kamira from ever using her abilities, had used her own gifts in sorcery on occasion to help people. It was one of the few things she admired about her mother. To mask her healing sorcery, she used salves concocted of beeswax, scented oils, and dried herbs made with the rarest healing plants. It was the most dangerous thing her mother ever did, because the ability to heal marked her as a Legion—a Sorcerer of all four elements.

Kamira recalled when her own abilities revealed themselves at the young age of seven. Her parents had thrown her a grand birthday party with mountains of presents and a pony. Luckily, the only ones in attendance were her mother, father, and brother, Adonis. Being taught at home by her mother until the age of eighteen hadn't given Kamira the opportunity to make many friends.

She could remember every minute detail of that very morning. Her father had brought out a massive lemon cake drizzled with beautiful yellow icing and surrounded by spring flowers with seven candles arranged in a ring—their flickering flames glowing like beacons welcoming her into a new year of life. When he set the cake in front of her, she closed her eyes and made her birthday wish. When an unfamiliar tingle coursed through her, it invoked an excitement that her wish had come true. The thrill was quickly extinguished when her mother screamed and her father cursed. The table cloth had been engulfed by flames, and the candles had not been blown out, but strengthened into bright strings of flame that blazed toward the ceiling. Kamira screamed alongside her mother and pushed herself away from the table. Adonis sent a wave of water over the table to drown the fire, drenching the cake and presents.

A flicker drew Kamira's attention back to the present as she looked to her left, where a lantern hung, fire dancing within its glass case. It was ironic how fire was the first element of her gifts to reveal itself, since it was the most unruly of elements and the only one that she still struggled to grasp. She couldn't even use it to light a candle. It was wild and angry—the polar opposite to the gentle fluidity of water. Water ebbed and flowed in rhythmic patterns whereas fire jerked and sputtered erratically. It scared her more than any other element.

Air had a current, a course, and direction—similar to the way water moved. Earth came most naturally to her after water. Not only was it made of dirt, but it combined air and water into a solid formation and could easily be manipulated.

The use of all four elements at once connected a Sorcerer to life itself. They could bring a person back from the brink of death or steal their ability to live. Her brother told her that long ago, it was said a Legion could even raise someone from the dead. The idea of that made her skin crawl, and she scratched at her arms, goosebumps rising along her flesh.

Kamira didn't think she would ever be able to make her gifts go that far. She hadn't heard of anyone being able to do so in hundreds of years. That much power only belonged in fairytales—like in the tale of the War of Four Kings. In that story, a master wielder of the four elements named Honoria raised an army of the dead from their endless slumber and ended the thousand year war for good—but it was just a parable created to teach peace and held no truth. It wasn't possible to *actually* bring something back from death. Death was an ultimatum. It was irreversible, and not even a Legion could change something so final.

That story was one of her favorites because of how colorful the elemental Sorcerers were depicted. She could picture them vividly in her mind.

The myth described the water elementalists as Udina with cerulean skin that made them nearly invisible in the water and varying shades of green hair like the kelp and seaweed of the ocean. The fire elementalists were called Salamanders—their skin described as blinding pink with hair ranging from orange to dark red, like a forever burning flame. The air elementalists were called Nymphs, their skin and hair as white as snow, and the earth elementalists were named Gnomes, their skin and hair able to change, replicating their surroundings. They had always seemed the most dangerous to Kamira since they could resemble any elementalist they wanted, blending into a Salamander army only to annihilate them from the inside. She shivered at the thought, wrapping her arms tightly around herself.

Kamira looked at her fair skin and wondered if the ability of the Gnomes to change their looks had simply been forgotten. If she or any other earth and Legion Sorcerer tried hard enough, could they become anyone they wanted? It would solve all of her problems. She could change herself into someone else, create an entirely new persona, and never worry about anyone finding her.

She huffed out a weak laugh at the thought, shoulders sagging as she watched the waves fanning out as the ship cut through the water. It was just a story, an ancient tale passed throughout history, and nothing more.

Kamira looked to the horizon. It was still dark enough that the sea and sky blended together, the stars the only distinction between them. If she didn't sleep tonight, she would pass out tomorrow and fall from the crow's nest to a watery death. She was hungry and exhausted, but tomorrow was a new day—a day to fully embrace her new life and be grateful for the fact that she still had a life to live.

The flame still flickered at the corner of her vision, dancing in its usual manic state. Kamira closed her eyes and blew out a breath, flicking her exhalation like throwing a knife at the flame. When she opened her eyes, the lantern was extinguished with smoke rising in its wake. She smiled and headed back inside, hoping to get a few more hours of rest before sunrise.

11

Kamira

Kamira's eyes shot open at the sound of shouting and loud movements above her. Empty hammocks swung around her, blankets and pillows littered the floor. Not a soul remained in the crew's quarters. Why had no one woken her? Possibly, the Captain had thought she needed more sleep after her late night escapade, but she highly doubted it.

She crawled out of bed, sprinting out the door and up the steps just in time to hear a voice yell out, "All hands to quarters!"

The crew swarmed the deck, barking orders, carrying what looked like gunpowder and large cannonballs. She grabbed onto a crew member's arm she had yet to learn the name of, stopping him in his tracks. "What's going on?"

"We're making chase to a supply ship." He nodded toward the ship's bow before pulling his arm from her grasp and walking on toward a cannon that another crew was preparing.

Kamira furrowed her brows, turning her gaze toward the bow where, sure enough, a ship could be seen in the distance. She spun, heading for the helm and the Captain positioned behind the wheel, a smug look plastered on his face.

"You're going to attack that ship?" Kamira yelled, taking the steps two at a time.

"We are going to *pillage* that ship," he corrected without hesitation.

"Then why are you preparing the cannons?"

"Curious as always I see." He chuckled. "The pirate who is unprepared for any outcome rests at the bottom of the sea."

"You aren't going to hurt anyone though, right?"

"That depends entirely on them now, doesn't it?" he asked with a wry grin.

It was as if all that had transpired between them the previous night was forgotten, and she found herself rolling her eyes at his response. What had she expected? They were pirates after all. They pillaged and plundered, probably causing more than one passing ship to sink. Hundreds of lives had doubtlessly been lost at their hands. Her breath quickened at the thought, throat constricting as she placed a hand over her racing heart, willing her breathing to slow down as black began to cloud her vision. She would not pass out on the helm for the whole crew to see. Kamira closed her eyes and blew out a shaking breath.

"Are you alright, boy?" The Captain shifted his gaze down to her, one eyebrow raised in curiosity. "Don't get weak knees on me, landlubber. This is the life of a pirate. You best get used to it now." He slapped her on the back and she stumbled forward, almost plummeting down the four rickety steps leading to the main deck.

She knew he was right. This was her life now, like it or not. It was the price she had to pay for what she had done. And she would take the life of a pirate over the gallows any day if it meant she had a life.

A thought suddenly sprung to her mind. What would she do when her monthly courses came? *Shit.* That would be a hard one to hide, especially since these were the only clothes she had. If an accident were to occur, well, she would be done for. Her ruse over. And what would they do to her then? "Bloody skies," she breathed.

"What was that?" Captain Doraan questioned.

"What should I do? How can I help?"

The first truly genuine smile she had seen on the Captain, spread across his face. It was strange how something as simple as a smile could transform him from someone harsh and threatening into someone trying to find their way in this world, just like her. Kamira swallowed the lump that formed in her throat, placing her cold hands on either side of her heated cheeks to cool them down. She wasn't sure she was ready for her first pillaging.

"Cabin boy, *you* will be our powder monkey."

"Your what?"

"You're in charge of making sure we don't run out of gunpowder if the time ever arises for us to use cannon and pistol."

"Great," she groaned. "An errand boy."

"Well, go on and get started, powder monkey. We've a pillage to prepare for. Head down to the ship's hold for the magazine and grab one of the barrels."

She tried not to roll her eyes as she left him and headed down to the main deck. They had moved considerably closer to the ship now—so close she could see the crew members running across the deck and hear the distant echo of orders being shouted. They were preparing as well, probably realizing the *Cursed Soul* was faster than their cargo ship.

Kamira sighed before taking the steps down into the belly of the ship. She wasn't exactly sure what the cartridges looked like. Hopefully they were labeled or easy to spot. She hadn't actually been down into the ship's hold yet.

As she continued her descent, a loud bang sounded overhead that shook the entire ship. She threw her arms out, pressing against either side of the passageway to steady herself. A chorus of shouting traveled through the snaking corridors. Who had fired first? She couldn't imagine a cargo vessel carrying much artillery, if any at all.

Suddenly, the walls vibrated as the ear shattering boom of cannons firing one after the other rang out, followed by the sharp crack of gunfire.

Shit! She hadn't expected an actual fight from what the Captain had told her. She assumed they wouldn't need a 'powder monkey' at all and that he had given her busy work to stay out of the way. "Shit," she cursed and hurried down into the ship's hold.

She found the magazine easily—a large brass lined room at the stern full of wooden barrels—she wrapped her arms around one, black powder spilling slightly as she hauled it out of the room and headed for the main deck.

With each step up the stairs, the shouting and cannon fire grew louder until she finally made it to the top. Just as she set foot on the deck, a high pitched hiss made her ears ring as a metal ball whizzed less than a foot in front of her. She squealed and dropped the barrel, gun powder scattering across the deck. "Blazing stars!" she screamed, bending to right the barrel before it poured out anymore of the flammable substance.

As soon as she gathered the powder, she surveyed the deck before her. It was utter chaos. Orders were bellowed left and right. Smoke filled the air and blood was splattered across the deck with no clue as to whom it had come from.

She spotted what looked like a severed finger just a few paces in front of her, cracked bone jutting out through ripped flesh. Kamira turned sharply, gagging uncontrollably as she brought a hand up over her mouth, dropping the gunpowder beside her. One of the crew jumped from the smog, ran over to her, and handed her a pistol before picking up the barrel she had so carelessly dropped. "Use it," he instructed before disappearing into the smoke.

This was warfare, she realized. That ship was no ordinary cargo vessel—it was a militia. The *Cursed Soul* was caught in the middle of a battle. The crew on the other ship were men in green uniforms with a golden sun embellished on their chests. Her eyes widened. She had seen that symbol many times before, in her northern hometown of Torheim. "The Emerald King," she whispered.

It seemed a lot had changed in the two years since she had been forced to leave her childhood home for Aksahri. From the looks of it, this self-proclaimed King had developed a full blown navy. Before she left, the King had configured a small group of rebels whose only goal was to kill and torture the Emperor's men in the smaller northern cities. There had not been any naval units. How had he even accomplished such a feat? This so-called King in the North was said to reside in Sumaaria, which was completely surrounded by the perilous Emerald Peaks. They didn't have any ways to access the sea.

Rumors of the King's ambition to gain full control over the large city of Sumaaria had spread like wildfire before she moved south. Had he finally taken the city? How else had he amassed a mighty force like this one?

If that was true, then it was only a matter of time before word of his power spread and the entirety of the North fell to him. Once that happened, he would come for the Emperor and conquer the South. Civil war was hovering just on the edge of the horizon.

Her brother's parting words to her sprang to the forefront of her mind. "*The Emerald King seeks revenge. When the first signs of war begin, you need to find a way to survive. Flee if you need to. Be smart and play the game of war and fate.*"

She watched from the top of the steps, just out of reach of the bullets soaring across the deck, wood chips flying as they embedded themselves into the *Cursed Soul*. They were losing. The crew could not keep up with the onslaught of the Emerald King's attack. They were severely outnumbered and they would all die if something wasn't done.

They needed help. They needed a Sorceress.

Kamira closed her eyes and rolled her shoulders back, standing tall. Opening her eyes, she took a deep breath, cracked her knuckles, and walked into the fray of war.

12

DORAAN

Black bloody fucking sails. Was he bad luck? Was he some kind of bad omen? This was the second ship in the past eight months that looked like nothing more than a merchant ship on the outside, yet housed a full company of soldiers. This one looked even more unassuming than the last. It was a simple brigantine vessel, one of hundreds he had seen before. Who were they? They weren't Aksahrian men. They wore colors he had never seen before, and they were strong.

A well trained militia.

The cannon fire barely ceased as they were bombarded with blast after bloody blast. That kind of ship shouldn't have had more than seven, maybe eight guns. Yet this one had double that, if not more. How had it even been constructed to hold so many? Doraan had never seen anything like it. It was absurd—a vessel created specifically for decimation—any ship that went up against it wasn't meant to sail away.

To make things worse, it had begun to piss down buckets of rain so heavily that he could hardly see his own limbs.

Waves crashed into the ship causing just as much damage to the *Cursed Soul* as the bloody cannon fire. The only reprieve was that the storm had slowed the attack of their green and gold foes down considerably. Doraan could just see their ship through the haze, taking on more damage as the onslaught of crashing waves pummeled them with a vengeance. It was almost as if the sea itself was angry with them for attacking the *Cursed Soul.*

Doraan glanced across the deck. Jorne lay unconscious, blood gushing from his head. Flashes of his own mangled leg, blood pouring from it and splintered bone jutting through the skin flew through his mind. *No, not again.* His chest constricted, making it hard to breathe. *No one will die, not in this crew.*

Doraan rubbed at the spot just above his heart and was about to call out the command to cease the attack and flee when he noticed a small figure standing on the railing of the ship's broadside, hands raised into the air.

Zev. Any breath he had left in his lungs vanished.

"Zev! Get down from there!" What in the bloody seas was the boy doing? He was standing like a target for the enemy to practice their aim. Doraan could make out more than one pistol aimed directly at the boy.

Doraan tried to get to him, tripping over debris and his own limbs. "Zev!" he yelled again, just as Cormac locked his eyes on the lad and sprinted toward him, but neither were fast enough. A deafening blast echoed through the mist and rain. Doraan froze, watching in horror as Zev was thrown backwards by the force, hitting the deck of the *Cursed Soul* with a thud that Doraan felt in his bones.

Doraan didn't take a second to think as he clambered back up to the helm and spun the wheel, yelling out commands to his crew as they fled, sailing further into the storm. His mind reeled. *Zev would be alright. He wouldn't die, not on his watch. He couldn't.* Doraan's head pounded, his heart racing as he clutched at his chest. *No one else could die.*

The further they got away from the ship, the more the storm eased and faded like a ghost, disappearing as if it had never existed. The clouds opened overhead, revealing clear blue skies and the bright morning sun as it shone down on the cerulean sea.

Doraan ignored the strangeness of the storm, waiting until they were far away from the ship before he stumbled down the steps to join the rest of the crew huddled around Zev.

The cabin boy lay in a crumpled heap upon the bridge, blood seeping into his linen shirt, spreading out like spilled wine. Jorne was pressing his hands to the wound in a feeble attempt to stop the bleeding. Doraan rushed to the lad and knelt before him. The boy's face was drained of its color, the life slowly seeping out of him only to be replaced by the pale tinge of death.

Doraan pushed Jorne's hands away and tore the lad's shirt down its center for a better look at the wound. A cloth was wrapped around the boy's chest, wet and sticky with his lifeblood. *Was he already injured before?*

It looked as if the bullet had pierced the right side of the boy's chest, but the cloth binding was so saturated with blood it was hiding the wound from view. He pushed Zev onto his side, Cormac's hands came into view as he helped to hold the boy still while Doraan looked for an exit wound, tearing through the cloth binding.

The crew gathered around, watching as Doraan revealed the bleeding hole where the bullet had exited and they loosened a collective sigh of relief. Another crew member hadn't been lost today.

The lad would need stitching, but the bullet was far from any vital areas. He would be fine as long as they could get the bleeding under control.

Doraan's fingers moved quickly as he finished shredding the binding, but as soon as he pulled it free, he froze. His eyes widened in shock as they fell upon the lad's chest.

The boy had breasts.

Zev was a girl.

13

DORAAN

"What was that ship, Cormac?" Doraan paced the length of his quartermaster's room. The boy—who was actually a girl—was currently unconscious in his quarters.

He wanted to know who she was, why she had pretended to be a boy, and what in the flaming seas she was doing up on that railing.

Cormac shook his head in response to Doraan's question. "I don't know."

"That's the second military ship this year that has been disguised as a merchant vessel."

"Something is brewing in the realm." Cormac's brows drew together.

The soldiers had been wearing a uniform Doraan had not seen before, green with a golden sun. Who were they and where did they come from? There was no indication of their origins or allegiance.

"They were well trained men. Strong," Cormac added, hands clasped behind his back as he watched Doraan continue to pace.

Cormac was always so bloody calm and poised. There was nothing that seemed to fluster the man or make him bristle. He was a stone wall—solid and unreadable. It was something Doraan had always admired about the man. Cormac always stood the voice of reason when Doraan's mind ran frantically, when anger and anxiety struck, which they often did. And right now, he was not only angry and anxious, but something far worse. He was scared.

"Something isn't right, Cormac," Doraan growled. "There is a foreign army sailing in Aksahrian waters. Do you think my father knows? Does Aksahri know?"

Doraan's visit home had been unpleasant for many reasons. If only he could have reached out, showed them that he was alive and wanted to come back home, but he couldn't—that was a truly wretched piece of the curse. What use was it to see your friends and family knowing they had no idea you were there? It only sufficed to bring suffering and heartache.

He had tried once before, on his thirteenth birthday. After a hard year at sea trying to come to terms with the curse and his new seabound life, he couldn't wait until he was able to go back home, even if it was only for a few hours. They had docked their boat behind Crescent Rock, paddling their small skiff to the shore, but the instant his foot made impact with the solid ground, his entire body shifted and became translucent in the moonlight. He brought a hand up only to look directly through it to the palm trees lining the beach. It was enough to make him jump into the boat and go straight back to the *Cursed Soul*.

Another unpleasant discovery he had learned during his visit home was that his father was ill. He no longer sat at the helm of the Empire, but was instead bedridden with fever. Doraan hadn't stayed long enough to see how truly bad the illness was, but the Emperor being ill with war looming wasn't good.

"Did you see or hear any talk of a rising foe against the Empire while we were in Aksahri?" Doraan asked Cormac. He hadn't heard or seen anything during his short visit that suggested they were preparing for war. If he was being completely honest, everything had looked pretty much the same since he had left all those years ago.

Cormac shook his head again with a sorrowful sigh. "Nothing."

"Me either. I overheard many conversations while moving through the palace, and I didn't hear a word about a rising enemy." He grunted. "They were more concerned with the week's dinner menu. They didn't seem like an

Emperor and Empress preparing for battle, securing the Empire."

Doraan came to a halt, rubbing the relentless pain in his thigh. "This isn't good, Cormac. That was no mere rebel force or newly formed militia—that was a navy ready to attack. We are lucky to have gotten away with as little damage to the ship as we did and no casualties. If my father doesn't know anything about this…" he paused, rubbing a hand down over his face, "We need to do something, warn them, help them."

With the Emperor ill and no apparent heir to replace him, the kingdom was fragile. If this enemy was even remotely aware of Aksahri's vulnerability, they would strike soon.

In his father's absence, Aksahri was being run by the Peregrine Council, a group of power hungry idiots too concerned with their own social standings to care about things such as border and naval patrols. Anyone could enter the capital from the Aksahrian shores with little to no defense stopping them. If the Aksahrian military wasn't prepared, then the Empire's capital was little more than a sitting duck. The city wouldn't survive an attack. Aksahri was so crowded with people that civilians outnumbered soldiers fifty to one.

His father had never seemed concerned about an attack on his city. With the Sorcerers gone, he would say, *"The people rejoice! The Sorcerers are gone. There is no threat to our Empire. We won.*" He was too proud to realize that even if the Sorcerers were gone—which was highly unlikely—not all the Ungifted agreed with his dictatorship. The possibility of an uprising could never be completely ruled out.

But what his father had always seemed to ignore was that many of the Sorcerers had simply gone into hiding after being forced from their homes and slaughtered on the streets. Many had found other ways to survive. Even with the military groups specifically created to snuff out any Sorcerers, there would always be some that survived. Who knew how many were hiding right under his father's nose? This new enemy could very well be those survivors.

Doraan thought about the storm that had come almost out of nowhere during the attack. The sea and skies had grown angry in a matter of moments—almost as if they had been coaxed or created. Was this new enemy building an army of Sorcerers? If that were true, the entire Empire would have no chance of survival. The only reason his father and the Ungifted rebellion had worked all those years ago was because of the element of surprise. The Sorcerers had no idea the Ungifted were planning a mutiny. If war really was just over the hill and they had an army of Sorcerers ready to attack, it would be a bloodbath.

Doraan closed his eyes, rolling his neck from one shoulder to the other in a feeble attempt to relax them. He didn't have the ability to help. He could do nothing but sit and watch the onslaught. The only thing he could do to try and help his people was to break the curse, and he had to do it now. He couldn't just sit and watch his people, his home, crumble to ash in front of him. There was only one hope he had left. A single spark that, if ignited, could change everything.

The Temple of Gorria.

It had to be real. History told of a powerful assembly of Sorcerers known as the Tetrad. Legend depicted them as the most powerful Sorcerers to ever live—even more powerful than Forcina herself. If anyone could help him, it was them. And when he was done with them, curse broken and forgotten, he would finish them off before they could take back the Empire.

The only problem was there wasn't any concrete proof of the Tetrad or the Temple. He was basing his entire plan on myth. His own father had laughed in his face whenever he mentioned the Tetrad and the Temple, telling him to stop daydreaming about fantasies.

If anyone had information about them, where they were, if they were still alive and hidden in the realm, it would be the Brothers of the Spring. The Brothers were a known religious cult buried deep in the forested hills of the North. They weren't Sorcerers, but Ungifted who believed Sorcerers to be the children of the old gods, and beings to be worshiped. The Brothers believed the old gods to have birthed the Sorcerers from the Spring of Zjanoak, an underground water system full of rich minerals and supposed healing properties. They bathed and drank from the Spring in sacred rituals, believing it to grant them gifts of their own as well as a longer life span. Doraan had learned all about them in his history classes. They were hunted just as rigorously as the Sorcerers because of their beliefs.

"We need to find the Spring of Zjanoak and speak to the Brothers. We need answers, Cormac."

The quartermaster's nostrils flared, the only show of emotion he would ever let slip. "We cannot, Doraan. It's on land. And even if we could, no one knows its exact location. It might not even be in the North like your history books have told you. There are also rumors that it's buried beneath the ruins of Barrum, in the sand dunes just above Aksahri. No one actually knows where it is. "

"We have to try."

"Even if we were to try, to attempt to find someone to help us, we wouldn't be able to speak with them. We have never been able to interact with anyone on or off this ship except for..."

"Zev," Doraan finished for him. "Do you think we can use her, Cormac? Maybe she could go on land and speak to someone? Somehow extract the information we need."

"There's no way to tell if she has fallen under the curse. She might not be able to anymore."

Doraan shrugged. "Only one way to find out."

Cormac cast an uncharacteristic smirk at him.

"What? Why are you looking at me like that?"

"I like the lass. She's not afraid to get her hands dirty and she's worked as hard as any of the men since she's been here."

Doraan snorted and turned toward the cabin door. "I think I liked her more as an unruly boy than a headstrong woman."

Cormac laughed. "I've always known she was a woman, since the very moment you brought her out from below deck."

Doraan spun, nearly losing his balance and toppling over, "Come again?"

"Honestly Doraan, most of the crew knew. You would have to be blind not to have noticed. She's a sweet thing with a lovely face and a petite stature. Young boys don't typically have curves like a woman. She attempted to hide hers under those baggy clothes, but it didn't cover her frame fully." Cormac chuckled, shaking his head at Doraan's bewildered stare. "Plus, I've never known a young lad with as quick a wit and sharp a tongue as her."

"And none of you thought this might be important information to tell me?" he grumbled.

"It didn't matter. She wanted us to think she was a boy, and what we saw was a truly frightened woman who needed a place to stay. Lucky enough for her, she stumbled upon the only pirate ship that would have the heart and honor to help her. So we played along, letting her pretend to be a boy, hoping she would feel safe and comfortable around us."

Doraan listened to Cormac's words, realizing the truth of them and the kindness he had been surrounded by all these years. He was thankful for them, for this crew he didn't deserve by his side. These men who didn't deserve what had happened to them.

He watched as Cormac's face transformed into a look of sorrow. "She reminds me of Fiona."

Doraan frowned at the change of tone in Cormac's voice as he mentioned his daughter's name. Fiona had only been ten at the time the curse took root, pulling them away from their former lives. Cormac had missed practically every important moment of his daughter's life. He knew that was a big reason why Cormac had taken Doraan under his wing and been a father to him during his time of need. He was forever grateful that Cormac was the one on the docks that day Forcina cursed them. He couldn't imagine the last ten years stuck on a ship with one of his father's cocky admirals or lazy naval captains.

During their visit home, Cormac had been able to go and see his little girl for the first time. Although Doraan supposed she wasn't little anymore. She was a grown woman now.

"She's getting married," Cormac said with a weary sigh, hands clasped tightly behind his back as he looked down at his boots. "I've not wanted to give you any false hope, Doraan. I don't want to see you hurt any further or completely dejected if there is no other way to break the curse."

Doraan held his breath as Cormac lifted his head and ice blue eyes bore into him.

"But if we can do it, if the girl can help us... I want to be able to walk my little girl down the aisle." He closed his eyes for a long moment, and swallowed hard before opening them once more and continuing, "For the first time since the curse bound us all together, I feel hope. I don't think the girl being here is by chance, Doraan. I think it's fate."

His words wrapped around Doraan like a warm blanket, melting a layer of tension from his shoulders. Cormac was the most important person in his life, and he was giving Doraan his full support. It wasn't until this moment that Doraan even realized how much he needed those words to come from Cormac. The weight of his previous disapproval had been so heavy, but now he felt so much lighter. He felt energized for the first time in forever.

Doraan reached out his hand as a wide smile spread across his face. Cormac returned the smile in full, the corners of his eyes crinkling and grasped Doraan's forearm before pulling him in for a crushing hug. Doraan laughed, returning the embrace just as firmly before they both broke away and Doraan said, "It's settled then. Set a course for Torheim. It's the closest northern city to us.

Let's hope we find what we are looking for there." His chest rose with a heavy sigh before he added, "I've an imposter to question."

14

KAMIRA

Kamira moaned as she forced her eyes to open. She felt like she had been tied to a team of horses and dragged through the cobbled streets of Aksahri. Every muscle in her body ached.

She groaned while attempting to push herself up into a sitting position, gritting her teeth as pain shot through her torso. She yelled out, falling back against the pillow with a loud curse, gripping her side. It was then she startlingly realized that her binding was no longer holding down her breasts. *That couldn't be right.* She grabbed them just to be sure, "Bleeding stars."

"Bleeding stars is right." The Captain was leaning against the doorframe, arms crossed over his chest, a single brow raised in interest.

She instantly released her breasts and pulled the bed sheet up to her neck. Well, on the bright side, she wouldn't have to figure out a way to hide her monthly courses anymore.

"Captain, I can…"

He didn't give her a chance to continue. "What were you doing standing on the railing in the middle of a battle? Were you trying to get yourself killed?"

She froze, stunned by his first choice of questioning. "No…no, I was trying to help," she stammered.

"You had no weapon, no protection, no nothing. How exactly were you expecting to help? Did you think that by just standing there waiting to be shot you would miraculously save us all? That it would somehow make the other ship stop firing?" He frowned and stepped into the room, coming closer with each spoken word.

"No! I don't know…" She wouldn't in a million years tell him she was a Sorceress and had only been trying to help by using her gifts of water and wind — that she had been the one to invoke the storm and the massive waves of the sea in an attempt to cease the enemy fire.

"It was dimwitted and foolish! This is the exact reason I should have never let you stay aboard this ship. It's too dangerous. I've lost too many men, too much blood has been shed upon the boards of the *Cursed Soul*. Too many lives lost. If something had happened to you… I've had enough bloodshed on my hands. If I had known you were a…" He stopped his eyes slowly traveling down the length of her body, and sea and sky help her, she could feel the heat climbing to her cheeks and knew they were bright red with her embarrassment. The shirt she had on suddenly felt far too thin, and the sheet she held over her hanging breasts felt invisible under his piercing gaze. She tucked the bedsheet under her armpits and crossed her arms over her chest to hide them from view.

The Captain sighed heavily and rubbed his weary eyes, his body sagging as if the weight of the entire ocean sat upon his shoulders. He collapsed and took a seat in the chair beside her bed. "Why did you board this ship?"

She opened her mouth to speak, but he held up a hand. "Before you say anything, I want to know the truth. There is no use lying."

She stared at him for a long moment, emotion rising like a burning ember up her throat causing her eyes to water. "I—I had no other choice. I had to get as far away from Aksahri as I could."

"Why?"

She opened and closed her mouth several times before the tears spilled free and she choked out, "I can't say."

The Captain remained calm and said, "Why not?"

"B—because it's too awful!" she sobbed, bringing the sheet up to dry the ceaseless waterfall of tears spilling down her cheeks.

She blinked to clear her blurry vision and saw the Captain slowly close his eyes and take a deep, steadying breath. He rose, walking to his dresser and revealed a handkerchief tucked into the top drawer. He offered it to her with a weary smile before settling back down into his chair and resting his elbows on his knees, "I'm trying to stay calm here, but you are trying my patience."

Kamira blew her nose into the handkerchief and watched as his jaw clenched, nostrils flaring.

"If the reason is as awful as you say, then you being on this ship has put the entire crew in danger, do you realize that?" His voice was rising, his movements growing more agitated. "If someone is after you, you need to tell me now so we can prepare for whatever might be coming."

The tears had finally slowed enough for her to speak more coherently, "I—if I tell you, you'll want me off the ship and I've nowhere else to go."

The Captain rubbed at his Temples. "Do you think we are the type of men to do that?"

"I don't know, are you?"

"I promise you," he said through clenched teeth. "No matter what you say, we won't throw you off this ship or leave you to fend for yourself. Happy?"

"Shake on it." She held out a hand, still holding the sheet up to her chin with her other hand.

The Captain grunted and grasped her hand, his rough skin brushing against her palm.

"Now that we have that out of the way, tell me, what did you need to get away from so badly that you went so far as to stow away on a ship full of pirates and disguise yourself as a boy?"

Kamira closed her eyes tight against the fresh set of tears, and with a shaky breath, whispered, "Murder."

His entire body went as rigid as a statue. Then, ever so slowly, his jaw tensed and his brows drew together. "You murdered someone?"

"Yes," she squeaked, gulping at the admission.

"Who?" His expression didn't change. He stared at her with those intense eyes, his brows knitted together into a frown that creased the skin around them.

"My–" She looked away from him, lip quivering as she brought trembling fingers to brush her throat, remembering the feel of large hands squeezing as she choked. The events of that night were burned into her mind like a branding iron.

"Zev?"

She let out a shuddering breath, the memories scattering away. "My husband."

She glanced at the Captain again, who didn't move or even blink an eye before he sputtered, "Y—you're married?" and pushed up from the chair he was sitting in to pace the small perimeter of the room. "To whom?" he finally asked, pausing his stride.

"To Lord Tarkiin Asharr of the Emperor's Peregrine Council."

The Captain's eyes went wide and he swayed, grabbing onto the back of the chair to steady himself, "Y—you killed Tarkiin?"

Kamira raised a brow at the way he said Tarkiin's name, as if he had known the man personally. As if they had been close enough for the Captain not to call him Lord.

The Captain sat down with a heavy thud into the chair once again, slouching as he crossed one arm over his broad chest, bringing the opposite hand over his mouth, and let his head fall back to rest on the back of the chair. "So you are fleeing for the murder of your husband, who just so happens to be one of the Emperor's most trusted advisors, the head of house Asharr, and the fifth most powerful man in the Kingdom? Did I get all of that right?"

"Yes." She wanted to tell him why. She wanted him to know that it was in self-defense and not out of malicious intent, but she supposed it didn't matter. She had killed him nonetheless and she wasn't sure how to even voice the reason why. The words were stuck in her throat like thick honey, unmoving.

"Why?" he questioned.

She thought about that for a long moment before saying with a shrug of her shoulders, "It was either him or me." It was the only thing that felt right to say, and it wasn't a lie. It really had been her life or his. She didn't have the courage to tell the full story just yet. Not with it still so fresh.

Kamira waited for more questions, for him to yell at her, or take her up to the bridge and punish her with some awful task. She wouldn't fault him for it—she was a fugitive hiding out on his ship and had put all their lives at risk.

She was taken aback when he burst out into a chorus of boisterous laughter. It was so out of place and uncharacteristic that she couldn't help but chuckle in return, instantly regretting it when pain shot through her torso. Her humor quickly turned into a series of agonizing coughs.

"Don't laugh," he said, wiping away the tears that had pooled in his eyes. "You'll tear your stitches." He stared at her with an odd look and then shook his head, a smile spreading across his lips. "Well, Ze...actually I haven't even bothered to ask, what is your name? I take it Zev isn't your real one."

She smirked, shaking her head. "It's Kamira."

"Nice to meet the real you, Kamira. You can call me Doraan."

She nodded, her smile stretching a little further.

"Well, someone was bound to kill that fat, pompous bastard one day. He had it coming to him."

Kamira almost choked on her own saliva. "Y—y—you know him?" she stuttered. "I find it hard to believe a pirate would know Lord Tarkiin outside of the gallows."

"I didn't say it was a friendly acquaintance," he said with a wink. "I didn't need to know him for long to realize he was a clod of a man. I don't blame you for killing him."

"It was an accident," she whispered. She couldn't bear anyone thinking of her as a careless murderer who went around killing men for sport.

He was quiet before turning his large light-brown eyes on her, "Can I ask what happened? Why did it come down to the survival of either you or him?"

She looked away, suddenly feeling cold and far too exposed. She pulled the sheets up over her head, covering herself completely, "Another time, maybe."

"Fair enough," he offered.

She brought the sheet back down to reveal her eyes, watching as a small smile quirked on the Captain's mouth.

He cast his gaze down toward his feet then, the smile fading from his face. A long silence stretched between them, and she could see the cogs of his mind churning with whatever he wanted to ask her.

When he finally looked at her, she didn't expect him to say, "I have a favor to ask of you."

She furrowed her brows, bringing her full face out from behind the sheet. "A favor?"

"Yes."

Why did he look so damn serious all of the sudden? She almost preferred the scowl. "What sort of favor?" she asked hesitantly.

"We need you to go ashore once we get to our destination."

She cocked her head as questions swam through her mind, and she finally settled on, "I'm confused."

Doraan rested his elbows on his knees and leaned forward, clasping his hands tightly together in front of him.

"We need information. A certain kind of information." He paused, clearing his throat. "It...it could be dangerous."

"Um, okay...I'm still not following. Why exactly am *I* the person you need to go get this information? Why don't you or one of your crew go and get it yourselves? I'm fairly certain any one of you would be a far better choice than me," she said, raising a brow. *Why was he being so cryptic? What a strange conversation.*

"We can't."

"You can't or you won't?"

He closed his eyes, shoulders rising with tension as he sucked in a breath but never exhaled, "We can't."

"Why not?" Kamira queried.

"We can't go on land."

She snorted. How stupid did he think she was? Who couldn't go on land? Were they famous outlaws? Actually, the more she thought about that the more plausible it seemed. "What did you all do? Accidentally steal from one of the Emperor's personal ships?" She chuckled.

He laughed but there was no humor in it. "No, we physically can't step foot on land."

She didn't say anything, just stared at him. They couldn't physically go on land? Why the blazing seas not? What happened if they tried to? Would they explode or something?

When he didn't freely offer any further explanation, she finally said, "Well, are you going to tell me why or just continue to stare at me as if I might bolt out the door at any second?"

He brought a hand up to cover his face and leaned back in his chair again, dragging the hand down to his neck with a sigh.

"Well?"

"We are cursed," he huffed.

She waited for more, but he stayed silent, which only made her roll her eyes. "Seriously, that's the response you're going with? You couldn't come up with anything better to tell me, so you devised some absurd explanation to avoid the truth? You asked *me* to go and get some kind of dangerous information, but you won't tell me the actual reason you need me to get it?"

"That is the actual reason."

She glowered at him for a long moment, watching as a small bead of sweat gathered at his hairline before dripping free and rolling down his forehead. "No," she said.

"No, what?"

"No, I won't go ashore and get you your mysterious information. Not until you tell me the truth," She lifted her chin.

"I am telling you the truth!" He groaned, rubbing his eyes with his thumb and forefinger before leaning toward her, resting his elbows on his knees. "Okay, listen. I know it sounds insane, but I'm not lying to you. You can ask any one of the crew and they will tell you the same thing. We were all cursed ten years ago by a Sorceress named Forcina. She cursed us to never walk on land again. We can't do it even if we tried. For ten years, we haven't even been able to take the ship closer than ten miles from shore."

Kamira's eyes glazed over. Cursed by a Sorceress? She had never heard of such a thing. That would mean that the Sorceress could control her words as if she were controlling an element, binding them into existence. There was no possible way to do that.

"A Sorcerer can't curse someone. I don't think their gifts work that way. I've never heard of anything like that," she said, her eyes finally coming back into focus.

He huffed a laugh. "I assure you, they most certainly can. This entire ship has been cursed. We can easily prove it to you."

"Why?"

"Why were we cursed?"

She nodded, eyes narrowed on him.

He looked away from her, his expression shadowed in sadness. "She cursed me as a punishment to my father for killing her son. She wanted him to feel the same pain, only worse. She wanted him to know I wasn't gone, but trapped and never able to come home."

"That seems a harsh punishment for you, who did nothing. Why didn't she just curse him?" She didn't believe this curse scenario for a second. Something else was going on here, but she would placate him to find out whatever information she could.

"It wouldn't have had the same effect I suppose. As the saying goes, an eye for an eye," Doraan shrugged. "She wanted it to be equal. A son for a son."

"So, your crew is cursed too?"

"When she cursed me, she cursed this ship, which was docked on one of the smaller Aksahrian piers. She cursed all those who were on that pier at the time, too. There used to be twenty of us, but now there are eighteen, plus you." He looked at her with squinted eyes, biting his lower lip as if she were a puzzle to be solved.

"Why are you looking at me like that?"

"Because until you, no one has been able to board this ship."

She huffed. *Sure they couldn't.* "Well, that *is* weird," she said slowly.

She had been so fortunate that night to stumble across the ship, she hadn't thought twice about boarding it or how she had even gotten next to it. The last thing she remembered before the *Cursed Soul* had loomed above her was drifting alone in the open sea. "The night I fled, I rowed as far out to sea as I could, until my arms nearly fell off, and then, suddenly, your ship was beside me, almost as if it wanted me to come aboard. To save me. If I hadn't come across your ship, there's no knowing what could have happened. I probably would have died in the middle of the ocean or been caught by the Aksahrian guard." She shrugged before ending with, "Maybe your ship knew I needed help and saved me."

The corner of his mouth curved upward. "Maybe it did."

She thought about all he had said and mulled over it in her mind, drawing her own conclusions. "So, you think since I was able to board your vessel, and I wasn't cursed with you, that I can go on land? Do I have it right?"

His eyes were alight with something akin to excitement. "Exactly."

"So, what sort of information do you need me to get for you?" She supposed since they had done so much for her, she needed to repay them, and if this is what they needed she would do it.

He took a deep, shuddering breath before saying, "I need you to go to Torheim and find out any information you possibly can about the location of the Brothers of the Spring of Zjanoak."

Kamira froze. She tried to swallow the lump that had begun to clog in her throat. That was one of the first places the Aksahrian guard would come looking for her. Not only that, if she went home, she would find out what had happened to her parents due to her actions. It almost felt better *not* knowing. Had her father lost his position? Had they lost the house? Were they even still alive after what she had done? The Empire had been known to punish others for the acts of a family member.

She pushed the thoughts away as soon as they sprung forth. She didn't need to go to Torheim to find that information for them, and she knew for certain her parents were fine. They were survivors and would find a way to avoid the Empire's blades.

Kamira chuckled. "Tonight might just be your lucky night, Captain Doraan."

He arched a single dark brow, cocking his head slightly, "Why is that?"

"Because I already know where the Brothers of the Spring of Zjanoak are."

15

DORAAN

The further north they sailed, the rougher the seas became. Whitecaps as tall as the ship's hull slammed into them, spraying icy water onto the floorboards. The wind howled like wolves, swirling through the sails and rigging with a vengeance. The cold was biting, burning his skin with its chill, practically sucking the moisture from the air.

It had been two days since their encounter with the disguised war ship and Kamira had been injured. They continued their trek northward but were no longer stopping at Torheim. Kamira somehow knew where a group of the Brothers of the Spring were located. When Doraan had asked her how, she only gave him a vague, clipped explanation about how she had eavesdropped on a confidential meeting. When he questioned her further about what sort of meeting it was, she simply shrugged her shoulders, keeping her mouth shut, not willing to provide anything else. He wasn't buying a word of it, but it was better than nothing, especially if it meant them getting closer to breaking the curse.

So now they were headed to the hills of Neilmaar. Kamira said a large group of the cult were hidden there beneath the city. Neilmaar was the worst possible location she could have said because it was on the eastern coast of Emmoria. They were currently off the west coast, and they had already sailed too far north. Turning around to travel through the easier, calmer, and safer southern oceans would take them an extra week, if not longer, and time was of the essence. They had to get to Neilmaar as fast as possible, break the bloody curse, and get back to Aksahri to warn them of this new enemy before anything catastrophic happened.

Now that they had sailed so far up the west coast, they would have to come around the top of Emmoria along the frigid northern coast, which they had never done before. It would take a little over a week to get to Neilmaar that way if everything went to plan, which was far better than turning around to face an extra week of sailing via the southern route.

They were getting closer to Torheim and would pass its shores in three days' time, which would be the furthest north they had ever sailed. They had no idea what to expect once they passed it, especially so late into the year. It was already considerably colder than the last time they were in these waters. They weren't prepared for the drastic change in weather, but they would make due with the supplies they had. If nothing else, the crew of the *Cursed Soul* was resourceful.

They had to be to survive.

Doraan shivered as a blast of icy wind blew past him. Once they passed Torheim, it would take another three days to make it to the tip of the Emerald Peaks. He would be lying to himself if he said he wasn't apprehensive. His mind couldn't stop wandering to the merchant frigate that was actually a mysterious enemy war ship. There was no knowing what waited for them on the Northern seas. They could be running headlong into an entire fleet of military ships. If they came upon a fleet, they wouldn't survive. There would be nothing they could do. That thought made him think of Kamira again.

Doraan had left Kamira to rest and recover in his quarters over the past few nights, which left him to sleep with the crew. The hammocks down there were far less comfortable than his bed. He cracked his sore neck from side to side and rubbed at his thigh. A deep ache had set in with the cold that wouldn't leave no matter what he did. It was a persistent, uncomfortable throbbing that he hoped would go away once his body got used to this new climate.

"I hate the north," Cormac muttered beside Doraan, pulling his thick wool coat fully closed and buttoning it all the way down to the frayed bottom edge that hung at his knees. "The wind steals the breath from your lungs."

Doraan grunted his agreement. "It's only for a few weeks, and then we will be in Neilmaar, hopefully gathering answers. Then, sea willing, we can head back south with the curse broken."

Cormac frowned. The old man hadn't fully conceded to Doraan's plan. He was willing to do it, but he was still skeptical. "You trust the girl?"

"We don't really have any other choice, do we? It's absolutely implausible that possibly one of the only people in existence to know where the Spring is—besides the Brothers themselves—wound up on our ship, but it's the best lead we've ever had. The *only* lead we've had and the only chance we've ever had to actually make contact with land."

"The tides of fate are shifting. The sea wants change," Cormac mused, nodding his agreement..

"If this isn't the answer we've been searching for, then all hope will be forever lost. I know hope has gotten us nowhere these past years, but something about this feels different. It feels real, Cormac. So I think I do trust her to a certain extent. I think she does know where the brothers are, and she'll keep her word to help us."

"That's the only reason you could get me to come this far north. Fate is alive and kicking us in the direction of freedom, that's for sure." Cormac looked out over the rocky seas. "This is real."

"I think the crew knows it, too. They haven't said one word about our destination. They feel it too."

"Is that ice?" Cormac suddenly exclaimed, pointing to a large white pointed rock sticking up from the ocean, waves crashing against, blocks of frozen sea falling from its surface. "Seas beyond, this is my nightmare," he mumbled before turning the wheel, steering the ship as far away from the solid chunk of ice as he could.

Doraan chuckled. "As we get close to the coast of Torheim, stay as far from it as possible. There's no knowing how many of those warships are this far north. I fear a fleet may be waiting for us."

"I fear you might be right. Something is definitely brewing in the North, and it doesn't look good."

"I'm going to check on Kamira." Doraan shivered. It would be his turn to helm the ship later, and he wanted to stay as warm as possible for as long as he could before then.

"Last I saw her, she was in the galley looking for something sweet to eat."

Doraan groaned, "She's supposed to be resting. One of the crew can bring her what she needs." He shook his head, smiling softly before making his way down to the kitchen.

It had been two days since they had discovered the cabin boy was actually a woman. *Kamira*—it was such a pretty name, and now that he knew she was a woman, he couldn't figure out how he had ever thought her to be a boy. He could now clearly see her features were delicate and soft; granted, she had hidden her breasts quite well, but even the curve of her hips had suggested a feminine frame. Funny how it had taken him seeing her fully exposed to finally realize it.

He made it to the galley just in time to see Kamira eat the last biscuit. "Didn't save any of those for the crew I see." Doraan smirked.

Kamira spun in her seat, wincing and clutching her side for a split second before swallowing the biscuit fully. "They were half gone already when I got here. Someone got into them long before me."

Doraan rolled his eyes. "You should be in bed, resting."

"I can't just lay around in bed all day. I need to stretch my legs, move around a bit."

"Out," he said, pointing toward the doorway. "Back to bed."

"You don't have to be so rude about it. Didn't I tell you if you keep scowling like that your face is going to freeze that way? Well, that still holds true. Life is too short to spend it with a perpetual scowl on your face." She crossed her arms over her chest and raised her chin at him before scurrying out the door.

"How did I ever think you were a fourteen year old boy?" he mumbled, shaking his head as he followed her out into the hallway, but one wrong step had him suddenly lying face down on the floorboards. "Bloody sails!" he growled.

"Are you alright?" Kamira was instantly beside him, gripping his arm, but one pull and she was doubled over on the floor beside him. "I didn't think that through."

Doraan couldn't help but laugh. "Skies, look at us, two invalids."

"We aren't invalids. We are just two people learning to deal with our injuries."

He looked into her blue eyes. They were like the sea on a calm cloudless day, sparkling and wide. "I hadn't thought of it that way." Curious, but he honestly hadn't thought of it like that. Ever since that terrible day he woke up without a leg, he had thought of himself as *less*, as flawed. Like he was no longer the same person, even though he knew that really wasn't the case.□

Kamira slowly pushed herself back into a standing position before extending a hand, her other hand grasped against her chest where the bullet wound was still so fresh and blood seeped into her linen shirt.

He swatted her hand away. "You've torn your stitches."

She reached her hand out again. "I'm fine. Would you just take my bloody hand, you bumbling idiot?"

He arched one eyebrow before taking her offered hand, and she yanked until he was steady on his foot once again. "You don't seem like the type of woman who would be mistress of a fine upstanding house like Lord Tarkiin's."

She snorted, heading up the steps at the end of the hallway. "I'm not sure whether to take that as an insult or a compliment."

"What I mean is, I can't imagine many noble ladies such as yourself who would board a pirate ship, cut off all their hair without a care, get shot in the middle of a battle, and then go scavenging for sweet treats barely even two days after said injury."

"I wouldn't say I cut off my hair without a care. There were certainly tears involved." She looked back at him with an amused smile. "And little good it did me. I was found out in what, three days on this ship?"

"For what it's worth, you had me fooled. Well, for the most part," he added with a wink.

She swatted his shoulder in the most familiar way, as if they were old friends reunited. It took him by surprise. It had been a long time since he had someone near his own age to banter with.

It was refreshing.

When they made it back to his quarters, Doraan's heart felt lighter than it had in years. He had a friend. Technically, his entire crew could be called friends, but not like this—this was something else. Talking and interacting with Kamira was what he had been missing for so long, and he didn't even know it. It was comfortable. It was nice.

"I've been meaning to ask you—how many of those Sumaarian warships have you come across? Are there a lot of them? I was surprised to see the Sumaarians had formed a navy so quickly. I thought it was a cargo ship like you had said, but that army was definitely Sumaarian."

Doraan went very still and blinked at her in confusion. "A what?"

"You didn't know that was a Sumaarian military ship?"

Since when did Sumaarians have ships and a military like that? They were secluded, wealthy people who only cared for trade and money—or so he thought. Was it true? Had the Sumaarians decided to revolt? Had they amassed a rebel army in secret? "I..."—his gaze drifted to the worn floorboards, unseeing—"did not."

"I didn't notice it when it was far away, but up close with its flags and the green uniforms with the golden sun. That's the Emerald King's sigil. He must have finally taken over Sumaaria like he's attempted for so many years, using their wealth and resources to amass an army and build a naval fleet."

Doraan's head whipped up to meet Kamira's eyes so fast he just about gave himself whiplash. "The Emerald what?" he gasped, rubbing the back of his neck from the quick movement.

"The King in the North," she cocked her head to the side. "I suppose if you aren't from the north you've most likely never heard the rumors of the King or seen the evidence of his rise. But seeing as he has a navy, I would think his existence would be more broadly known by now. Although, now that I think about it, I can't say I heard those rumors at all during my time in Aksahri." Kamira frowned. "How did he manage that I wonder? To remain a secret to all of Emmoria."

"How do you know this? Where have you heard these things?" he asked in a rush, uncaring how anxious and angry he sounded.

Kamira leaned away at his tone, looking at him with surprise. "I—I know I told you I'm from Jaaria, but I'm actually from Torheim. I lived there my whole life at the base of the Emerald Peaks on the southwestern border. The King in the North had always just been a rumor when I was a child. There was no proof of his existence, but in recent years, the true evidence of him has been seen throughout every northern town, especially in Torheim. There have been multiple attacks on the Aksahrian military units there. They've burned down their barracks and slaughtered soldiers in the streets, leaving them with the mark of his golden sun painted on their faces. Just in the past few years, there have been very few and scattered sightings of ships bearing his colors seen sailing near our shores but nothing like that military vessel we encountered the other night. I think, originally, when I was young, the rumors of the King were just that, embellished tales, but sometime in the past ten years or so, someone decided to take on the name of the Emerald King and use it to grow an army of rebels to rise up against the Emperor."

Doraan stared at Kamira unblinking. He had no idea how to process this information and all he could think to ask was, "Who is he?"

She laughed. "I don't know. No one does. He stays hidden somewhere in Sumaaria, commanding his troops from afar. Honestly, we ignored the whispers of his attacks until we saw his rebels taking action in Torheim. Like I said, I think someone took advantage of the rumor, of the name and what it means, to make it real and take action. It's smart if you ask me. So many were already on the side of the rumored King, and by taking on the title, they were guaranteed followers. The first attack on the Aksahrian troops in Torheim was about seven years ago."

"How big is his army? How many military units and warships does he have?"

"I have no idea. We only saw a few ships with his banners over the years, definitely not a full navy of warships. I suspect that was because Aksarian patrol ships were always docked in Torheim's harbor. Their attacks on the city would always be on land, coming down from the mountains in the cover of night," she said with a shrug of her shoulders. "If he had a large fleet of warships, I would assume he would have launched an attack on Aksahri by now. It's been so long since I've been home; who knows what he has accomplished in that time."

"Hmm." Doraan frowned. "You might be right. If there were a large fleet of those ships, they would annihilate Aksahri, and if what you said is true, they would have already done it years ago. There would be no point for them to wait. Aksahri is in a vulnerable state right now with their Emperor ill. Now would be the perfect time." He stopped and nibbled his bottom lip, eyes glazing in thought. "Maybe they were waiting for something like this to happen—a chink in the Emporer's armor."

"And they would have most likely heard by now that the Emperor's council is missing one member." She looked away from him as she said it, clasping her hands tightly behind her.

Doraan ignored her comment, noticing her change in body language. "Not to mention we haven't come across another ship these past two days. Are you sure there aren't any of those ships at Torheim? Could they just be slow-ly making their way south, hitting Torheim's naval ships first?"

Kamira sighed. "It is possible. But as I said, I haven't been to Torheim in nearly two years. If something like that had happened, my father would have mentioned it. I saw him a few weeks ago, just before..." she stopped, growing agitated and twisting her shirt anxiously.

"Kamira," Doraan said, placing a hand gently under her chin and lifting her gaze to meet his. "You did a good thing in Aksahri. You saved yourself. Don't ever feel ashamed of your actions, for saving the most important person, yourself."

Her face softened, a small smile spreading across her lips as she looked at him with tears in her eyes and then wrapped her arms tightly around his waist to rest her head against his chest.

He froze, caught off guard and not entirely sure what to do. When she only squeezed him tighter, he breathed out and relaxed into her embrace with a smile of his own before wrapping his arms around her and pulling her close enough to rest his chin atop her head.

"Thank you, Doraan," she whispered against his chest.

He knew what she was thanking him for and instinctively placed a kiss on the top of her head before they released their embrace. Heat rose to his cheeks at that sudden sign of affection, and he quickly brushed it aside to say, "Come on. Let's get you back resting. I need to go speak with Cormac about all of this."

She nodded, and he watched as her face relaxed from his gentle smile. Her blue eyes shifted from storm clouds to calm pools of cerulean. She offered him a soft smile in return, and there was a happiness in her expression that he hadn't seen in her since she boarded the ship. Doraan grinned, a boyish lightness filling him at being the cause of that happiness.

But it was quickly replaced by a heaviness as the reality sunk in that there was a rising threat to his people. A war was coming for them—one they couldn't win—and Doraan wasn't there to help. That thought made the heaviness sink further into his heart, and he knew it would stay there until the curse was broken and he could go home once again.

16

KAMIRA

It had been two days since Kamira had given Doraan her impromptu hug. It was completely out of character for her, and she still couldn't believe she had done it. If her mother could have seen her at that moment, she would have been scolded and sent to her room without dinner.

There had just been something in his hazel eyes that drew her closer. The green in them had brightened in earnest as he spoke, as if they were the most important words Doraan had ever said to anyone. To her, they were exactly what she needed to hear—the most perfect thing he could have said to her. Tears welled just to the point before spilling free to trail down her cheeks, which caused his face to soften with compassion. No one had looked at her like that or shown they cared since her brother, Adonis. So, she couldn't help it. She threw herself against him, wrapping her arms around his waist and squeezed him tight, putting all her thanks into that embrace.

She hadn't expected him to return the hug, but he squeezed her just as tightly, if not more so. She felt different, like her soul was lighter than it had been in years. She felt like herself again. Even if it had only been a week, she felt like she truly belonged with these people, and with him. All the years spent preparing for marriage—the rules, the propriety, the boredom, and the loneliness—had left her little more than an empty husk of herself. The time she had spent on the *Cursed Soul* was bringing her back to life. Once pale and lifeless, her blood flowed through her more freely now, as if her circulation had been cut off for so long.

She breathed in the musk of the sea air, taking it deep into her lungs, the movement pulling at the skin sewn together at her side. She winced from the tightness, blowing a breath out in a garbled wheeze. She had, in fact, torn her stitches the night of their embrace. Doraan had called for Lindor, who was the closest thing they had to a surgeon on board.

He was a large man, with hands triple the size of hers, and she'd found herself wondering how he was able to hold something so small and delicate as a needle between his fingers without snapping it in half. She shouldn't have worried, though, because his hand was steady, and he worked with such precision that she knew he had done it many times before.

The experience had made her glad she wasn't conscious the first time around. It was far more painful than she expected, and even with the few swigs of rum Lindor had given her before starting, she was still able to feel every single prick of the needle piercing her skin and each pull of string through her flesh. By the time he was done, she was shaking from head to toe.

Doraan was kind enough to make sure she was as comfortable as she could be, completely relinquishing his quarters to her and sleeping in the crew's quarters instead. She'd offered them back to him a few times over the past few days, but he wouldn't hear it and just shook his head and put up his hands. The room was hers now, and, if she was being honest, she was relieved to never have to sleep in the crew's quarters ever again.

Kamira having a room to herself allowed her to practice her sorcery in private. She was getting better each day—all four of the elements coming a little more easily to her, except for fire. She wasn't sure she would ever become adept in that element, but she continued to try—safely, of course, with plenty of water waiting on hand *just* in case she lost control.

She didn't want to burn down her freedom.

She had even used her sorcery to help move the *Cursed Soul* quicker through the water these past few days. Just little pushes and current changes to help the ship cut through the waves. That was until she heard Cormac questioning Jorne, the ship's navigator, on how they had made it to the coastline of Torheim an entire day ahead of schedule. Jorne had been just as baffled, rambling on about how it made no sense considering they had been sailing against the wind for the past two days, and the recent shift in the currents as they got closer to the Uskdar sea should have slowed their progression.

Kamira stopped using her sorcery to guide them immediately, realizing the danger. She didn't want any suspicion coming her way, especially not from this Aksharian crew without any knowledge of their thoughts on sorcery.

Kamira breathed in deeply as they passed the familiar bend of land that marked her journey home as almost complete. Her heart raced in her chest. It has been nearly two years since she had seen her home. The scent of pine and lemongrass filled her senses, bringing a smile to her lips as the cool breeze whipped through her short curls.

A thought came to her so suddenly she choked on a gasp. It was as if the sea breeze whispered in her ear, *use your sorcery.* Doraan had told her that they couldn't move the ship closer than ten miles from shore. If that were true, maybe this sorceress was using her gifts, somehow filtering a constant flow of her power into the sea around the vessel, pushing them away from Emmoria's shores and making them believe they couldn't touch land.

If she could use her own gifts just enough to counteract Forcina's sorcery, then maybe she could bring the *Cursed Soul* to land. She laughed, surprised the idea hadn't come to her earlier.

Kamira peeked at the crew behind her, ensuring no one was watching her, before she drew in a deep calming breath, reaching into herself and letting her sorcery roam free. She called on all the energy around her, feeling its power move through her, and used it to change the water's current, pushing the ship slowly closer to land. Little by little, she felt the water as it moved to the portside of the ship and pushed just as she instructed.

She chanced another look at the crew. None of them had even noticed what she was doing. A smile spread across her lips as she pictured the surprise and bewilderment that would be plastered on all of their faces when they passed that ten mile barrier Doraan had mentioned.

The excitement made her push just a little bit harder, willing the currents faster until it stopped. Kamira frowned and pushed the currents again, but nothing. The ship wouldn't budge. She cocked her head, looking down at the sea below and then out in front of her. She reached out a hand, thinking there might be some kind of barrier, but she almost fell into the waves below.

Shit, she inwardly cursed, steadying herself.

Kamira narrowed her eyes and huffed. It didn't make sense—there was nothing there. Her hand moved easily through the air and yet the ship was stuck.

Another thought sprung to mind, maybe Forcina was an air elementalist, and was instead using the air surrounding the ship to keep it from land. She had read once that sorcerer's gifted in air could create impenetrable pockets of wind around themselves or larger objects. The most powerful ones could even fly, using the currents of the winds to propel themselves through the air and glide just like a bird. If this Sorceress Doraan spoke of was powerful, then she could also be using her air sorcery to keep anyone from boarding this ship. It was also possible that this Sorceress was a Legion just like Kamira, using both air and sea against them, and that was the reason that only Kamira had been able to come aboard the ship. It could be that Kamira had somehow pushed through whatever power source Forcina may have put around the vessel.

She grunted, trying once more to push the *Cursed Soul* past whatever force was holding it back. This time funneling the power of both water and air, blending them together with a strength that could fell a hundred trees at once, but the ship stayed in place.

"Blazing biscuits," Kamira breathed. Doraan was telling the truth. Their vessel couldn't sail any further. How was that possible? A tingling scattered across her forehead as she tried to comprehend it. She scratched at her skin, suddenly feeling an eeriness course through her. Her brain hurt just thinking about it. Kamira swatted the thoughts away like a pesky fly.

She sighed heavily, rubbing at her eyes as she leaned against the starboard railing of the ship, looking out at the towering evergreen trees that surrounded her home. Any moment now she would be able to see the gray stone turrets of the city buildings peeking through the treetops and the small harbor town along the black sand beach. Darkness was falling quickly and she just wanted to catch one small glance before the sun tucked itself beneath the horizon.

She truly missed her home. She missed the beauty of the forest on a quiet morning, the sounds of birds singing and animals roaming freely through the trees. She could even say she missed the snow that would come down from the mountains and the cold winds from the sea that would freeze everything in the winter time so that the entire city sparkled in the sunlight.

A part of her wished that she could stop her journey here, disembark and live the rest of her life in the town she loved so dearly, but she knew it was the first place the Aksahrian guard would come looking for her. She wasn't stupid enough to think that she wasn't their number one suspect for Tarkiin's murder. He was dead, and she was gone. She was most definitely their *only* suspect.

Honestly, she was in the safest place she could be—in the middle of the ocean, on a ship that couldn't even dock near land if they tried. It might as well be a ghost ship.

Movement and a sudden flash of white caught her eye, pulling her vision along the distant treeline to where a person stood, sparking a fading memory from the night she had fled, one of shimmering white hair and someone hidden in shadow standing at the top of a hill behind her.

Kamira gasped, squinting through the haze of the falling evening, but the man was no longer there. She shook her head, frowning and rubbing at her eyes. That evening was still so heavy on her subconscious, she wasn't even sure it had been real. The past week felt more like a dream than reality. She looked back up to the trees now blanketed in shadow with no one in sight.

Night had fully fallen, the moon just a small sliver in the sky providing little light for her to catch that single fleeting glance of her home. Kamira blew out a weary sigh and sank further against the railing, letting her arms dangle over the side as she watched the ripples the ship was making as it sailed slowly through the water. Her eyes were playing tricks on her—maybe she should go to bed for the evening. She hadn't rested much over the past week—first from attempting to sleep in a room full of snoring pirates, then from the many uncomfortable nights of trying to sleep with a hole in her side. Last night was probably the only decent rest she had gotten in a week, and it wouldn't be long before they made it to Neilmaar, where she was to engage with the Brothers. She needed to think about how she would even find them upon arrival.

Doraan still hadn't told her why he wanted to seek out the Brothers of the Spring. He only said he needed to find something important, and he thought they might be the only ones who knew where it was. No doubt it was something to do with the so-called curse that he claimed was cast over them.

Kamira still wasn't entirely convinced that the curse existed. She had assumed the crew had simply created an entirely outlandish and extreme scenario—not being able to step foot on land—to overcome some traumatic event. It was always easier to believe in something incomprehensible, pushing away a past event, than to face it head on. She could understand that. She would love for the memory of the night she murdered Tarkiin to shift into something whimsical and eccentric in her mind.

She feared it would haunt her forever.

But she now knew that wasn't true. They really couldn't sail into shore. However, the idea of a Sorceress being able to mold their words in order to bend fate didn't make any sense. A Sorcerer's powers lay in the elements alone, giving them the ability to change and alter their environment. They couldn't bind someone's life force to a specific fate.

Could it be that this Sorceress was just that much more powerful than Kamira? She supposed that was probably the case. After all, she was still only learning.

Kamira closed her eyes and groaned; her mind was spiraling out of control.

She was ripped from her musings by Cariin, the boatswain's sharp cry of "Sail ho!" from the foresail. Kamira looked up to see him pointing toward the bow of the ship. She whipped her head around, spotting a handful of lights glimmering in the distance. With each blink of her eyes, the lights multiplied until the entire skyline was illuminated. It wasn't just one or two ships she was seeing, but an armada, and they were sailing directly toward the *Cursed Soul.*

"All hands about the ship!" Cormac cried out, his command reverberating across the deck as he spun the ship's wheel hard to the left, sending the ship careening. Kamira was thrown off her feet, skidding across the deck and slamming into the port side railing with an agonizing thud. She bit back a curse as white-hot pain radiated through her body, and she screamed as the frigid waves rose quickly toward her. Instinctively, she threw out her arms and wrapped them around the railing just in time to save herself from being thrown overboard.

"Douse the lights!" another crew member yelled as Cormac spun the wheel back to the right, leveling the ship once again.

Kamira steadied herself and sprinted for the lanterns closest to her, sending out a blast of wind and extinguishing three at once. She spun to see three more still lit on the starboard side and extended a hand out to smother the flames with her sorcery, but just before she could, Doraan stumbled onto the deck.

"What's happening?" he yelled.

"The light! Put it out!" Kamira howled, pointing to the lantern just beside him at the top of the steps. His dark brows drew together in confusion, but he soon noticed the hurried actions of the crew around him and turned, dousing the flame with one nimble motion.

She spotted the faint orange glow of another lantern perched several feet away. Doraan stumbled toward it, his foot catching on something hidden in shadow and he slumped against a nearby barrel. It was then she looked down and realized why he had been hopping. He only had one leg to stand on. He wasn't wearing his wooden appendage.

Kamira rushed to his side, lifting his arm gently and draping it over her shoulder. With one swift breath, she blew out toward the final lantern, guiding it the entire way until the flickering flame became a puff of smoke. Her anxious gaze darted to Doraan, but his eyes were focused solely on Cormac at the helm.

"Come on," she said and led him to the steps that ascended to the quarterdeck.

Doraan gripped the railing. "I can take it from here."

She raised a brow in doubt. He relented with a sigh and leaned his weight into her as he said, "Fine, it would be faster if you helped anyway."

Kamira only shook her head and snorted as they climbed the steps.

"Cormac, what's happening?" Doraan released Kamira and jumped to the helm, grabbing onto the wheel that Cormac held firm.

The Quartermaster nodded to the long line of lights illuminating the murky horizon. Doraan turned in the direction of Cormac's gaze and his dark skin drained of its color. He stared, unmoving at the lights, eyes wide.

"Are...are those ships?" His voice was strained, barely above a whisper.

"A fleet," Cormac stated.

Kamira noticed how Doraan's throat bobbed, his entire body tensing. His lips drew into a thin line, and his jaw quivered, hinting at clenched teeth beneath the skin.

"There's a small cay of rocks there." Cormac pointed directly in front of them where a shadowed mass could barely be seen. "Jorne spotted it before sunset. If luck is on our side, they haven't seen us and we can hide out there until they pass."

Doraan's breathing quickened, nostrils flaring as his entire body grew as taught as a bowstring.

"Doraan," Cormac said and reached for him, but it was too late. Doraan was already hopping toward the steps, his movements hurried and frantic as he stumbled, grasping the railing hard as he went.

Kamira moved to help him but Cormac gripped her elbow, pulling her back. "Let him go."

"What, why? Is he okay?"

"He needs to be alone right now. There is nothing we can do to help him."

"Is he worried about the crew or worried the fleet is going to Aksahri for war?"

"Both, but he knows Akshari isn't prepared for an attack, and the fact that we aren't there makes it all the worse."

Kamira looked toward the distant lights again, wondering how many ships there were. They were getting closer but didn't look like they had changed course toward them. She reached out to gauge the sea surrounding the fleet, sensing their course and any shifting direction. They were steady on their course, so she was certain they hadn't been seen, but she closed her eyes, pushing against the currents around them and shifting them to guide the *Cursed Soul* faster toward the enclave of rocks.

Cormac steered the ship expertly behind the cay so that they were completely out of sight and Cariin, along with a few other crew members, dropped the anchor. The black sails of the *Cursed Soul* blended into the darkness well enough that they didn't need to furl them.

There was a small section in the rock that was just large enough to see through to the other side. Well-hidden and settled behind the rocks, Kamira and the crew watched as lines of ships passed by. With limited range, it was impossible to count how many, but she guessed at least twenty, if not many more.

There was no doubt in her mind they were headed for Aksahri. The King in the North was going to claim the South. After many years of unrest, war had finally come to Emmoria.

She didn't stay to see how many more ships passed. She wanted to check on Doraan, so Kamira ventured into the belly of the ship in search of him. After looking almost everywhere, Kamira realized he had most likely gone to the place he felt most comfortable—the very room she had lived in the past week. Kamira stood outside the room and knocked. "Doraan? Are you in there?"

Silence followed, and she knocked once more. "Doraan?"

An incoherent sound came from the other side.

"Can I come in?"

Another muffled reply.

When she opened the door, she was greeted with the pungent sweet scent of rum. It coiled around her, making her eyes water. A discarded amber bottle rolled along the floorboards.

Kamira coughed. "Skies, did you bathe yourself with that bottle of rum?"

"Wha' do you wanth?" he slurred, pushing himself off his bed into a standing position, instantly stumbling straight into her. She caught him, but his weight sent them tumbling to the floor.

"Oof, Doraan! Get off of me!" She pushed with all her might, but he didn't budge, his weight and size far greater than hers. Breathless, she grunted, "Will you roll over? You're too heavy." He began to laugh and she yelled, "Doraan! Get off!"

He rolled to the side, flopping over on his back beside her. "I can' belieth I thought you were a lad."

She turned her head and glared at him. "I think my disguise was rather good, thank you very much."

He guffawed, rolling back and forth with hysterics. "Even a boy of fourteen would be stronger than you."

She sat up and punched his arm. "You take that back! I am stronger than any boy of fourteen."

He only laughed harder, wheezing from the lack of breath, tears running down his face.

It was so youthful, so infectious, that she couldn't help but laugh right along with him, and then a thought sprang to mind that made her laugh just as hard as he did. "I can't believe I cut off all of my hair only to be found out only a few days later."

That sent them both into a fit of uncontrollable laughter that lasted until their stomachs hurt with the effort and they began to come back into themselves. When they were both silent again, Doraan still on his back, Kamira sat beside him and leaned her back against the cabin wall.

He asked, "How long was your hair?"

She smirked, looking down at her hands clasped on her lap. "Down to my waist."

"Bleeding skies, you cut off all that? You should have headed to Jaaria instead, hidden yourself there and avoided the need to blend in on this ship all together."

She huffed a tired breath, exhaustion beginning to take over as she finally had a moment to sit. Doraan sat up beside her, shaking his head slightly. No doubt the room was still spinning from the amount of rum he had drunk.

"I think this was a better option in the end. Even on horseback, I don't think I could have made it far. The last place they would think to search for me would be on the sea. It was either this or face the gallows in Aksahri. I'd cut my hair off any day to stay alive."

"Will you ever tell me what happened? What forced you to do what you did?"

She studied his glazed eyes, lids heavy from consumption. "Only if you tell me what made you so upset it drove you to drink an entire bottle of rum."

He grunted, falling back against the hard wood of the floor. "I might need to sober up first."

She nodded and remained quiet for a long time, debating whether to confess. "It was our wedding night."

Doraan sat up again and turned to face her, the haze in his eyes clearing as he gave her his entire focus.

"We had finished our supper, and I should have gone up to my rooms, but I found myself curious and wandering the halls of the manor." She sat up a little straighter before continuing, "I found Tarkiin's study. It was massive, the entire room lined with rows and rows of bookshelves. I couldn't help it, I scanned them looking for something that I might enjoy reading, but then I heard voices coming from the hallway just on the other side of the door."

Kamira took a deep breath before shaking her head and breathily chuckling, "Any sane person would have politely made themselves known and left, but for whatever reason, I hid behind a large leather reading chair."

Doraan smirked. "That certainly does sound like something you would do. Hiding behind things, boarding ships in the dead of night, and sneaking around places you shouldn't be."

She glared at him. "Do you want me to continue or not?"

"Sorry," he said, raising his hands in defense before motioning for her to continue.

"Tarkiin and two men I'd never seen before came into the study. They were speaking in hushed tones, but I heard one of them say something about a will being settled and stamped with the Emperor's seal. Tarkiin laughed, a truly heinous sound." She scrunched up her face in disgust, an involuntary shiver racking through her at the memory. "Tarkiin poured them all a drink and said '*A toast is in order, men. Our hard work has paid off. After years of the Emperor refusing to name a new heir, he has finally named one in writing and given it his official stamp of authority. To the legally binding will that has sealed our fates!*'"

Doraan's eyes were wide. He was growing more sober by the minute.

"The Emperor is sick, you see, and I took their words to mean that, somehow, Tarkiin got the Emperor to sign some kind of will stating that he was the new heir to the throne and stamp it with his royal signet ring. I don't know how he did it, but they all seemed to think it was set in stone. But then, he said the words that showed him for the true monster he was." She paused, adjusting her position on the hard floor. "He said, '*Now we can give the old man the final dose, and once he takes his final breath, the will shall appoint me as rightful heir, and I will become the new Emperor of Emmoria.*'"

Doraan had gone very pale, and Kamira wasn't sure he was even still breathing.

She placed a gentle hand on his shoulder. "Doraan? Are you alright?"

"Y-yes," he stammered. "Please, go on. What happened next?"

She narrowed her eyes suspiciously at him before continuing, "I couldn't believe what I was hearing. Treason of the highest form. Tarkiin was the reason for the Emperor's sudden illness and he was ready to finish the job. I must have made a noise or something, because when the two men were dismissed, Tarkiin knew exactly where I was and came straight for me. He yanked me up by my hair and threw me against the wall, his hand came around my neck, and he squeezed so tight, I saw stars. He asked me what I had heard, and I wasn't about to give him the satisfaction of my fear, so I simply said 'you treasonous pig' and spat in his face."

Doraan looked at her, the color returning to his face. "Is that why you killed him? Because of what you heard?"

"Yes and no. He was choking me. I couldn't breathe, and I began hitting and kicking him as hard as I could, but his grip didn't loosen. I knew he would kill me, so I grabbed the heaviest thing I could reach—a small marble bust from the shelving just next to me—and hit him over the head with it. It took him by surprise and he let go, but the blow also caused him to lose his footing and he fell backward, hitting his head on the edge of his desk. Blood pooled so quickly around his limp body, I knew if I didn't flee, I would be strung up for all to see in the Aksahri square. It wouldn't matter what I heard—only those two men knew of Tarkiin's treason—and they would deny it all. No one would believe the ramblings of a woman who just killed her husband in cold blood. So, I fled to the sea."

Doraan drew his brows together in thought. "Do you realize what you've done? Without the final dose of the poison Tarkiin was giving him, he might recover. You did good. You saved the Emperor's life, Kamira."

She didn't smile, but cast her gaze solemnly at her feet. "I don't know, it might be too late."

"Kamira." Doraan's warm, calloused hands cupped either side of her face. She blinked, unsure what words were going to come from him next. "Because of you, and only you, my father is still alive. You are amazing. Each time I talk to you, I am more in awe of the person you are. Your strength and determination are admirable. You make me believe that anything is possible. How in all the realm did you end up here in my life?"

"I think it was..." but she didn't get a chance to finish as Doraan's lips descended on hers, hard and searching. Kamira's eyes went wide as his tongue shot into her mouth. She moved her mouth with his, waiting for a spark, a flicker, anything, but none came.

Doraan broke away suddenly and dropped his hands from her face, pushed away from her with a frown. "I'm so sorry, I—I just got caught up in the moment and the rum didn't help. I'm…"

Kamira was dazed, but then his words prior to the kiss registered. "Did you say father?"

17

DORAAN

Had he really just done that? *Bloody seas*. Doraan raked a hand from the back of his head, and pulled it down over his face. The room was spinning around him—his senses felt slowed and his movements loose. Why had he drunk so much rum? He knew he would regret it, but he wanted to drown his thoughts and the crippling anxiety that seemed to be a constant in his life these past weeks. He wanted to forget everything just for a little while, so he just kept drinking, one swig after another, until the bottle was completely empty. Not even one drop left.

Doraan groaned. He would definitely feel the nasty after-effects in the morning. He looked over at Kamira who was staring at him, concern sparkled in her blue gaze.

His eyes darted to her parted lips, and he groaned again. Skies, did he kiss her? Why did he do that? It felt like kissing his cousin. He knew it had been the alcohol that sprung him into action. Ordinarily, he would never have made such a forward move. In all honesty, he never really had the chance. It was ten years since he last kissed a girl and he didn't remember it feeling like *that*.

She continued staring at him with a strange look. It wasn't that she wasn't pretty—with her rosy cheeks and freckles dotted across her nose and under her eyes—but there was just nothing there. No feeling outside of friendship.

"I'm so sorry," he muttered and began rambling about the rum, apologizing for his rashness and not controlling himself.

When she smiled at him, he realized that she had asked him something earlier and he had completely ignored her. "Wait, what did you ask?"

She snorted, giving him an incredulous look as she said, "I asked if you just referred to the Emperor of Emmoria as your father."

Flaming stars. "I—" he stopped. There was no use in lying to her. She was bound to have found out at some point if she remained on their crew. "Yes."

"But..." she huffed, growling. "The Emperor doesn't have any children. His only son died..." Kamira breathed in sharply and put a hand over her mouth, eyes as wide as the wheel of the ship. "Captain Doraan. You—you're Doraan, *Prince* Doraan?"

"In the flesh," he said with a mournful half-smile.

"But...they said you died ten years ago. Th—there was a burial. There is even a statue made in your honor that sits in the city center of Aksahri. The entire realm mourned your loss. How are you...how?" She stopped trying to find the right question to ask, because there wasn't one. "Why would the rulers declare you dead when you clearly are not?"

Doraan looked at his missing leg, shoulders sagging with the grief of all he had lost, of all he wished to get back, and sighed, "I mean what would have happened if they told Aksahri *'our son was cursed by a Sorceress'*? My father's entire rule has been dedicated to forcing the Sorcerers out of Emmoria and saving the Ungifted from being enslaved to them. To tell the people that he had been bested by one would have been political suicide. It would have caused kingdom-wide chaos. If the Emperor couldn't even keep his only son and heir from a Sorcerer's grasp, how could he save all of them? How could he rule?"

The more he thought about it, the more what his parents did made sense. They needed the people to believe he had died in some tragic accident because his father's entire rule was at stake. But that didn't mean it still didn't hurt. And it didn't forgive the fact that they could have still tried to help him. He supposed the fact that his father hadn't selected an heir in his stead meant something—perhaps they were still hoping for his miraculous return from the dead.

Kamira cast her eyes to the floorboards, her gaze absentminded and distant until her head suddenly popped up. "Do you agree with your father? That sorcery should no longer exist?"

Doraan had thought about that many times over the years. His mind constantly jumped back and forth between hatred and kindness toward them, especially when he thought back to his mother's fondness for Sorcerers and how she told him most of the Gifted didn't want to harm, but help. However, the only experience he ever had with a Sorcerer proved his mother wrong, and he didn't think he would ever get past it. Cruelty and sorcery were the same in his mind, and no matter how much he had once loved his mother and trusted her every word, she had proved to be just as cruel as the Sorceress that cursed him. He had expected his father to cast him off, uncaring whether he returned or not, but not his mother. Now that he had seen the truth, it was like a beacon illuminated the reality of his situation and guided him to his rightful path. He would break the curse, go home, overthrow his pig of a father, and finish what his father never could—eradicating the Sorcerers from Emmoria once and for all.

He looked Kamira in the eyes and said, "Look at what good sorcery has done to me." He motioned around the small quarters and then to his missing limb. "I believe Sorcerers are nothing more than a stain on our Empire, one that needs to be washed away completely for Emmoria and its people to thrive."

Kamira bristled at his words and turned away. He knew what he said was harsh—to destroy an entire population of people would never be his first choice—but the hard truth was that Sorcerers were too dangerous, and unfortunately, the only way to get rid of them was to execute every last one.

"You don't think there is a way for them to coexist with us?" she asked quietly.

"How can you coexist with people you can never fully trust? We have no defenses against their powers. The only thing we can do to fight against them is to kill them so they can never use their abilities again."

Kamira's face fell. This world they lived in was vicious and he knew that the people of his realm never truly felt safe. They were in a constant state of agitation, the entire Empire was full of unrest, and it was only a matter of time before things escalated into civil war. The evidence of that had just sailed past them, and he would do anything to prevent war from happening.

"Kamira." Doraan cleared his throat, but she didn't look up at him. Her eyes were fixed on a small piece of frayed thread sticking out of her trousers that she was twirling around a finger. He waited, but when she still didn't look at him, he sighed and continued, "The safety of Emmoria is the reason why I need to make contact with the Brothers of the Spring of Zjanoak."

She snorted, still not looking up from the small piece of thread. "What can the Brothers do to help you keep the entire Empire safe? They are just a cult of idiotic zealots who believe in things that never even existed."

Doraan's eyes grew wide at the vehemence in her tone. "I need help in figuring out how to break this curse. It's the only way I can go home and help them."

"And you think the Brothers will know how? You sound just as foolish as them."

Doraan frowned. Her entire demeanor had changed. She had become closed off and distant, acting as if talking to him was painful for her.

"Are you alright?" he asked, placing a gentle hand on her shoulder.

She stiffened under his touch before shaking him off. "Yes, I'm fine. So tell me, why do you think the Brothers can do anything for you?" She finally looked into his eyes. The normal teal of her irises had turned gray and stormy. She didn't seem to harbor the same dislike for sorcery as he did.

Hopefully their difference of opinion didn't change her mind about seeking out the Brothers for information. That would certainly make things more difficult for him. He fumbled with the idea of telling her the truth or fabricating a story to keep her compliant. In the end, the truth was always the better option, he supposed.

"I believe they know the location of the Temple of Gorria."

Kamira furrowed her brow, nostrils flaring. "Why?"

"It's well-known that they worship the Sorcerers as children of the gods. They know everything and anything there is to know about Sorcerers, and the only way to break this bleeding curse is through a Sorcerer." He was growing agitated, almost as if her change of mood was rubbing off on him. He didn't want to seek out the Temple, but he had to out of necessity, out of survival.

"They're lunatics!" Kamira laughed, a hard sound without any humor. "Nothing they say can be believed. They will probably tell you the Temple is in the bloody center of Aksahri, right under your father's nose." She almost spat those last words.

Doraan closed his eyes and leaned his head against the wall behind him. He could feel his temper rising. He took a few calming breaths before saying in an even tone, "Will you help me or not?"

Kamira stared silently at the wall where a small painting hung, depicting a beautiful field of wildflowers, white capped mountains along the horizon, and a setting sun that cast the whole scene in a warm shade of amber. When he was first cursed, he would stare at that painting and weep, knowing he would never be able to run through a field like that in his lifetime. He had never even been outside the sands of Aksahrian and was barely able to leave the palace most of the time. He always longed to travel the realm and experience the different atmospheres and cultures, but now all he could do was look at them from afar and imagine what it was like in those cities.

He had nearly given up hope on Kamira answering and was about to ask her to leave him alone in his room for a while when she suddenly said, "I'll help you."

Doraan raised a skeptical eyebrow. "Are you sure?"

"You'd be wise to not give me the option of backing out, Doraan."

He chuckled, but noticed how her shoulders sagged and the sad frown etched across her face.

"Look, you don't have to agree with my views, but you have to understand that my entire life was completely flipped upside down and shoved into a deep dark hole because of sorcery. I cannot allow such terrible acts of hatred to be cast on anyone else in Emmoria. This will end with me."

Kamira took a deep breath beside him. "It just doesn't make any sense. Have you heard of any Sorcerer in all of our history being able to do something like what that Sorceress has supposedly done to you?"

Doraan bit his lip in annoyance. She still didn't believe him. She was so dead set on Sorcerers being unable to perform certain acts. But what did anyone really know about

Sorcerers? Had the Ungifted ever truly known the extent of their powers? It was highly unlikely. Did the Sorcerers even know the limits of their own gifts? If they were smart, they would have never shown their full set of skills to the Ungifted.

"The history books don't know everything, Kamira. Different ones say different things. There is no exact knowledge of anything." He moved himself up, wanting to get off the hard floor when a sudden sharp pain so intense he was certain he'd been struck by lightning shot through his leg and all the way up to his lower back. He yelped, wincing as he lowered himself back down. He had sat for too long in this position without moving, and stiffness had settled in, creating a prickling ache and stabbing pains through his lower half.

"Are you okay?" Kamira's tone shifted from detached to worried in a split second, and she moved to her knees, hovering beside him.

"Fine," he ground out as spasms moved through his muscles.

"Does it hurt you often?" she asked, leaning over him and trying to get a glimpse of the stump of his missing limb.

"It comes and goes, but the further north we get the more it aches."

She furrowed her brow and cupped her chin in thought. "It's the drastic drop in temperature. It causes sudden changes in the body as you adjust to the new atmosphere putting pressure on those nerves around the injury."

"Is there anything you don't know?" He half grunted, half laughed. Honestly, this woman seemed to have an answer for just about everything. He could ask her why there were fish in the sea and she could tell him the exact reason for it.

Surprisingly, she huffed a laugh in return. "There are many things I don't know, but I told you my mother was a healer. I learned a lot by watching and listening to her while she worked."

"Well, I hope my body acclimates soon. I don't think I've slept in two days because of the constant, gnawing pain."

"I can help with that. Well, with the pain. Unfortunately, I don't think I can make you sleep."

He smirked, happy she was coming back to the helpful and cheery person he had known these past weeks. He knew that she still wasn't pleased with his words, but it seemed like she did understand why he felt the way he did, and that's all he could really ask for. Even so, doubt and fear crept into his mind like fog climbing its way up a mountain. If they succeeded, what would become of him? Would he be able to go home and ascend the throne? Would he be able to finish what his father started? In his eyes, this quest to break the curse was like killing two birds with one stone. Not only would they hopefully be able to shatter the curse, but he would know where a large remainder of the Sorcerers lived. If Kamira learned of his double motivation for finding the Temple, there was no way she would help him. It was a secret that he wouldn't even tell Cormac.

But that was all based on the slim chance that Kamira was actually able to find the Brothers and that they actually knew where the Temple was. He was stressing over hypotheticals. Nothing was discovered yet, and he wouldn't sit here and get his hopes up just for them to be crushed into a millions pieces once again.

Right now, he hoped Kamira could help with his pain. "How?" he finally asked, looking at her incredulously.

"Wait here. I'll be right back." Kamira stood and reached out a hand to help him. "You'll be more comfortable on the bed."

He nodded, reaching and clasping wrists with her as they pulled against one another until she was able to yank him up to balance on one leg. He instantly regretted it as the room spun around him and his stomach roiled. He stumbled, placing a hand on the trunk beside him to steady himself.

"Can you make it to the bed okay?" Kamira asked, still holding onto his wrist.

"I'll be alright. Go ahead and get what you need."

Kamira sprinted from the room. He quickly hopped to his bed, and fell onto it with a heavy sigh of relief. Why had he drank so much? The sight of all those lights headed straight for his home had sent him into a panic, and all he could think to do was drink the thoughts away. Drink until he forgot about the ships, until he forgot about everything and passed out until it was all over.

It had been a very long time since he was a part of the Aksahri council— offering input and listening to conflicts—but when he sat beside his father, learning what it was to be ruler of the realm, they never seemed concerned with an uprising. No one had ever brought up a concern of war. There had only been talk of units in the Aksahrian guard being sent to keep the peace throughout the realm. Maybe they knew of the King in the North and had been preparing. It was entirely possible that these past ten years, his father had been preparing for a moment like this, and he hadn't allowed Doraan to see it. From what he saw during his short visit, not much had changed, and there was definitely not a fleet of ships in their harbor as large as what was coming for them.

Doraan groaned, pressing the palms of his hands into his tired eyes. He couldn't think about all this now. There was nothing he could physically do. His main focus needed to be breaking the curse, and that was enough to worry about for now.

"Alright," Kamira said as she walked briskly back into the room.

Doraan sat up on the bed, propping himself against the wall.

"Are you ready?" She had a bowl in her hands with a thick green substance inside.

He cringed, pointing to the paste. "Not if it involves that."

Kamira rolled her eyes at him. "Trust me, it will be worth it. You'll be thanking me after."

He glared at her before conceding. "Fine, but if my leg turns green because of that stuff, I'm throwing you overboard."

Doraan smirked at her, his smile spreading into a gleeful grin when she graced him with another annoyed eye roll before sitting at the foot of the bed. That same lightness that seemed to settle over him every time Kamira was near enveloped him in a warm embrace that chased away the dark thoughts that plagued him. Doraan sank further against the wall behind him, finally relaxed and at peace enough to fall asleep for the first time in two days.

18

KAMIRA

Kamira breathed in deeply. The room smelled like almond and fresh mint leaves mingled with the herbs she had ground down for her ointment. She sighed as she mixed the mint and herbs in beeswax to create a paste, trying to settle her tightly wound nerves.

That had not been how she wanted that conversation to go. He had such a deep-rooted hatred for Sorcerers and she could completely understand why. A Sorceress had ripped him from his life—torn it apart for something that he had no part in.

At first, she was going to tell him she would no longer help him. Partially because she didn't actually think he was cursed, but mostly because of his extreme prejudice toward her people. But there was something in his face, hidden behind his hazel eyes, that showed her he wasn't fully convinced. That, maybe, a small piece of him didn't really want anyone to die—that, ultimately, he just wanted to go home again, to walk on land once more.

She wanted to believe she had actually seen those feelings in his gaze because if she had, then maybe she could prove to him that Sorcerers weren't all bad, that they simply wanted the same thing that all of Emmoria did. Peace.

The realm didn't need another dictator to eradicate an entire race of people. It needed a savior. It needed something to bring complete peace to the realm, and maybe, just maybe, if she could convince Doraan, and show him that it was possible, he could be Emmoria's savior.

The bringer of peace.

Kamira had practiced her gifts everyday since boarding the *Cursed Soul,* and every time she did, she pushed herself a little bit further, gently prodding the well within her, gauging how far she could take her sorcery. She had never really been interested in power and politics, but maybe that was her true purpose in life. Maybe this was her way to help the ones she loved, as a Sorcerer consort to the Emperor. Was it fate that brought them together?

Kamira looked over at Doraan, noticing the fatigue through his heavy-lidded eyes and the way he was slumped against the wall. "You should lay down," she said. "If you fall asleep like that, you'll have pain in other areas of your body tomorrow morning."

He smirked and scooted down, resting his head upon the pillow she had been using for the past week. Kamira gestured to his pants that were still covering his injury. "May I?"

He propped himself up on his elbows, nodding.

Kamira gently rolled Doraan's pant leg up to reveal his limb. He watched her intently to gauge her reaction, but she kept her face completely void of emotion. It wasn't pretty, she could admit, but she knew the difficulty it caused him for her to see it. The skin at the base was deeply scarred. She could see several jagged, puckered pink lines where someone, probably Lindor, had tried their best to sew the flesh together. She glanced up at him with a frown noticing his face scrunched into a sneer of self-loathing before he fell back against the pillow.

"How long ago did this happen?" she asked.

"Almost eight months."

"The scars and tissue have probably not fully healed yet on the inside. It takes time. That's likely why you are still feeling a lot of pain."

Doraan only grunted in response.

Kamira took the herbal paste and began to rub the mixture gently into the scarred flesh. Doraan groaned at the pressure, but made no move to pull away. The ointment was truly only a ruse—something to distract from the actual work that she was doing with sorcery. The paste would simply cause slight tingling, along with a cooling effect due to the ingredients she used, but it did little more than make you smell good for a bit.

The type of sorcery she was about to use was challenging. It was something that only a Legion could perform. Growing up, Kamira had asked her mother question upon question about her healing process. She wanted to know how she did it—how to use the elements together as one, where she learned to use her sorcery, and anything else she could try and pry from her mother's mind. Eventually, she was forbidden from asking any questions at all, left only to observe and learn through her eyes alone. She used what little she had learned to practice on Adonis and the occasional creature.

Once, she had helped a rabbit who was trapped in a snare, foot bleeding and skin torn from the wire trap. She had melded the elements together, using their combined power to stitch the torn skin of the rabbit closed. It was an amazing feat that she still couldn't believe she was able to do. Another time, she had found a small sparrow with a broken wing that surely wouldn't have survived another day without her kindness. That had been one of the most difficult uses of her sorcery to date. Mending bones was complicated work. It required patience, persuasion, and extreme mental and physical focus to move the fragmented bone back into place before weaving the pieces back together. Skin was more forgiving and much more pliable.

What Doraan needed was neither of those things. She wasn't going to move the scar tissue, or tear and knit it back together in a more pleasing way. And she wasn't going to mend something that was broken either. What he needed was the movement of fluid and gasses in the body—a release of pressure building on the nerves around his knee and severed limb.

Kamira forced heat into her hands as her fingers massaged over his skin. She took a long, steadying breath before she closed her eyes, feeling the swelling of his muscles and the thickness of the fluid surrounding the area that was causing him the most discomfort. Kamira pushed the warmth through him, leveling his internal temperature, while at the same time moving the fluid build-up away from his leg and distributing it evenly all throughout, restoring balance in his body.

Doraan moaned and his entire body relaxed as the pressure released, easing his pain. She continued to knead soothing circles along the base of his leg until he closed his eyes, and she heard the telltale heavy breathing of sleep. Kamira gently rolled Doraan's pant back down and grabbed the blanket folded at the end of the bed to lay atop him before smothering the lantern flame and quietly exiting the room.

She slowly closed the door behind her and just about jumped out of her trousers when a deep voice spoke beside her from the shadowed hallway. "Kamira."

She turned quickly to see Cormac standing there. "Skies, Cormac. You scared me. I didn't see you standing there."

He always stood in a proper sort of stance, hands clasped tightly behind his back, no doubt from his days as a Navy Admiral. This must be his casual, at ease stance.

"May I speak with you privately for a moment?" he asked. There was an earnest expression on his face that sparked worry in her chest.

"Is everything alright? Did the fleet fully pass us?"

"Yes, we are preparing to set sail. I have another matter to discuss with you. Please, let's speak in my quarters," Cormac said in a low voice, walking the few paces down the hall to his room and pushing the door open, motioning for her to step inside.

She furrowed her brows but headed into the room anyway. Cormac followed, closing the door behind him. "Please, sit," he said, lighting the lamp beside the door.

Kamira sat in the chair at Cormac's desk and anxiously squeezed the armrests so hard that the wood creaked beneath her grip. "So, what's this all about?"

He didn't respond, but simply walked to the opposite corner of the room, where a second chair was propped against the wall. Cormac pulled it out, setting it in the center of his room to face her, and sat.

Kamira squirmed like an unruly child in her seat. "Alright, you're starting to make me nervous. What is it? Just tell me already."

"I know you're a Sorceress," he said calmly.

Kamira froze, raising her eyes to meet his unwavering blue-gray stare. His face revealed nothing of what he was thinking—no hint of emotion or quiver of interest. Was he upset? Did he want her thrown off this ship? She opened her mouth to speak, but he put a hand up to silence her.

"There's no use denying it. Your secret is safe with me. I have no issue with Sorcerers and don't hold the same opinions as the Emperor."

She blinked a few times at his words, surprised that he didn't share Doraan's hatred, before blowing out a shaky breath. "How did you find out?"

"I've been around long enough to understand what it means when unexplainable things begin to happen." He finally allowed the corner of his mouth to twitch up for a split second before falling back into that steely expression he always held firm. "My suspicions started the first morning you spent on the ship, when the whirlpool you claimed you hadn't seen appeared on one of the calmest sea days we'd had in weeks. The second clue came during the attack on that merchant ship. The storm that allowed us to get away with our lives showed up out of nowhere, just as you stood on the railing—unwisely, might I add—and disappeared shortly after you were shot."

Kamira gulped audibly, sinking further and further into her chair as he spoke. She had been so stupid and careless.

"But the final straw was the fact we reached Torheim a full two days ahead of schedule. The fastest ships in the realm couldn't amount to such a feat, even with the wind and currents on their side. That's when I knew for sure that you are a water Sorceress."

"I—stars, I just wanted to help, and the only way I knew how was with my gifts." She closed her eyes, letting her head fall back against the back of the chair before opening them again and sitting up. "Do the other crew members share your views, or do they side with Doraan when it comes to Sorcerers?"

"It's an even split. I know Doraan informed you of the curse. Of the reason we're stuck roaming the seas. Most of the men can not forgive those who use their powers. They have only seen and experienced the pain it causes. There are those, like me, who have experienced the opposite."

Kamira sighed, slumping in her chair once again. "I understand. I mean, I don't like it or agree with it, but I can see where they are coming from. I'll stop using my sorcery. I'll be better."

"I actually had another notion in mind," Cormac said, leaning forward in his chair and resting his elbows on his knees.

She cocked a brow at his expression. Curiosity was etched into his features and a sense of excitement she'd never seen from him before.

"And that is?" she inquired.

"I was hoping you could use your gifts to cut our trip to Neilmaar in half."

Kamira's eyes widened in surprise, unsure if she heard Cormac correctly. He wanted her to use her sorcery after all? "But wouldn't that cause suspicion in the crew? They would know something strange was happening."

"Desperate times call for desperate measures. We need to reach Neilmaar as soon as possible. If anything, that fleet made the urgency of our trip increase ten-fold." Cormac clasped his hands together, still leaning his elbows on his knees, his pale blue eyes locked onto hers. "Jorne will be able to come up with some explanation about the luck of the currents and the angle of the winds to keep the crew from asking too many questions. He remembers before, when we lived freely with the Sorcerers. He knows that most are kind and good."

Kamira looked at his clasped hands, watching as his knuckles turned white. He was hiding his agitation well. He needed her to say yes.

"So, only you and Jorne will know what's actually going on?"

He nodded. "Yes, just the three of us will know the truth."

"What about Doraan?"

Cormac sat back against his chair, placing a hand on either knee, and Kamira watched as red replaced the white across his hands as the blood rushed back to them. She waited as he seemed to mull something over quietly in his mind. "It is imperative that Doraan not know you are a Sorceress. He cannot even have an inkling of suspicion."

Kamira nodded. "Agreed. But how do we keep it from him? He's bound to think something is amiss if we make it to Neilmaar days ahead of schedule."

"I will handle Doraan. Don't worry."

"But what will..."

Cormac reached over, placing a large calloused hand on her knee. "He won't find out. Trust me."

Cormac's tone was laced with desperation—a hitch in his voice that took Kamira by surprise. In the span of several minutes, Kamira had seen more emotion flash over Cormac's features than she had during the entire almost three weeks on the ship, and it was all surrounding Doraan. He loved Doraan like a son, she realized, and would do anything to protect him. That thought had her noddin g."I trust you, Cormac."

He pulled his hand away, shoulders relaxing with a sigh of relief. "Thank you, Kamira." She smiled at his relief, but anxiety washed over her when he added, "There is one more thing."

Her eyebrows rose in anticipation of his next words, "Yes?"

"Forcina, the Sorceress who cursed us. She…well, she visits us sometimes, with no warning at all. She can show up at any time."

Kamira frowned at that. "How? We are in the middle of the sea? How does she find the ship?"

Cormac shook his head rather frantically. "She is the most powerful Sorceress I've ever seen. I don't know how she does it, but that's not important right now. What's important, well, it's more than important—it's absolutely imperative she does not know you are on the ship."

Kamira bit her lip, frowning. "Why is that?"

"Because there is a reason that you were able to go outside the confines of her curse and board our ship when no one else could. I think you are what we need to break it. If she saw you, she would know something is wrong. She would realize the same thing I have and kill you in a split second. She will not hesitate to do it. Do you understand?"

"Y—yes, I understand." Kamira's heart began to race in her chest. Just how powerful was this Sorceress to have Cormac so out of character and frantic? She hoped this Sorceress stayed far away until she was off this ship, and their curse broken.

She still wasn't completely convinced that this curse existed, but her test with her gifts from earlier and Cormac's words were beginning to change her mind. She wondered if there was far more about her people and the power in her veins that she didn't know.

"We will find a way, Cormac. I will help you all go home for good."

19

DORAAN

"The Emerald Peaks," Doraan whispered. A light snow had begun to fall as they sailed through the frigid Uskdar Sea. There was a deep silence this far north. A calm that came with the snowfall. Doraan looked out over the sparkling white dusted mountains. They stood like sentinels, towering high above them as a reminder of their strength and protection over Sumaaria. The clouds were thick above them, blanketing the tops of the peaks and hiding any glimpse of the city within from view.

Cormac stood beside him, his thick beard collecting snowflakes. "We're getting close," Doraan said, his voice low and gravelly. "These waters are more treacherous than any we have sailed before. We also don't know if any of those Sumaarian ships are hidden here. We need to stay on high alert."

His quartermaster nodded solemnly. "They'd be daft to dock their ships out here, but you're right. We have no idea how many there are or if they are hidden within the caves lining these mountains. They could be anywhere."

As they sailed further north, the snowfall grew heavier, to the point they could barely see a few feet beyond the bow of the ship. The strong wind whipped across the sails and pushed the *Cursed Soul* as Doraan fought to keep the wheel steady, turning against it. The cold air bit into their skin, burning to the point of agony. Doraan could see the crew shivering against it, but they were almost through the worst of it. Just another few days and they would be to their destination. He would stop at nothing until they made it to Neilmaar.

Suddenly, a high pitched cackle cut through the air. Doraan spun around, his hand already on one of the pistols at his hip. That laugh never brought anything good with it. "Forcina," he growled, as she prowled out of the dense fog behind them. She had known exactly where they were. She was following them, tracking their movements.

"Where are you going sweet Doraan?" she purred. "You are very far away from home."

Doraan said nothing, only crossed his arms over his chest, glaring at the unwanted visitor. She had made an appearance too many times this past week. He didn't like it. She had a reason for it, and that thought made his skin crawl.

She chuckled. "Not going to tell me, hm?" Her thick, fur-lined cloak boasted a hood of wool and black fur, leaving only her face and the end of her braided dark-red hair visible.

She opened her mouth but closed it again, cocking her head and narrowing her eyes at him. "Something feels different here." She turned in a circle, cloak billowing out around her, looking at each member of the crew. "You're all a bit more on edge than usual. You are hiding something from me, aren't you?"

"The only thing we are hiding is a hull full of rum."

Forcina laughed—a malicious, grating sound that rattled his eardrums. "Oh, Doraan, you know I can smell a lie from a mile away." She smirked, taking a few steps closer to him. "But I'm not here to play games this time. I have news for you."

Doraan cast a quick glance to Cormac, who was staring at Forcina with an unwavering look of disgust. "What kind of news?" Doraan asked.

She smiled a toothy grin that looked more like she was baring her fangs. "Well, I suppose it might be quite sad news for you. Although, happy for many others."

"I've no interest in your news, Forcina. Leave and let us be on our way." He waved a dismissive hand at her, tired of her perpetual games. He couldn't care less about whatever she was trying to do, but one thing was for certain; he needed her off this ship so that she didn't see Kamira. If she knew someone had been able to board the ship, she would not only ruin his entire plan, but there was no knowing what she might do to Kamira.

"Oh, no? You don't want to know about dear old mom and dad? You don't want to know what they have been up to since your ghostly visit?"

"Frankly, I couldn't care less about what they are up to. They proved they are no longer my parents, so I am no longer their son."

Forcina flashed a sinister grin that made her features appear feline, as if she were ready to pounce at any moment. "More lies, my dearest Doraan. You are such a fool. Must we constantly talk in this endless loop? Why can't you ever just be honest with me?"

"Because you are nothing more than a cowardly snake!" he roared, unable to hold down his temper any longer. "You could've helped your people. You could have saved them and figured out a way to overthrow my father long ago, but instead you cursed his son—a son he doesn't even care about. So who's the real fool, Forcina? Because it's pretty clear to me."

Forcina's face twisted into something far more deadly—eyes like sharpened blades, mouth set in a hard line, the vein on the right side of her neck twitching with her ire as she lifted a hand. Cormac stepped in front of him shielding Doraan from the anger she was about to unleash. He pulled the gun free from the holster at his hip and pointed the barrel towards her face, no more than an inch away. The air sizzled between them.

"You've terrorized the lad enough, witch. Go back to whatever dark pit you crawled out of and leave us to live out the rest of our days on the sea in peace."

Doraan's heart pounded in his chest. Cormac had never spoken to Forcina that way. He always treated her like a delicate flower made of glass, careful not to make her crack, or far worse, shatter. The hatred-filled gaze she cast upon Cormac resembled what Doraan imagined death incarnate would look like. Her eyes were painted a terrifying shade of gray-blue—dark enough to be mistaken for black—and they bore into Cormac with an icy resolve as if she might reach into his soul and consume him.

"It must be killing you to have missed all these years with your family, Cormac." She spat his name as if it were the worst thing that had ever come from her mouth, taking a step closer until the tip of his pistol was pressed into the flesh between her eyes. "Not able to see them grow into adulthood, get married, and have children of their own."

Cormac growled, a low rumbling hum that made Doraan flinch from its ferocity as he cocked his gun.

"Oh, look who's finally fighting back after all this time. I must say I do like this side of you, Cormac. Where have you been hiding it?"

"Right under your ugly nose," he said, just as he pulled the trigger. The shot rang out through the quiet of the snow storm, echoing around them, but the bullet missed its mark. Forcina was fast— able to manipulate the wind to propel herself at unnatural speeds. They had never been able to land a shot on her, and not for lack of trying.

"Good try, old man. I commend you for actually getting close for once."

Cormac's nostrils flared as both he and Doraan spun to find Forcina standing in the middle of the main deck. She pulled her hood to the side, revealing where the bullet had pierced the fabric just beside her Temple.

Cormac wasted no time angling his pistol at her again, but before he could pull the trigger, Kamira sprinted up from the hull and froze on the last step when she spotted Forcina.

Forcina's brow creased as she turned round to see who had stumbled up behind her. "Who is..." she began, but Cormac gave her no time to finish as he took his shot once more and, for the first time in ten years, the bullet pierced through flesh. Red blood sprayed out onto the icy wooden boards of the deck, the droplets freezing upon impact.

She shrieked, spinning back around and gripping her shoulder where blood seeped between her fingers. Her chest rose and fell with stilted breaths, and she slumped forward, pinning Cormac with her feral gaze. She bared her teeth, growling at him, and took a hitched step forward.

Cormac remained stoic as he reached over and pulled a pistol from Doraan's hip, immediately firing on Forcina a third time. She roared in frustration, stopping the bullet with a gust of wind before disappearing in a haze of snow and fog.

"Skies above," Kamira breathed, eyes wide. "Was that Forcina?"

"Yes," Cormac said, as Doraan stared at the spot where Forcina's blood still lay, a frozen red puddle upon the deck. "And we've just made her very angry. We have to get to Neilmaar, yesterday."

20

KAMIRA

An endless landscape of sprawling rural hills lay before them. They had finally made it to Neilmaar.

Cormac had docked the ship on the north side of the hills, which meant Kamira had quite the trek ahead of her. The plan was for her to row one of the boats to the closest shore, which just so happened to be the furthest northern piece of beach, sandwiched between the bubbling Kryystal Cove and the roiling Estdar Sea, before taking the long hike over the verdant hills to the city.

At least they had made it to this point quickly. In less than two weeks, the *Cursed Soul* made it from the boiling beaches of Aksahri to the frigid peak of the Uskdar Sea. Kamira was to thank for this, of course. She pushed the ship—probably quicker than she should have—guiding it as it sliced through the icy waves with fluid ease. As they sailed, she would reach out to sense any frozen barriers obstructing their path and shatter them into millions of shimmering pieces. She was able to get them to their current location a full three days ahead of schedule, which definitely hadn't gone unnoticed by the crew. She was worried she might have misinterpreted Cormac's insistence in getting to Neilmaar as fast as possible, but he reassured her countless times that she was doing good, and he would take care of the crew. He kept good on his promise because by the time they made it to this spot, the crew were as excited and carefree as could be, ready for Kamira to go ashore. She just hoped she wouldn't let them down.

The entire crew had been on edge since Forcina's visit. Everyone was jumpy, anxious that she could show up at any moment and enact her wrath upon them for what transpired all those nights ago. Doraan had spent that night scrubbing away the evidence of Cormac's actions—as if getting rid of the blood meant it had never happened.

Kamira gazed at the peaks of the hills shimmering in the morning light, mesmerized by the grass swaying in the swift breeze. Beyond those verdurous peaks, she knew the city would be gleaming, and she couldn't wait to see it in all its glory.

She had never been to Neilmaar, but her brother often spoke of its wealth and beauty. Some of the richest men in the realm lived in the city. It was also the oldest city in all of Emmoria, containing knowledge of the Empire that stretched back thousands of years to the first inhabitants of the realm.

Adonis had also told her that many who lived here still worshiped the gods of old—the very gods that the Brothers of the Spring believed bestowed the Sorcerers' their powers. It made sense that the Brothers would choose this city as their home.

There wasn't much about the old gods in the history books back in Torheim or even in Aksahri. They had been long forgotten by most of the realm. The only reason she knew of them was because of her brother. Supposedly, they were powerful beings who lived in the sky, and it was believed that one of these gods created them all, both Gifted and Ungifted.

Kamira didn't quite understand how there could be strange beings that lived in the sky, so powerful that they created life and an entire world all on their own. But who was she to judge what others believed? She had never seen the need to believe in anything but herself, really. She believed in what she saw around her—the sea, the forests, the mountains, the sky, and all the living things in the realm. Many believed that the gods would grant them eternal life after death if they prayed to them, offering up gifts and sacrifices. A life by their side, reborn as a god themselves.

Kamira honestly didn't really care what happened after life. She was content to live in the moment.

Even the Brothers of the Spring didn't make much sense to her, although their beliefs made a whole lot more sense than the existence of gods. The Brothers believed first in the Spring of Zjanoak and its supernatural waters, but ultimately they believed in the power of knowledge.

Their doctrine was created on the idea that all things followed the Pyramid of Koruum. The pyramid consisted of four tiers, the lowest tier being life. If you are given life, you must feed it–taking care of yourself and surviving–treating all other life with respect. This was followed by the tier of earth.

Just as all people were given life, so was the earth. It provided all beings a place to live, and it must be taken care of, and one must use it to fully understand life itself and how to further it. The third tier was synergy. This involved combining one's own essence with all those around them, becoming one with all living things, and only then could one understand the true meaning of life.

The fourth and final tier, topping off the pyramid. was ascension. Those who had mastered the first three tiers could ascend, discovering the ultimate knowledge of the world by bathing in the Spring and drinking its waters, grounding them in the world and binding their being to the elements around them to connect with life itself. Ascension and the waters of the Spring granted them powers that surpassed the Sorcerers of Emmoria, giving them the ultimate knowledge of the old gods.

Or so the legend went.

The entire thing sounded oddly like how the early Ungifted lived. When they first came to Emmoria, they practically worshiped the Elementalists, thinking that if they did strange things like drink the blood of a Gifted, or sleep with one, they would gain their knowledge and abilities and become just as powerful. History always seemed to repeat itself in one form or another. That thought brought her back to the reality of the Emerald King and the impending war.

It was a known fact that war was inevitable. There would always be some extremist able to rally followers to their cause and spark a revolution. This time, it was the King in the North. She didn't disagree with all he was doing. The Sorcerers should have never been sent into hiding, and the number of her kin murdered in the Emperor's name was something she didn't like to think about often. But this self proclaimed king didn't just want freedom for the Sorcerers, he wanted justice, and that was something that she didn't stand behind. His goal had never been peace and that is what Kamira believed in. That's what she truly wanted.

There was a small part of her that always hoped being the wife of Lord Tarkiin would have allowed her a chance to push for change—that she could whisper her beliefs and ideas into his ear and he would take them to the council. But she never had the chance, and what she discovered about Tarkiin in their short twenty-four hour marriage was that he cared for nothing but himself and his own thirst for power.

Kamira knew peace could be spread throughout the realm. With the right ruler at its helm and an overhaul of the vicious, harmful laws put forth by the Emperor, unity could happen, demolishing the Brother's belief in the pyramid of Koruum. She would love to see their pyramid come crashing down around them.

The more Kamira discovered of Doraan and the closer they became, the more she truly thought that he might be the one able to do it. His passion and love for Emmoria was evident, but the only thing that stunted him was his hatred of sorcery. There was a bold determination that resided just behind his eyes—a resolve and a fight that not many had. If she could prove to him that Sorcerers were not a stain on this world, but rather a potentially powerful ally, then she could get him back home to sit at the helm of the realm.

"Are you ready?" Doraan came up beside her, following her gaze to the rolling hills, snaked with fog and pops of yellow spread throughout.

She huffed, looking at him with a shrug. "As ready as I'll ever be."

"Kamira." His voice deepened, growing quieter. "I want you to know that doing this for me means everything. It..."

She placed a hand on his arm. "I know, you don't have to say it. I know what it means, and if I succeed, I know what that means, too. I am with you."

His eyes widened, a sparkle in them giving way to the emotion he felt at her words. He turned his head away and brought a hand up to his mouth, clearing his throat. "The sea is rough here, we can move a bit further along the coast to where it's calmer."

"I'll be fine," she assured him.

"Right, then." He raked a hand along his scalp, still not looking at her. "The skiff is ready for you."

Kamira looked over the railing and down to the small boat waiting for her far below in the rocky Uskdar sea.

"Listen," Doraan said, gripping her shoulder and turning her to look him in the eye. "If you feel unsafe, if you fear for your life at any moment, come straight back here. Understood?"

"I can take care of myself, you know."

He brought his other hand up to rest on her other shoulder. "I'm serious. We know nothing of the Brothers. They are very secretive and they might not take lightly to someone poking around in search of them. If you ever feel in danger, leave and don't look back."

"Understood." She nodded, watching as relief washed over him.

"Good luck."

"Thanks," she replied before climbing onto the boarding ladder. Before she descended, she turned to him with one last thought. "If I succeed in this, I want you to give sorcery a chance. I'm risking my life for you and your crew because I believe in you, Doraan. You are my Emperor, you are the people's hope, both the Gifted and Ungifted alike. They need you. Emmoria needs you."

Doraan's gaze took on a far away look as his brows drew together and his chest rose with a deep, sorrowful breath before he looked back at her, locking onto her eyes with a fierceness that sent a chill through her core. "I will try."

Kamira offered him a small smile and nodded. It was as good an answer as any she would get from him. She climbed down the ladder, boarded the small craft, grabbed the paddles, and rowed herself out to sea. She didn't dare use her sorcery for help since they were all watching her every stroke as she got closer and closer to shore. She could see the worry on all their faces, the distress in their eyes. They didn't think she would make it. That thought made her curious as to what would happen when one of them tried to get close to shore. Did they run into a solid force like the ship did when she had tried to guide it to shore? Were they flung backward several feet? Or could they literally not will their own limbs to move, left frozen in place? She would have to ask when she returned.

Waves chopped against the boat from the strong, eastern current. She gritted her teeth and channeled her strength to row until the *Cursed Soul* was no more than a black blip along the horizon.

By the time she reached the sandy strip of land, she was heaving and gasping for breath. Kamira jumped out of the craft, shrieking at the bite of the icy water on her shins as it seeped into her pants. She grabbed the edge of the boat and trudged it fully onto land before collapsing into the sand, rolling onto her back, arms outstretched beside her, panting.

The heat from the bright sun above made her exposed skin tingle. She sheltered her eyes from the light with a sand-covered arm, sputtering as sprinkles of sand landed in her mouth.

Kamira pushed herself up to observe her surroundings. Squinting against the bright sun, she scanned the seemingly endless stretch of shore, searching for a spot to hide her boat and ensure she had a way to return to the ship. Tall dunes leading into grassy peaks were all she could see. There was no gift of a large boulder or small crevice to stash it, only the beach and plenty of it.

She took a deep breath and stared at the mounds of sand before closing her eyes and reaching down into her core, tugging against the well of sorcery she knew was there, and pulling forth that piece of her that called for the manipulation of the earth. It was like calling forth an old friend eager to help. It was the one element she hadn't touched while on the *Cursed Soul*.

She had practiced both water and air constantly, feeling more comfortable each day using those gifts. She continued to dabble with fire, only using it in small doses, and it was still as sporadic as it had always been. She couldn't figure out how to keep it under control—it was like trying to tame a wild beast that constantly bucked and reared with every command.

Now was her chance to at least *try* to move the earth.

She dusted the power off like an old book that had sat collecting sediment for years. The last time she attempted the use of earth sorcery was before she had married Tarkiin. She stilled her mind and centered herself in the nature around her, feeling its subtle ebbs and flows beneath her feet, so close to both water and air. Kamira grasped it, pulling on the sand around the craft. She opened her eyes as the grains moved at her command and watched the boat sink beneath the surface until it was completely hidden from view.

She smiled, letting out a sigh of relief. The element had come to her so easily. Practicing these last few weeks helped. Kamira could feel the spurring of a great power within her ever since she started using her gifts more. She felt like up until this point, she had only used a small spark of what she was truly capable of. Just tapping into the surface. She was still afraid to dig too deep, worried she would lose control and hurt someone, or herself. That was something she would deal with another time, attempting to use her full power when she was unhurried and alone, but for now, the morning sun was moving high overhead, and she needed to get to Neilmaar, quickly.

She dug her hands and wet boots into the dune, struggling to climb as sand fell away beneath her grip. "Bleeding Stars!" she shouted as she slid all the way back down to where she had started. Huffing, she collapsed to her knees on the beach, grumbling in annoyance. She was so tired.

Why had she agreed to this again?

Kamira groaned and turned to fall back against the sand dune, searching the churning sea toward where the *Cursed Soul* lingered—no more than a speck between the light blue sky and deep blue ocean. Waves crashed onto the shore and rolled toward her, stopping just before her feet as the tide pulled it back in.

They didn't know if more of the Emerald King's warships were on Neilmaar's waters so they had stopped just far enough away not to be spotted by any oncoming ships, or vessels docked close to the city.

If only she could blink and be there in the city's center. That journey through the rough white caps had taken more out of her than she had expected. Suddenly, an idea popped into her head that had her laughing for not thinking of it sooner.

Kamira pushed herself up, spinning to face the dune once again, one hand on her hip in determination, another held out in front of her as she pushed against the earth, bending it to her will. A staircase of carved sand emerged from the dune in front of her. With a satisfied smirk, Kamira ascended her makeshift steps until her feet met with the soft green grass of a wide open field covered in blossoms of yellow and orange. The wind brushed by her, tickling the field and sending the flowers dancing in a wave of color. With a flick of her wrist, the sand folded into itself to form a smooth dune once more.

Determined, Kamira huffed, shielding her eyes from the sun rays, and mapped a path toward the city that lay just beyond the humps of green ahead of her. She walked through the blossoming field, enjoying the feel of solid ground beneath her for the first time in weeks. Her body swayed back and forth, as if the tides of the sea still bobbed beneath her. She had grown accustomed to the constant rocking of the ship, and the sea had become especially rough over the past week as they sailed through the harsh Uskdar sea. Kamira was feeling its effects, and it made her slightly nauseous as she trekked onward.

By the time she made it over the gentle slopes of the grassy knolls, the entire city of Neilmaar was spread out before her in all its glory. It was so much more spectacular and breathtaking than she could have even imagined.

The city spanned from the Kryystal Cove to the Est-dar sea. Bordering its southern edge was the Neim Forest, which boasted monstrous trees with branches full of deep red and bright copper leaves. The entire city sparkled like a pearl beneath the sun, enriched with flourishing land-scapes and shimmering waves. From the red terra-cotta roofs, to the scattered cobbled lanes, and the naturally carved sandstone structures, history emanated from every nook. She wanted to learn its secrets and uncover myster-ies, all the while wondering how it would feel to live in such a spectacular place.

A swift breeze wisped around her, bringing the smell of crisp exotic spices and the sweet scent of nectar. The sun was beginning to lower in the sky, the red and cream of the city falling into shadow. She needed to get inside before night fell completely.

A barrier of weathered tan stone encircled the city, caging its beauty within. An obstacle that Kamira had not prepared for. She hadn't thought Neilmaar would be so heavily guarded, but it looked to be the only possible way into the city from her position atop the hill. With spears in their hands and swords at their sides, guards stood still as statues on either side of a worn and rusted iron gate. Black metal breast plates painted with the Emperor's sigil—a crowned bronze falcon—covered their ruddy red leathers, and winged russet helmets hid their faces. The large gate loomed behind them, steadfast and imposing—the thick bars resembling a prison cell.

As she approached them, she took a deep breath, feeling a twinge of unease. The guards eyed her suspiciously, their hands moving to the swords on their hips. Kamira was still dressed like a boy, so she knew she didn't look like a threat, but their hard stares made her feel like they could see straight through her disguise.

"State your business," the guard on the right said gruffly.

"I'm here to visit my brother," she squeaked, clearing her throat and clasping her hands together to keep them from shaking.

"Name?" the large guard asked.

"Adonis Nardisee."

The guard nodded, obviously recognizing the name, and yelled up to the guard stationed atop the wall to open the gate.

She didn't dare take a breath until she was inside the city walls. When she finally heard the solid sound of the iron gate clanging back into place, she let out a breath and turned to the city before her, eyes growing wide with bewilderment. She hadn't thought it possible, but the city was far more dazzling from within.

She had never seen so many people in one space in her life. Not even Emmoria's capital city of Aksahri was this full of life. The wealth and power of this place was painted not only in the streets but in the massive white stone buildings, in the clothes the people wore, and in the very air she was breathing. For a place so crowded, the air smelt as if a perfume of lavender and mint had been spritzed all throughout it. The white buildings were spotless, glowing under the sun rays, all of them massive structures that looked like castles built for a king. The entire city looked like it was connected, with bridges arching from one building to the next, creating tunnels beneath where townsfolk scurried back and forth.

It was huge—much larger than she thought it would be. She knew Aksahri was the largest of the cities in Emmoria, but the buildings there were not nearly as tall as these, and the ruddy tan of the Aksahrian structures made the entire city almost blend into the desert, hiding its true size from view.

How was she going to find her brother in a place like this? It would take her days to find him in all of this, and where did she even start? Adonis never told her where exactly the Brothers were, or where he was in this city for that matter. When he had left all those years ago, all he told her was that he was going to Neilmaar and had joined the Brothers of the Spring, a place where he could freely use his powers.

Kamira closed her eyes and whispered, "Sea and sky help me," into the crisp, sweet air before she stepped into the throng of people.

21

DORAAN

The floral scent of wildflowers mingled with the salty mist of the oceans spray as Kamira rowed to shore. Doraan held his breath, watching Kamira through the spy glass until she safely landed on the beach. He let out a sigh of relief. "She made it," he said, putting down the telescope as he turned to Cormac. "Now we wait and hope for the best."

Cormac nodded solemnly. "There is a shift in the wind. A storm may be approaching. I'll have the men prepare."

"Do you think she'll be okay?" Doraan asked, ignoring Cormac's words.

"She'll be alright. She's strong, a fighter like us."

"What if she doesn't come back? She could have been playing us this whole time. Using us just to get far away from Aksahri." The words tasted sour in his mouth.

"You know that isn't true, Doraan. You're spiraling. Reel in your thoughts."

Doraan sighed. He knew Cormac was right, but so much was riding on Kamira. Their lives were, quite literally, in her hands. He had to trust her.

He thought about her parting words to him, *'You are my Emperor'*. Those words pierced through something deep within him. He rubbed at his chest as if still feeling them in his aching heart. She believed in him, even though they didn't share the same views, and so he would show her the same respect. He would believe in her, too. She would find the answers they needed, and she would come back to them. To him.

But he couldn't shake that sense of unease gnawing at him, twisting his insides until he felt sick to his stomach. They still hadn't seen Forcina since the night Cormac shot her. She wasn't the type to ignore that kind of attack. Doraan felt like a sitting duck floating in the middle of the ocean, just waiting for a shark to bite.

Each gust of wind that whipped around him furthered the tension coursing through him like a molten liquid, setting his blood boiling. It was the waiting that made him most anxious, knowing that she could appear at any moment, and there was nothing they could do about it.

He was even more afraid of what she might do to Kamira if she got her claws in her. Forcina would definitely force her from the ship or, worse, kill her.

Doraan paced the length of the *Cursed Soul* as his men prepared the ship for the coming storm. He looked out over the endless sea behind them where gray clouds gathered, growing darker with each passing moment. There was something strange about it—the unnatural way the clouds moved sporadically, almost like a giant flock of birds following one another through the wind streams.

Doraan jumped at the sudden clap of thunder, startling when lightning illuminated the horizon.

He squinted into the looming storm. A dark form floated toward them at a frightening speed. With another blinding flash of lightning, Doraan's heart leapt into his throat. Panic overtook him and he gasped for breath, a choking wheeze gushing from his lips as he desperately tried to warn his crew. Grabbing his throat, he finally called out, "All hands to quarters!" stumbling as he rushed toward the helm.

Each of his crew turned to him, confusion etched in their features.

Doraan pointed to the quickening storm. "Forcina! Weigh anchor! Unfurl the sails!" That was all they needed to hear before they scrambled into action. Doraan joined them, sprinting as fast as his limping body could take him to the helm.

Cannons were readied and pistols were loaded for the impending onslaught that was drawing closer with every clipped breath. A thick blanket of darkness enveloped them like a falling shadow, blocking out sun and sky, bringing with it the bitter tang of sorcery. "The lanterns! Light the lanterns!" Doraan heard Cormac yell from somewhere below. Tiny lights flickered to life one after the other at his command, but it still wasn't enough as the wind swept around them, howling like a pack of hungry wolves, extinguishing the flames.

Fog wrapped around them like a sheet, sucking the air from their lungs. Doraan's heart raced to the point of pain in his chest as an ominous silence drowned out the ever present song of the sea. They each stood frozen, squinting through the mist, attempting to find Forcina in the darkness that surrounded them. Doraan wasn't sure anyone was actually breathing until there was a slip of a finger sparking a pistol to life, quickly followed by the *boom* of cannon fire ringing out through the haze. Doraan turned the wheel of the *Cursed Soul* sharply, sailing blindly while his men shot at air.

A violent gust of wind rocked the ship hard to the left as water sprayed across the deck and drowned out the yelps of the crew drifting toward him. Doraan spun the ship's wheel as fast as he could, saving them all just before the *Cursed Soul* capsized.

Suddenly, everything stopped. The *Cursed Soul* rocked back, flinging a few of the men overboard with its sudden force. The seas had calmed and the clouds parted to reveal a blue sky, the sun shining down on them, illuminating the damage the unnatural storm had caused.

The foremast of the ship had snapped, splintered wood scattered across the deck. The black sail and its mast were barely a shadow beneath the waves as they slowly sank to the bottom of the sea. The entire portside railing was gone, and the sail of the main mast sported a giant hole, making it completely useless and leaving them vulnerable, unable to fight back.

Doraan scanned the sky, but Forcina was nowhere to be seen. The air around him grew thick, sticking like sap to his skin, seeping into his lungs and clogging his pores until he could no longer draw breath. He was choking on air.

Doraan gulped in frantic rasps of the heavy air unable to pull it into his lungs. He tore at his chest and throat, stumbling as he desperately tried to breathe.

She was here.

She wouldn't kill him, but she would let him get as close to the brink as possible. That moment of wavering between the living and the dead.

Doraan coughed, spit sputtering from his lips as he pointlessly rubbed at his throat trying to work the clog free. The only thing that could fight against sorcery was sorcery, and Doraan had none. He cast a glance down to the main deck where Cormac, Jorne, and multiple other crew members lay unmoving. He tried to call out to them, wanted to go to them, but he could feel himself losing consciousness.

Pressure built along his forehead, as if someone had wrapped a belt around his head and was pulling it as tight as they could. That same build up of tension traveled down behind his eyes, blurring his vision. Just as darkness crept in from all sides, tunneling his sight, he saw a figure dressed head to toe in inky black leathers, gleaming in the sunlight. A cape billowed behind her like the obsidian wings of a raven as she floated down toward him, as graceful as a bird herself.

With a snap of her fingers, the thickened air evaporated, and Doraan fell to his hands and knees, wheezing with painful gasping breaths, coughing uncontrollably from the sudden rush of air back into his lungs. It burned through him as if a fuse had been lit, the flame traveling and scorching through every corner of his being. He bit hard against it, clenching his fists, nails biting into the rough wood below, flesh scraping against the splintered bark.

The distant creak of shifting wooden boards steadily drew closer as Doraan felt the vibrations of someone approaching beneath him. He didn't look up until Forcina's shiny black leather boots came to a stop just in front of him.

"Where is she?" the witch growled.

Doraan ignored her, pushing back onto his knees, finally looking up at her. The burning within him eased as he glared into her seething gray eyes. He always thought they looked like swirling pools of liquified silver—almost mesmerizing in their uniqueness.

Doraan had often thought about the strangeness of Forcina's features. The deep red of her hair was unlike any color he had seen on a person. It was unnatural, the color he imagined the Salamanders from the War of the Four Kings fairytale to have. But that was just a story and Forcina was real, standing in front of him with murder etched into the furious lines of her face. The silver of her eyes looked almost as if it was moving, shifting, and shimmering beneath her stark black lashes. He bit back against the shiver that threatened to rake through him. Forcina was most definitely unnatural. When she was near him, there was always a nagging in the back of his mind telling him she didn't belong here.

A memory suddenly flashed before him of something Kamira had said only days before. *'A Sorceress can't curse someone.'* The more he thought about it, the more he realized he had never heard of such a thing. Over the years, he had spent time off and on attempting to learn more about Sorcery and how it worked. He had never once read about a Sorcerer cursing something or changing the course of a person's life entirely. They dealt in the elements—fire, water, air, and earth. Suddenly, nothing made sense. His entire life flashed before his eyes and he had no idea of anything anymore.

"Who are you?" he heard himself ask just before cold air rushed toward him, whirling around him so fast it sliced his cheek. He reached up to touch it, biting back against the sting of the open flesh. His hands came away red with blood.

The swirling air picked up speed, howling as it closed in. And then he was no longer on solid ground. He floated, rising higher and higher as if he were no more than a feather caught in a draft. Forcina rose with him until they were both suspended in the air, held by nothing more than her sorcery.

"Who am *I*, Doraan?" She scoffed. "Well, I am your keeper, of course. Your owner. Your sovereign."

The wind wrapped around him tighter, his arms pinned to his sides until he was no longer able to move. "You are nothing but a depraved coward," he ground out. "If you really wanted revenge on my father, why don't you just kill me and be done with it?"

Forcina's nostrils flared, eyes like silver spitting flames. "Because I'm not done playing with you yet. Now, where is the girl?! I searched the ship and she isn't here. What did you do with her?"

"We dropped her off at Torheim, days ago."

The cocoon of air tightened until he was unable to draw in another breath. He moved a single finger and cried out when agonizing pain sprung forth. Blood slowly dripped down his hand from the fresh cut.

"I wouldn't move if I were you," Forcina purred. "Not unless you want to lose a finger. Now...." She floated so close to him that he could feel her hot, sticky breath caress his face as she said, "Where is the girl?"

He had never seen her this close before. At this distance, he could see every line carved into her skin, every hair, every pore, and with a newfound clarity that she was not what she seemed.

"What are you?" he breathed.

Forcina froze, those silver eyes growing dark, their shimmer lost to the blackness as she narrowed them. "*What* am I?" Her head fell back and she cackled hoarsely.

The sound grated in his ears and he angled his head away from it.

"It's funny how after all these years you have finally thought to ask me that question."

Sweat beaded on his brow, his heart pounding in his ears at the look of pure malice that spread across her face.

"I am something that you cannot even comprehend. Something that you will never be able to defeat."

And then he was falling, arms and legs flailing, desperate to find purchase to at least slow the fall, but there was nothing. Doraan had barely a split second to look down before he felt the biting smack of breaking through the cold surface as he plunged into the icy waters. By the time he had pushed through the murky depths of the sea, propelling his way back to the surface, Forcina was gone.

Doraan cried out in anger, slashing his hand across the ocean's wavy surface, and this time welcoming the sting against his skin as it slammed against the water, spraying salt into the air.

22

KAMIRA

"Hoy there, lad!" Kamira caught a glance of an elderly woman waving beside her, skin withered and wrinkled from countless years spent in the sun, hair stark white against the dark wooden door behind her. Kamira ignored her and continued down the cobbled street, eyes set on the sparkling cerulean hue of the ocean in front of her. Ships ebbed and bobbed at the docks, waves splashing against them in a spray of foamy white. She smiled at the sight. Weeks aboard the *Cursed Soul* had caused her to fall in love with the ocean. The more she thought about it, the more she found herself not wanting to find a life anywhere else but upon the sea with the crew she had formed a kindred bond with so quickly. They had become like family to her, and she knew that she would do anything—even risking her life as she was now—to help them.

Suddenly, a looming figure stepped in front of her and blocked her view. Kamira squinted up at them, using her arm as a shield for her eyes against the sun's glare.

"You look hungry, lad. How 'bout a stop in for a bit o' fish pie?" the old woman said in a thick low-born accent.

"No, thank you." she said, peering around the woman to the ocean just a few paces away. She stepped to the side to go around her but the woman followed, smirking down at her.

"Ain't from 'round here are ye'? Best be fixin' for a warm bed to sleep in. Don't want to be 'round these parts when the sun goes down." She motioned to the street they were on and down to the docks where several large stern looking men were prowling.

The sea breeze swept toward them, bringing the delightful scent of freshly baked pastry and smoked meat. She leaned into the smell, following it through the air like a dog. It had been a long time since she had a delicious home cooked meal. Her stomach gave a hearty rumble, and the woman smiled down at her. "Come take a load off, lad."

She really was famished, and night would fall soon. She didn't want to be on the streets when it did, and maybe she could test out this place, ask a few questions surrounding the Brothers while she was there.

Kamira looked up to the wooden sign swinging in the breeze on rusty hinges. It read *The Ale and the Wench Inn & Tavern* in faded white letters. If worse came to worst, she could at least stay here for the night, gain any information she could and continue her search in the morning.

She glanced behind her, eyes darting across the city square. Her gaze caught on a glimpse of gleaming red hair and she spun back around. *Was that Forcina? No, it couldn't be.*

Red hair was rare in Torheim and Aksahri, but she had never been to Neilmaar, so maybe it was more common here. It was probably best to get out of sight, just in case.

She smiled at the woman and said, "Might you have a room available for the evening? And anything other than fish pie?" Kamira had eaten her fill of fish during her time on board the *Cursed Soul* and she wasn't sure she could stomach more. The thought alone made her belly queasy, unwelcoming bile rising in her throat.

The woman only laughed, putting a hand to Kamira's back, leading her into the worn wooden door. "We have plenty, lad."

As soon as Kamira stepped inside the small tavern, she was smacked in the face with the pungent scent of sweat, grease, and rum. She almost winced at the putrid smell, putting a hand up to discreetly cover her nose. It smelled like the musty, cloying scent of a wet dog—if said dog had rolled in a vat of animal grease and then jumped into a bucket of spiced rum.

A number of heads turned at her entrance, most with careless expressions, turning back to their tankards, but a few looked as if they wanted to peel the flesh from her bones. She quickly looked away from them, shivering with unease. *Maybe this wasn't a good idea after all.*

The woman pointed to an empty table in the corner. "Take a seat and I'll bring ye a plate 'er food."

Kamira nodded and took a seat to observe the cozy seaside tavern.

Laughter and the sounds of clinking glasses filled the space. There were two long tables in the center of the room, each with several sailors sat spread out on stools along them, their rough voices echoing through the rafters. Behind those tables were several smaller ones, hidden in shadow, where a few patrons lingered and one large man sat with a woman—dressed in with the least amount of clothing Kamira thought she had ever seen—giggling on his lap, stealing kisses, and allowing the man to touch her in the most obscene ways for a public setting. Kamira averted her gaze, looking to the other side of the room where a high-top bar was, and the kitchen could just barely be seen through a small window behind it.

Kamira continued to study those within the tavern, trying to discern if anyone might be approachable enough to discreetly question them about the Brothers. Adonis had never actually told her where they were within the city—only that a large group of the brothers resided here, and he was going to join them.

A good number of the patrons were definitely drunk and would probably be completely unhelpful, and a few others looked like they would rip someone's head off if they were to be disturbed.

She didn't get the chance to finish her perusal before the elderly woman brought over a plate full of smoked meat, a hearty array of roasted vegetables, and a thick slice of fresh baked bread. Kamira's mouth watered at the sight, her stomach rumbling in anticipation. The smell of the meal completely drowned out the horrid stench of the patrons surrounding her, and she sighed in relief.

She barely waited for the woman to set the plate down before she dug into the feast, groaning with each steaming hot bite. Almost all of the meals aboard the ship had been cold, and while she was grateful for the food they had, she had very much missed a home-cooked supper like this one.

Kamira had practically inhaled the first half of her heaping pile of food before looking up and locking eyes with a man across the room. He was smirking at her, his deep set brown eyes dancing with amusement, illuminated by the flickering candle on the table in front of him.

His skin was a few shades darker than her fair complexion, his hair so dark it was almost black, but there was a hint of copper that shimmered when he tilted his head to the side. It was long on top and short along the side leading into the shadow of a beard.

She would have spent time studying his handsome features further if her view hadn't been blocked when a stranger moved in front of her. She looked up, craning her neck to find a barrel chested man with blond hair grinning down at her with a gnarly smile.

"Are ye a lass or a lad?"

Kamira raised a brow. Should she be offended by that question? Granted, she was still dressed in Doraan's old clothes, but she was no longer actively trying to hide her identity. Her hair had grown a bit over the past weeks, now curling behind her ears and annoying her to no end. However, she supposed its length still presented her with a boyish look.

"I'm not really sure why that matters to you, kind sir," she replied, going back to her dwindling plate of food.

As she was about to spear a vegetable with her fork, the man's hand came down hard against the table and the remains of her meal went flying from the plate in all directions.

"I asked yer' a question," he growled.

Kamira calmly set her utensils down and was about to tell the man exactly where he could stick his questions when a deep, velvet voice lilted toward them. "Don't you know it's rude to ask a person whether they are a man or a woman? Honestly, Logan, it's a wonder how you have ever gotten a woman to sleep with you after a question like that."

The blond-haired man, Logan, stiffened at the voice, his red face contorting into a snarl as he turned to face the owner of the voice.

It was the man she had locked eyes with only moments before, that same smirk still plastered across his face as he slowly walked toward them, his eyes never leaving hers. He was all broad shoulders and lean muscles, almost a full head taller than anyone else in the *Ale and the Wench*. It wasn't until he was beside the blond man that he finally broke their eye contact and turned to Logan. "Besides, anyone could see that she is obviously a lady." He cast her a quick glance and winked before facing Logan once again.

Kamira's heart skipped a beat and she looked away quickly, heat coloring her cheeks. She chanced a glance back at the two strange men, who were now caught in a silent staring battle, Logan's eye twitching with the strain of it. A slight movement had her looking down to find Logan's hand balled into a fist just before it arched up straight at the handsome stranger's face.

Kamira pushed up from her chair, mouth ajar, a breath away from warning the dark-haired man, but the words never came. Logan's fist hit the man across the jaw, his head whipping to the side, and then the entire tavern erupted into chaos.

Skies above. Kamira ducked beneath the flying limbs of the brawling men, hoping to make her way to the door and secure her escape, but she couldn't help herself.... she looked back once more toward the man who had tried to help her. Their eyes met with an almost electric force. His russet eyes went wide, and he yelled out to her just as a fist flung out from the crowd and hit her square in the nose.

The entire tavern froze as if stuck in slow motion. Pain flared through her skull. She reached out blindly toward the nearest table as she fell, grappling for something to grab onto. In a blurry haze, she caught the handsome stranger's gaze once again as he sprinted toward her, shoving patrons from his path until he was just inches from her. She desperately stretched out her hand to meet his, their fingertips brushing briefly against one another just before everything faded to black.

23

KAMIRA

Kamira's eyes flew open. She sat up, instantly regretting that decision as her head seared with a pounding pressure from the sudden rush of blood. She brought a hand up to her forehead, pressing against the pain before moving it gently to her throbbing nose, wincing.

"You should lie back down."

She froze, remembering that soulful, almost rhythmic voice, and then it all came crashing back to her. She looked beside her and was greeted by that same boyish smirk and honeyed brown eyes from when she was in the tavern.

"You took a nasty punch to the nose and hit your head when you fell," he said, wincing as if seeing it again in his mind. "I tried to catch you, but...well, I obviously didn't make it in time."

It was so quiet with just the two of them in a small room. Kamira blinked a few times, recalling a brush of rough flesh against her fingers and then nothing.

She looked down, startling as she realized she was on someone's bed. She jumped up to her feet, swaying slightly, and grabbed her head as the room spun around her. She felt as if she was rolling downhill in a rum barrel. She stumbled, placing a hand on the wall beside her.

The man was quick to stand in front of her, placing his hands on her shoulders, and steadied her before she could even comprehend his movements. His touch seared her skin—as if he had just placed them into a pit of burning embers.

"Don't touch me!" she yelled, pulling away from his grasp and slapping one of his hands.

He released her instantly.

"You should really lie down. I'm not going to hurt you." His voice was like a warm blanket on a winter night. It wrapped around her, making her feel safe. *Skies, how hard did I hit my head?*

Kamira sighed and collapsed back onto the bed, closing her eyes against the dizziness that hadn't yet subsided.

"Are you okay?" the stranger asked. "I was just about to go and find the physician."

"I'm fine. There's no need for that." She opened her eyes and looked up at him. There was actual concern on his face. He was worried about her, even though they didn't know one another.

□"Are you sure? You haven't had a chance to see your nose."

□She frowned. "What's wrong with my nose?"

□"Well." He screwed up his face, passing a hand mirror from the bedside table to her. "See for yourself."

□She glared at him, snatching the metal handle of the mirror from his grasp. The man brought a finger up to his mouth, biting onto the knuckle of his pointer finger in anticipation. "Skies, it can't be all that..." Kamira looked at herself in the mirror and screamed. "My nose!"

□She almost passed out all over again. Her nose looked as if someone had removed it and placed it a half inch to the right of where it should be. It was swollen to an enormous size, already turning an ugly shade of purple beneath the dried blood caked on her face.

□"Put it back!" she screeched, flinging the mirror onto the bed as if it were a cobra about to strike. She turned to the man, desperate. "You have to move it back!"

□He snorted, crossing his thick arms over his chest. They were covered in a bushy layer of hair as dark as the hair atop his head. She had a mind to go over there and rip some of those hairs out of his skin. "Why not?" she shrieked, frantically standing up and rushing toward him. "Please!"

□"No way." He put his hands up in front of him, backing away from her and staying just out of her reach. "I'm not going to be held responsible for doing it wrong and possibly making it worse. I'll go get a physician."

□"It already is your fault!" she yelled, flailing her hands out in an attempt to show her frustration.

□"I'm sorry, but how exactly is it my fault?" He raised a single black bushy brow at her. "I didn't punch you."

□"If I remember correctly, you're the one who started the whole thing." It was her turn to cross her arms over her chest in defiance, and she threw an eye roll in for good measure.

□"Me?" he scoffed, putting a hand to his chest. "I was helping you."

□"I don't remember asking for it," she growled.

□He narrowed his eyes at her before huffing loudly. "Fine. You might have a point, but I'm still not going to touch your hideous nose."

□Kamira's eyes widened and her mouth dropped open. "How dare you! It's only hideous because of the brawl you started in that tavern." She stepped closer, stabbing him in the chest with her finger. "Bleeding stars, I shouldn't even be here right now. I should be out there looking for the...OUCH!"

□She bit her tongue, unable to finish her thought as the man's hands flew up and his thick fingers grasped her nose, tugging sharply. A sickening crack was followed by searing pain that laced through her entire face, causing tears to well in her eyes, threatening to spill free.

"Bloody blazing skies! You bastard!" She put a hand on either side of her now much more straight nose.

"The name's Jaario, actually." His lips twitched into a brief smirk. "And you're welcome," he added with a wink.

She glared at him with all the annoyance she could muster. "You couldn't have given me some warning first? That was almost worse than getting shot."

His brows instantly drew together at her off-handed comment. "When were you shot? Actually, the more important question is probably *why* were you shot? Are you a traveling thief?"

Kamira snorted and then groaned, gripping her throbbing nose. "No, I'm just...I'm a pirate."

He stared at her, mouth slightly ajar for a long moment before bursting out into a full bellied fit of laughter, his entire body shaking and tensing from the effort.

She only continued to glare at him. "What's so funny about that?"

Jaario swiped a finger beneath his eye, wiping away the tears that his laughter had caused. "You aren't like any pirate I've ever seen."

She tilted her head up, crossing her arms over her chest to prove her point. "I'm just as good a pirate as any other."

He chuckled. "I'm sure you are...uh, what's your name by the way?"

"Kamira," she huffed, gingerly prodding her aching nose.

"So what brings you, a *pirate*," he emphasized with a crooked smile, "to Neilmaar?"

"I'm looking for someone," she said quickly. "Which reminds me, I should really continue my search." Kamira turned toward the door and stomped her way over, placing a hand on the door latch, but stopped when Jaario's voice rumbled behind her.

"Have you any idea where the person you are looking for is?"

She didn't turn around or lower her hand from the latch. "No."

"I can help you."

She dropped her hand, spinning with narrowed eyes as she met his dark gaze. "How? You don't even know who I'm looking for."

"I've lived in Neilmaar for a long time. I know everyone and everything that goes on in this city," he said, crossing his arms over his chest as he casually leaned a shoulder against the wall beside her and winked.

Kamira frowned and glowered at him for a long moment before finally grunting in annoyance. "Fine, but I highly doubt you will know the person I'm looking for."

□He grinned, eyes dancing with anticipation. "Try me."

□"I'm looking for Adonis Nardisee."

His smile widened into something far more devilish.

She looked at him incredulously. "Don't tell me you actually know who I'm talking about?"

She didn't think it was possible but his grin widened even further. "As a matter of fact, I do."

A snort of disbelief echoed from her, followed by a groan of pain as a sharp pain ricocheted through her entire face.

"You should really stop snorting like that," Jaario said before pulling open the door and directing an arm out into the hallway. "After you."

She rolled her eyes. "I'll have you know that if this is some elaborate plan to steal my belongings and gain some coin, I don't have anything worth your time or effort. I'll even let you check my bag." She held the rucksack out for him to take.

"Don't you think if I wanted to rob you I would have done it while you were passed out on the bed?"

Damn him, he has a point. She cast him a final stabbing glare before huffing and walking out into the corridor.

His heavy footfalls followed her out, the door closing with a soft thud behind them. Her skin prickled from the way she felt him watching her movements as they descended back into the tavern. She forced herself not to look back at him.

A few tables were overturned, tankards spilled on the floor. The old woman mopping up the mess didn't even look up at them as they hurried past and out the front door. She would be upset too if she were the elderly woman. Kamira hadn't meant for a fight to break out, it had all just sort of happened, and really, it was mostly Jaario's fault. She finally chanced a glance back at him, the dying sunlight brightening his eyes so she could see their true color. They weren't brown after all, but a strange hue of dark gray—like a surging storm cloud. He cocked his head to the side and bestowed her with a smug, crooked smile.

"Do you want to go in front of me since I have no idea where we are going?" she asked, frowning at him and motioning for him to lead the way.

He chuckled, elbowing her lightly as he walked past. "Come on, it's this way."

They were headed toward the town square when he suddenly stopped, spinning around. She ran directly into him, face colliding with his solid chest. "Ouch!" she squealed. "What are you..." but she didn't have a chance to finish before he, quite literally, picked her up by her shoulders and spun her around, pushing her quickly toward a small shadowed alcove between two buildings. It was barely wide enough to fit one person, let alone two, but he shoved her inside and followed right behind her, pushing them both far enough into the darkness so that they were completely hidden from anyone peering into the cramped space.

"Jaario..." she growled, struggling as she turned around to face him, but that only caused him to pull her close against him, wrapping a large arm around her so she could no longer move and clamping his free hand over her mouth.

Kamira squirmed trying to dislodge his grip.

"Shh...stop struggling," he whispered.

She finally looked up and noticed the look of alarm in his eyes, and the worry lines carved into his face. Something had frightened him, and whatever it was, he was trying to protect her from it, too.

She angled her head, peering around his arm toward the city street beyond, desperate for a glimpse of what he was shielding them from. Her eyes widened when she glimpsed a red streak past the alley opening. The woman came back slower this time and turned in a circle before pausing to peer into the dark alcove. Kamira gasped against Jaario's hand, still clamped over her lips, and he instinctively pulled her closer.

It *was* Forcina. She hadn't been imagining it earlier before going into the tavern after all.

She wrapped her arms tightly around Jaario's waist and leaned her head against his chest, closing her eyes in anxious anticipation of what was about to happen. This was it. Forcina had seen her on the ship and had come after her—probably to kill her—ensuring Doraan and the crew were forever stuck on the sea.

"Kamira," Jaario whispered in her ear.

She peeked up at him. He was tall—so much taller than her that she had to crane her neck all the way back just to look him in the eye.

"Are you okay?" he asked.

"Is she gone?" she breathed.

His brows knit together. "How did you know who I was hiding from?"

"Why are *you* hiding from her?"

He huffed, and that characteristic smirk spread across his lips, easing the tension in his features back into the carefree demeanor he had worn since the moment they met. "I've been hiding from Forcina for a long time."

"But why? Did you do something to her?"

He sighed. "She thinks I did. She's been out for revenge ever since. On a journey to destroy me and any happiness I've ever known."

"That seems to be a common theme of hers," Kamira said solemnly.

Jaario chuckled gently, and it was only then, when the vibrations of that laugh rippled through his chest and directly into hers, that she realized they were still holding one another. She pushed away from him, which only made him chuckle more.

"How exactly do you know Forcina?" he asked.

"I'm pretty sure she is looking for me."

He cocked a brow in interest. "Why would she be looking for you?"

Kamira sighed. She barely knew this man and yet here she was just giving away little pieces of information she had no business offering. "It's a long story and honestly not mine to tell. Can you please just tell me where Adonis is?"

"Alright, but I won't forget about this. I want that story at some point. Anyone who's on Forcina's bad side is a friend to me and I'll help them anyway I can."

"Why?"

"Why what?"

"Why would you help someone you don't even know? Why did you even help me back in the tavern, and why are you helping me right now?" She was genuinely curious. Not many strangers would offer or do what he had done willingly and so readily. He hadn't even taken a moment to think before saying he would help her find Adonis.

His expression darkened, growing somber and distant. "I did many things in my past that I am not proud of. Helping people is my way of attempting penance for all that I have done. It's the one thing that keeps me going, that makes existing a little more palatable and not so damn daunting."

Kamira frowned at his phrasing, not entirely sure how to respond to something so raw and honest. It had her thinking about Lord Tarkiin and what she had done to him.

"Come on. It's almost sunset, and we better find Nardisee before it gets too late." Jaario peered into the streets, pulling the hood of his blue sleeveless tunic over his head. "Come on, the coast is clear," he said, continuing on straight through the city square to a road on the opposite side.

Kamira followed, watching as just before they cleared the square, Jaario reached out quickly and pulled a hooded green cloak from a nearby cart. It was so quick and expertly done that she almost didn't even notice what he had done. She hurried, sidling up to him.

"Did you just…"

"Here," he cut her off, flinging the cloak against her chest. "Put it on. You don't want to be spotted by Forcina if she's still lurking nearby."

She glared at him and then huffed annoyingly, taking the cloak and throwing it around her shoulders, pulling the hood on. "Why did it look like that wasn't the first or even second time you've done that?"

He smirked at her offering a quick wink before striding down the darkened cobbled lane.

She had to almost jog to keep up with Jaario's long stride, trailing after him as he winded through side streets and alleys, down stone staircases, and through dark tunnels carved through the base of buildings. Kamira couldn't help but gape in awe of the beauty around her. She could practically feel the history oozing from every crack and crevice—from the smooth stones beneath her feet worn from centuries of townsfolk walking these roads to the ancient carved archways leading to every building and alley entrance. It was truly extraordinary.

She tilted her head back to look up at the sky. Night was falling, casting a vivid array of colors across the light blue like a painting. Deep purple faded into pink and orange as the sun slowly sank behind the city while they trekked deeper into its winding streets. She thought the buildings would never end. The roads were far less crowded here, with only a few people milling about, and the buildings grew more cramped, their outer walls darker and more weathered with age. Crawling plants snaked their way along the facades, almost like they were knitting the buildings together.

"This is the original city," Jaario said, as if sensing the train of her thoughts. "Neilmaar has grown immensely over the past thirty years. It's now a huge hub for traders and merchants."

"This part of the city is breathtaking. It's so lush and well-preserved. How old are these buildings?"

"This city is hundreds of years old. These buildings have survived countless uprisings and wars over the centuries. It's the only city with its original walls still standing since the War of the Four Kings."

She almost laughed at him. "That's just a story."

"Is it?" he queried, looking back at her with a raised brow as they made their way toward an opening just ahead.

She was about to say if it was real, there would be more evidence of its existence in the realm, but she didn't have the chance as her breath caught in her throat upon walking into another smaller town square. It was brimming with life, overflowing with flower gardens and people.

"Welcome to the Back Water market," Jaario said. "The place for locals, and those who don't have what you would call "acceptable wares," to sell at the main market square."

Kamira let her gaze wander, taking it all in. Flags were hung between roof tops, crossing far overhead. Many of them she didn't recognize, but she saw the Emperor's tell-tale red and black—the two-headed bronze falcon embellished in its center mingled among the rest. And to her surprise, there was a single green flag swinging in the breeze, the Emerald King's sigil etched upon it. His influence was here. That flag was like a small symbol of what was coming.

Kamira looked away from it, eyes drifting to the fountain in the center of the square.

A statue of a woman was raised in the middle of it, depicting not only water, which was flowing from her mouth, but all of the elements being worked by her. It was subtle, but if you studied it closely, you could see the ode to each element. The torch lit aflame in her right hand, stone spirals depicting air circling around her body, and the stepping stones at her feet, carved to look like earth protruding up from the fountain itself. She smiled at its beauty, at its ode to sorcery.

But her smile quickly faded, replaced with a confused frown as her gaze caught on a figure standing just behind the fountain. She recognized those upturned honeyed eyes, and the bulbous red nose just above a set of thin pink lips. She shuttered, letting her stare travel down to his protruding belly, the evidence of too many nights spent drinking his fill.

"Tarkiin?" she whispered, looking back up to his face, startled to see him staring directly at her, but no, it couldn't be. Flashes of red pooling like spilled wine around his head came into her vision, a gash oozing blood along his forehead. It wasn't him, couldn't be. He was dead, she was sure of it.

"Kamira?" A large hand clamped over her shoulder, making her jump and pulling her from her trance. Jaario was looking down at her with concern. "You look pale. Are you alright?"

"Yes," she shuttered, glancing back at the fountain, but the man was gone. It was just her eyes playing tricks on her. "Let's go."

He nodded and grabbed her hand, pulling her through the crowd to a quaint side street lined with potted plants in full bloom. Their purple flowers exuded a strong fragrance that made her dizzy.

Jaario stopped abruptly just as they had gotten to the end of the street. "Are you sure you're alright?"

She opened her mouth to answer, but was stopped short when she watched a hand clamp around Jaario's mouth and the butt of a sword slam on to his head as he crumpled to the ground. Kamira spun, the beginning of a scream at the tip of her tongue just before a hard blow came down upon her own head and, for the second time that day, the world went black.

24

KAMIRA

Kamira's head pounded, her vision blurry, as she attempted to search her surroundings. She was in a dimly lit stone wall room with no windows or furnishings other than the candlelit sconces along its perimeter. Was this some kind of dungeon?

She rolled her shoulders back, moving her sore neck from side to side, shifting her weight uncomfortably in the chair she was sitting in.

Looking down at her lap, she noticed that her hands rested there, unbound. She quickly pushed herself off the wooden chair with a mind to search for a way out, but as soon as she stood up, dizziness and nausea overtook her. She bent over, spilling the contents of her stomach onto the packed dirt floor beneath her. The water and bile seeped into the ground eagerly and she grabbed the back of the chair, leaning heavily on it.

Kamira closed her eyes as the room spun around her. She supposed this was what happened when someone hit their head twice in the same day. At least, she thought it was the same day, but she really had no way of knowing in this dark, enclosed room. Her stomach roiled again, and she bit back against it, willing the room to still.

The longer she stood, taking in deep, calming breaths, the more the nausea subsided, and the room steadied itself just enough for her to pry open an eye and slowly let it wander across the walls. A wooden door on her left allowed light from the outside corridor to spill through the gap beneath it, but it was suddenly obscured by a shadow just before the door creaked open on iron hinges. A man swept into the room, black robes swirling behind him with each quick stride.

"Please sit," the man said, turning his back to her as he closed the door behind him. "I'm here to question you on how you came to find this place."

Kamira looked up to the man's face and blinked. Skies, how hard had she hit her head? First, she thought she had seen Tarkiin in the square and now this.

"Adonis?" she whispered.

He frowned and cocked his head, studying her before recognition dawned and his eyes went wide. "Kamira!" he rushed to her. "What are you doing here?" he asked, pulling her into a tight embrace before pushing her away and placing a hand under her chin, tilting her head up so he could look at her more clearly. "What on earth happened to you?"

"It's a long story." She attempted a smile, but it didn't reach her eyes.

Adonis noticed, pulling her against him once more, stroking her hair. "It's alright. You're with me now. Whatever happened, you're safe now."

She relaxed into him, tears welling in her eyes. He smelled like Torheim—like fresh pine and lemongrass. He smelled like *home*. "I missed you."

"I missed you, too." He backed away, letting his hands travel down her arms and clasped her hands in his. "You should sit. Gods, Kamira are you alright? How did this happen?"

He helped her take a seat back in the chair before releasing her hands and motioning to her nose, which she knew had to look even worse by now.

"I'm alright. It was just an accident," she said, touching the back of her head, where her fingers came away red with blood. "Although, whoever brought me here could have been a bit gentler."

Adonis' nostrils flared, a darkness falling over his features. "They will be dealt with, I assure you."

Kamira ignored that statement. Adonis had always had a bit of a temper. "Where are we?"

"The catacombs. It's a system of tunnels hidden beneath the city," he said, suddenly taking her hand in his once again, placing his other hand atop it. "Kamira, why were you traveling with that man? Is he the reason for your nose?"

"Jaario?"

"Yes, did he kidnap you?"

"What? No! He was helping me find you! Why would you think he kidnapped me?" That suddenly had her mind reeling. "Where is Jaario? What did they do to him?"

"Nothing, he's fine," Adonis said, giving her hands a gentle squeeze.

She furrowed her brow. "Why did they bring me here?"

"To question you. They want to know why you were lurking outside our gates and why you were with Jaario."

"Where is he, Adonis?"

"He's fine, Kamira. I promise you. He and the Brothers just have a history. Don't worry, they won't harm him." He dropped her hand and sighed. "Can you please answer my question? Why are you here? *How* are you here?"

"I..." She looked into her brother's face, the perfect mix of both their father and mother, and suddenly the entire weight of everything came crashing upon her. Tears fell into her lap, soaking through her pants. "I left Tarkiin."

"What?! Why? What did he do? Do mother and father know?"

"I...he was a pig. I just couldn't be with him. He was a truly horrible man, Adonis." She paused, wiping the tears from her cheeks as she regained some of her composure. "I thought I saw him in the square earlier. But it couldn't have been him. He's haunting me because of what I did."

Adonis kneeled in front of her and gently asked, "What did you do, Kamira? What made you come all this way?"

She looked him in the eyes, his love and concern shone brightly in the deep blue of his irises and she couldn't do it. She couldn't tell him the truth and watch that love turn into disappointment. She had killed a man, taken someone's life, and she would live with that for the rest of her own, but she couldn't live with her family's disappointment, too.

She sighed. "Nothing, I just had to see you." She smiled and brought a hand up to his cheek, rubbing her thumb along it. "I need your help."

He frowned slightly, but didn't pry further. He had always been good about giving her space and letting her come to him when she was ready to talk about something. "With what?"

"The crew I traveled here with, they need something."

His frown deepened and he narrowed his eyes. "Why would they send you for what they need?"

"They need to know where the Temple of Gorria is, and they think the Brothers might know."

Adonis backed away, rising to his feet. "They don't," he said quickly. "I don't know what I expected you to say, but that certainly wasn't it. Why do they wish to go to the Temple?"

"It has to do with why they couldn't come here themselves. They are stuck in the ocean, some kind of curse from a Sorceress."

He turned his back to her. "Curse? What does that even mean?"

"They think this Sorceress made it so that they can never walk on land again. It didn't make any sense to me either, but they really can't. They have been stuck on the sea for ten years."

Adonis spun back around, his long robes slapping against the wall behind him as they twirled around him with the quick movement. "I've never heard of something like that. How well do you trust these people? Are you sure they aren't lying to you?"

Kamira looked down at her clasped hands resting on her lap. Even though it hadn't been long, she had formed a deep kinship with the crew of the *Cursed Soul*. They had welcomed her with open arms and saved her life. She was certain they weren't lying to her—they really did believe they were cursed—it was just figuring out *how* they were cursed that was the problem. "I trust them with my life. They are telling the truth."

Adonis arched his brow and then frowned. "Well, if they truly can't go on land, is it possible this Sorceress is controlling the water or atmosphere around them and their ship? You could possibly help counter it, push back against her sorcery."

"I've tried, but there is nothing to fight against. As far as I can tell, there is no sorcery being used against them. I tried to move the ship to shore, but it wouldn't go past a point. It was like there was a barrier my sorcery couldn't get through. Nothing I've done has worked."

She watched as her brother's face contorted into many expressions as he attempted to understand what she was saying. "This Sorceress must be very powerful."

"She is," Kamira confirmed.

He was quiet for a long time, eyebrows drawn together, deep in thought, and then he turned so quickly Kamira's nausea threatened to make another appearance. "Come with me."

She didn't question him, only followed him out the door and down a long narrow stone hallway that ended at a 'T'. He took the left corridor, which turned out to just be another long stone tunnel, dimly lit with pockets of deep shadow every few feet. "Where are we going?" she whispered.

"You'll see. I want to show you something." He continued on, turning right, then left, until on the final left turn, they wound up at the top of some questionable looking stone steps that spiraled around an ominous curve. "Careful, the steps are narrow," Adonis said before disappearing into the darkness, the sounds of his footfalls growing distant.

"Blazing biscuits," she sighed before placing her hands on the cold walls on either side of the stairwell and slowly following him down. The steps weren't only narrow, but surprisingly steep, to the point that she had to step down one foot at a time onto the next stair.

"Are you coming?" Adonis' voice echoed up to her.

"Calm down, I'm coming. I would prefer not to fall to my death, thank you." She quickened her pace, noticing a bizarre glow illuminating the final few steps. When she finally stepped off the final step and looked up, she sucked in a breath and her eyes went wide in wonder.

They were in a cavern, rocks piled like stepping stones around them, stalactites hanging from the ceiling like ice cycles of mineral and stone. But what had taken her breath away was what was in its center—a luminous pool of violet water sat there, unmoving. Kamira almost didn't think it was real, and then it dawned on her. This was the Spring.

She took a few steps closer, almost entranced by its strangeness. "Why is it glowing like that? And why is it purple?"

"The Brothers believe it was created by the old gods."

Kamira laughed. "The old gods? Sure, just like they created you and me, and everything else in Emmoria.

There is a logical explanation for everything, Adonis." She rolled her eyes. "It's probably some plant or something in the cave feeding into the water."

Adonis chuckled, shaking his head. "You haven't changed a bit, Kamira. Still as skeptical as always."

"You can't tell me you actually believe in the existence of the old gods." She raised a brow. "What do you *really* think causes it?" She knelt, looking suspiciously at the luminescent water from a different angle.

"I believe whatever the Brothers tell me to believe."

Kamira balked, shooting up to a standing position and glaring at her brother. "You seriously follow them so blindly? What happened to you these past years, Adonis? You're no follower."

He rolled his eyes. "I do what they need me to in order to have free access to the waters."

Kamira frowned. "Why?"

Adonis took a cup from a small table just next to the entryway they came through and plunged it into the eerie water. "Here, drink it and you will see."

She scrunched her face in disgust. "No way! I'm not drinking that." She pushed the cup away.

"Trust me, it will be worth it. Drink." Adonis held out the glowing liquid to her once more.

She narrowed her eyes at him before hesitantly taking the cup and staring at its contents, swirling it around. "What does it do?"

"Just taste it and see, Kamira. Trust me, you will love the results."

She frowned. "What exactly do you mean by *results*? Am I going to grow a third arm or something? Because that really doesn't sound like the kind of *results* I would enjoy."

"Blazing stars, Kamira! Just drink it!" Adonis yelled, pushing the glass up to her mouth.

The violet liquid splashed onto her lips, and she swallowed. It tasted sweet, like honeyed water. "Adonis!" she roared, tossing the cup onto the rocks beneath her feet. "I didn't want to..." but she froze as the strangest sensation traveled through her, starting in her throat and coursing down to her toes and into her hands like a strong current. She stumbled backward, gripping her stomach as it bubbled. "What's happening?"

Adonis smirked, a glint of mischief in his eye. "Just wait."

And then, everything stopped. Every sensation vanished from her body, and all that was left was the urge to use her gifts. Not only that—it was as if her strength had tripled. She could more clearly feel the power locked within her. She knew at that moment that she could demolish entire cities if she wanted to, and it didn't cause her excitement or glee. It scared her.

No one should have that type of power, it was too much, and it was building.

"You feel it, don't you?"

She did and it was overwhelming, pushing inside of her to the point she needed to let it free, to use her sorcery to drain some of it before she imploded.

Kamira crouched down, closing her eyes and wrapping her arms around herself, hoping it would all just fade away, but it only grew stronger until she could no longer resist. The ground rumbled beneath her, and the purple waters began to bubble and swell as the air whistled in her ears, swirling through the small cavern like a tornado. Stalactites fell and shattered as they speared the rocky floor, sending shards of stone flying, only to be pulled into the wind storm and flung out like a spray of bullets, embedding themselves into the cave walls.

She screamed, unable to reign it all back in. The ceiling erupted in a river of fire as the flames in the sconces shot up, crawling their way along the roof like slithering snakes threatening to rain sparks down upon them.

Kamira cracked open an eye to see Adonis standing in front of her, black cape flapping like a rabid bird behind him, hands outstretched. His face contorted as he fought against her rogue sorcery with his own gifts. She watched as, slowly, the flames shrunk, slinking back into their sconces, and the wind died down to a whisper of a breeze. The pool of the strange liquid went back to its unmoving state and the rocks beneath their feet stilled.

The earthquake she had created was gone.

Adonis breathed a sigh of relief and grabbed her shoulders, hauling her back to her feet. "Shit, Kamira. I...that was...I had no idea you were that powerful." His eyes were wide with wonder. "I didn't know that would happen."

Kamira pointed with shaking fingers to the violet spring. "W—what is that stuff?"

"I don't know, but it augments our gifts. I'm so sorry, Kamira. I didn't realize the extent of your sorcery." He was looking at her as if he was seeing her for the first time.

Shouting echoed down the stairwell and Adonis jerked his head toward it. "We have to go."

She barely heard him, not even registering when he grabbed her by the shoulders and spun her around, hurrying her toward the stairwell. They ascended, Adonis practically pushing her the entire way up. He stopped her at the stop of the stairs and peeked his head out into the corridor. "There is no one. We need to leave before anyone sees us or where we have been."

"Why?" Kamira asked, finally coming out of her stunned stupor.

"Because no one is allowed to go to the Spring. Only those who have ascended," he whispered, grabbing her wrist and pulling her out into the arched stone hallway. A few robed figures sprinted past them, straight for the stairwell, and Adonis slowed, nodding politely. As soon as they disappeared into the entryway of the stairs, Adonis grabbed her hand and ran down the corridor, turning down multiple other hallways until Kamira was dizzy from the maze of this place.

"Where are we going?" she whispered, just as a loud scream came from a closed door beside her. It sounded like someone was in pain and she stopped, pulling her hand from Adonis' grasp. "What was that?"

"Nothing," he said, trying to grab her arm again, but she pulled away, inching closer to the door. Another cry of anguish emanated from within.

"Adonis, what are they doing in there? Are they torturing someone?"

There was a quick twitch of his eye, so slight she almost didn't catch it before he said, "No, now let's go!"

A dark thought wormed its way into her thoughts. "Is it Jaario?"

His nostrils flared, and she could see his temper rising.

"It is, isn't it? What are they doing to him? We have to..." She reached for the door latch and Adonis grabbed her around the waist, yanking her off her feet, hauling her down the hallway.

"Let go!" she yelped, flailing and punching his arms that were wrapped tightly around her. When they were far enough away to no longer hear the yells of pain, he put her down and spun her around to look him directly in the eye.

"Kamira, you don't know these men; you don't know what they are capable of. Jaario will be alright, trust me.

This isn't the first time he has been here. They won't kill him."

"What?!" Kamira screeched. "How can you say that?! They won't kill him, but they will torture him for how long? Just for another few minutes or just within an inch of his life? It doesn't matter that they won't kill him, Adonis. They are *torturing* him! How is that okay? I can't let it..."

"Kamira!" he growled, shaking her by the shoulders slightly. "You have to listen to me. We need to leave. The Brothers will know someone powerful has been to the Spring. You practically destroyed the place. They will come looking for you, and they will do far worse than what they are doing to Jaario. Do you understand me?" His eyes were wide—frantic, even. She had never seen him like this before. He was scared. "We need to leave."

"I...I..." She was overwhelmed, too in shock to understand what exactly he was saying. What did the Brothers want with a Sorcerer? And why were they torturing Jaario? "But Jaario."

"Listen," he said softly, placing a gentle hand on her cheek. "Once we get you out of here and to safety, I will come back for Jaario myself. I won't let them do anymore harm to him. Okay?"

His eyes glistened. They reminded her of sapphires, always shining, sparkling in the fire light. "Okay," she finally conceded.

He nodded with a sigh of relief and held out his hand, "Come on, we're almost there."

She took his hand and let him pull her through the maze of tunnels, until they finally stopped at a ladder going up several stories.

"Go ahead, climb."

She huffed, looking up at the height of the ladder and thinking at least she had gotten a lot of practice over the past week climbing up and down rope ladders.

"Can you go any faster?" Adonis called from below.

She looked down at him a few rungs below her and stuck her tongue out before pulling herself up rung by rung a little quicker.

"So helpful, Kamira." He scoffed and she could practically hear his eye roll. "Once you make it to the top, you are going to have to push hard to open the door. It's covered in sand, and I don't know how much might have accumulated over it recently."

"How heavy? Maybe you should have gone first."

"Well, it's a little late for that now isn't it? You will just have to use all your strength," Adonis grumbled.

Kamira groaned when she finally made it to the top and pushed against the small wooden door there. It didn't budge. "Uh, it won't move, Adonis."

All she could hear was quiet mutters beneath her. "What do I do?"

"Push harder."

"I'm pushing as hard as I can!"

"I seem to recall you are a Legion who is capable of moving earth? Bend the sand above it."

Kamira glared down at him and sighed, closing her eyes and feeling the earth just past the door. She pushed and heard the muffled shifting overhead as she moved the sand away. This time, when she pushed against the wooden hatch, it opened easily. A few tendrils of sand fell inward as she climbed out onto the beach.

Adonis coughed beneath her, cursing as he climbed that last few rungs, joining her on the beach before shutting the door and covering it with a heaping pile of sand once again. He shook his head, sand flying from his hair.

"Where are we?" She looked around at their surroundings. They were on a secluded beach, the ocean's waves crashed behind her sending ripples of water across the shore.

"We're on the eastern beach, about a mile outside the city. Come on, we need to get you back to the ship. You should go home, Kamira. Go back to Torheim, to mom and dad," he said, heading up the beach. "Your gifts have grown significantly. Mother can help you control them."

"Wait! I can't leave. I haven't gotten what I came here for."

Adonis stopped, shoulders sagging. "Right. The Temple. You're really going to go with this crew there? Join them on their quest for some curse that you don't even know if it exists?"

"I am. I promised them I would help and I'm not going to go back on my word."

He brought a hand through his auburn waves and sighed. "All right, listen, I can tell you where the Temple is, but you have to promise me two things."

"Anything."

"Once you are done there, you go straight back to Torheim."

"Okay," she said, narrowing her eyes at him. She wouldn't tell him that she would be dead if she went back there. She wasn't one to lie to her brother, but he didn't know what going home would mean. He didn't know what she had done. "What's the second thing?"

"You can't tell anyone at the Temple what you are. They can't know that you are a Legion. Do you understand?"

"Why not?"

"Just trust me and promise." His eyes were intense, like a ten foot wave threatening to crash down upon her.

"Okay, I promise," she said, looking away from him, not wanting him to see the lie on her face.

He sighed in relief. "Good. Now where is this ship you came here on?"

"North."

"Come on," he said, wrapping an arm around her shoulder and planting a kiss on the top of her head. "I've missed you, you little twerp. You know that?"

She chuckled, looking up at him. "I've missed you too, big brother."

"Now, it's important to note that the Temple isn't in any one place. It's why half the realm doesn't believe it even exists. Not only is it invisible, but it is constantly moving from one place to another. Sailing like a ship among the waves. It's actually quite extraordinary."

"Have you been there?" she asked.

"Once, last year. It's when I discovered it actually existed." He smirked down at her. "It wasn't easy. Only a Sorcerer can reveal it, and it only comes to those in great need. That's why it took me so long to find it. I wasn't in any great need until late last year when I was discovered on a ship while sailing to the Tower of Fajar." He snorted, dropping his arm from her shoulder and bringing a hand down over his face. "I was on a packet boat and did something so daft I don't even like thinking about it. One of the mainsail lines had gotten loose, the rope whipping around in the wind, and it almost hit a child on board. So, I didn't even think, I just used the wind to stop it and bring it toward me so I could grip it. A few of the crew members saw me and started screaming out 'Sorcerer'. I did the only thing I could and dove off the side of the ship."

"Blazing biscuits! Did they shoot at you?"

"No, I dove down far enough beneath the surface and used the water to propel myself as far away from the ship as I could. But then the problem was I was all alone, floating in the middle of the ocean. That's when I began to wish for a miracle. I was too far away from land to use my gifts all the way to shore. After about an hour of hoping for a miracle, the Temple appeared out of nowhere and opened its doors for me."

Kamira furrowed her brows. "So, if you are a Sorcerer in enough need, it just comes to you?"

"Kind of," Adonis grunted. "It's hard to explain, but it's almost like you use your sorcery to put a beacon out for help. The Temple hears it and comes for you. Listen, I still don't understand it all the way myself. I didn't stay there long. Those people are, well, they just aren't our people."

"What does that mean?" Kamira laughed. They were quite literally the only other Sorcerers left alive. "They are exactly our people."

"No, Kamira. They aren't," he snapped.

She was surprised by the vehemence in his tone.

"They don't even want to come back to Emmoria. They could care less about the fact that their home—*our home*—was taken from us. It's disgusting."

"Well, maybe they are just happy there?" Kamira placated. It did seem odd that they didn't want to come back home, but honestly, she understood it. Emmoria was a hostile place for Sorcerers. It was either stay hidden or get executed. Without peace, who would want to come back and live a life spent hiding their gifts?

He stopped and turned to her. "We deserve to be here as much, if not more, than the Ungifted, Kamira. This was our home first. You know that, right?"

"Yes, I know, Adonis. I'm just saying, if they are happy in their fancy hidden Temple, then why try to make them leave it?"

Adonis sighed, shaking his head."You always did love a debate just for the sake of arguing."

"I'm just optimistic," she said with a playful smile.

He hooked his arm around her neck and pulled her into his side, rubbing his knuckles in her hair.

"Adonis! Stop, I'm not a kid anymore!"

He laughed and released her. "You'll always be my little sister."

She glowered at him, rubbing her sore head.

"You should be safe now. It doesn't look like anyone saw us leave or followed us. Will you be okay from here?"

Kamira could see the bend up ahead that would lead to the northernmost point of Neilmaar, where her boat was buried under gallons of sand. "Yeah, we are almost to my boat. I'll be alright."

Adonis pulled her against him in a suffocating hug. "Remember what I told you. Don't tell anyone you are a Legion."

"Yeah, yeah. I got it," she said, squeezing him back just as hard before releasing their embrace.

"Be careful." He placed a hand on either side of her face, angling her eyes up to meet his. "For the Temple to appear, you have to be far enough from land so as not to be sighted. It won't come otherwise."

She nodded, and Adonis bestowed one final kiss on the top of her head before releasing her and placing a small vial in her hand with a black cord wrapped around it. "Take this, in case you need it. I love you."

"I love you, too," she said, looking down at the small bottle of violet liquid glowing in her hands. She placed the cord around her neck and turned away from Adonis with one final wave before she began the long trek back to her ship full of pirates.

25

DORAAN

I t was a new day, and the *Cursed Soul* was wrecked. They wouldn't be sailing anywhere any time soon. Doraan's teeth chattered as he wrapped his cloak tighter around him. An unseasonable bone-aching chill had swept in overnight, bringing a flurry of snow that had blanketed the ship in sparkling white.

Doraan looked out toward the shore where the snow fall hadn't reached and to where Kamira had not yet appeared. He didn't like her being out there alone. His stomach hadn't settled since she left—it was stuck in a constant roiling loop since the very moment she got off the ship.

Over the past week, Doraan had formed an attachment to her, a friendship that filled a gaping hole in his heart—one that his parents had ripped into him. She cared for him, cared about what happened to him, and he cared for her as well.

A helplessness settled into his limbs, keeping him constantly on edge since Forcina's visit. He knew she had gone to Neilmaar in search of Kamira. His only reprieve—which was minuscule in comparison to his overflowing unease—was that Forcina had actually seemed scared of what the reality of Kamira on their ship meant. He had seen just a sliver of fear wiggling its way beneath her surface, digging a pit of doubt in her mind, and that gave him just a bit of satisfaction. He trusted Kamira; he had to because that small chink in Forcina's armor had ignited his hope. Kamira would help them break free of the curse. She would come back, and they would all finally make it home, stepping foot on dry, solid ground for the first time in what felt like an eternity.

"The foremast is too far gone." Cormac came up beside Doraan, ice crunching beneath his boots. "We've switched out the aft and course sails with the old ones, which should be good enough for now, but they won't last much longer. The other sails will have to be mended."

Doraan closed his eyes, pinching the bridge of his nose against the throbbing that had pooled there. "Do we have enough supplies to patch them?"

He nodded, solemnly. "We'll make do, Cap'n."

Doraan knew what that really meant—the crew would have to give up whatever spare clothing they had left.

"Not all is lost," Cormac murmured, resting a hand on Doraan's shoulder.

"It is if we can't sail."

"We will make it work. We always do. We can sail without a foremast."

"At the pace of a snail," he grunted, pushing Cormac's hand off his shoulder and stepping over a splintered piece of the portside railing as he headed toward the hull.

"Where are you going?" Cormac called after him.

"To find any clothing that Kamira hasn't stolen yet," he huffed. "We need to be ready to sail by the time she gets back."

It had taken half the day, but they managed to get the *Cursed Soul* as ready to sail as they could. The sails were patched, the damaged masts salvaged—except for the foremast, of course—and the ship was still afloat. It would sail, but it wouldn't be pretty while doing it.

"Ahoy!" Doraan spun at Jorne's exclamation to see the orange-haired man waving excitedly to someone in the ocean below.

"Kamira," Doraan whispered, instantly dropping the rope he was tying and hobbling his way toward Jorne just in time to see a head of auburn curls pop up over the railing as Jorne helped her climb aboard.

Doraan didn't stop. He practically barreled into her and wrapped his arms around her. "Skies, I thought you weren't coming back," Doraan breathed, pulling Kamira against him, taking in the scent of lemon and sea breeze that clung to her. The tension instantly melted from him as his heart eased, settling back into his chest where it belonged.

"I've only been gone a day, Doraan."

"Two full days," he corrected.

"Alright, one night then. You didn't think it would take me just a few hours to find out what you needed, did you?"

"No," he huffed, breaking their embrace. "I was just worried."

She looked up at him smiling and said, "I missed you, too."

"Kamira! What in the bloody seas happened to your face?"

She chuckled. "I may or may not have been unintentionally involved in a tavern brawl."

He was speechless, the words frozen on his lips, as he tried to sputter a string of questions, but her eyes caught on something behind him. Her smile suddenly turned down into a frown as she gasped and pushed past him. "What happened to the ship?"

"Forcina," he said, solemnly.

She spun on him. "I saw her in the city. She was looking for me, wasn't she?"

His eyes widened. "She didn't see you?"

"No. I...I hid and she walked right past."

He sighed, glancing up quickly toward the sky, half expecting to see Forcina hovering there. "Did you find out anything about the Temple?"

"Yes. I think I can get us there."

He laughed, bringing a hand down over his face in disbelief, shaking his head. "Skies, you actually did it? You found it."

"Don't look so happy about it. I'm not entirely sure I can actually get us there. We need to go east to the Estdar sea." She looked at the disarray of the ship around them. "Can we even sail?"

"We can, but not at our normal speed. The foremast is resting on the ocean floor and we had to replace some of the sails with the ones you helped mend last week. They will do, but without the foremast, we aren't going to make much distance. We'll be lucky to go five knots in a day. We could probably go up to ten knots, but only if the winds are good, and right now, they are almost non-existent."

Kamira anxiously looked back at the shore. "When can we leave?"

Doraan placed a hand on her shoulder and she turned back to face him. "Forcina won't come back to the ship for a while. She thinks you are on land now. And if she does come back, I won't let anything happen to you, understand?" He meant it. He would make Forcina kill him before letting any harm come to Kamira.

She smiled weakly. "We should leave as soon as possible anyway. Just in case."

"I can't believe you actually found out the location. How did you do it?"

She smirked at him. "Honestly, it was all luck."

26

DORAAN

They had actually made it. After four days of sailing with patched sails and no foremast—a trek that should have taken no more than two days tops—they were finally in the Estdar sea, thirty nautical miles from the closest stretch of land.

Kamira had been at the bow of the ship all morning, barely moving, sitting upon the Grim Reaper's shoulder, arm wrapped around its neck. Its skeletal outstretched hand had been snapped off during Forcina's attack. Doraan wished the entire thing had fallen off. He knew Forcina had chosen this particular ship as his prison just for the irony alone. He was dead to the world, dead to his people, and the ghostly grim reaper had taken him and all the other cursed souls on this ship. They were wandering souls, stolen from life too soon. An intense anger suddenly washed over him, his mood changing into something foul as he looked out at the endless expanse of water before them.

Doraan stomped his way to the bow of the ship, grabbing a piece of rigging and leaning out over the side to look Kamira in the face. "There's nothing here," he seethed. "I swear to the sky and sea, if the Brothers lied..."

"Doraan." Kamira suddenly gasped, bringing a hand over her mouth as she pointed out at the sprawling sea in front of them.

Doraan pushed himself back onto the solid boards of the ship and looked out toward where she was pointing, the breath instantly leaving his lungs. In front of them was something out of a story book—it was as if a heavy fog had been lifted from his eyes to reveal a massive gate of shimmering marble where, only moments ago, there had been nothing but water. He looked from side to side, marveling at the sight. The same white stone extended farther than his eyes could see on either side. The wall was colossal. How was something this immense hidden out in the ocean?

To his surprise, the doors of the gate began to open with a booming echo that reverberated around them as the solid stone moved on invisible hinges. Doraan was about to yell out for his crew to hold tight as a tidal wave soared toward them due to the doors' displacement of water, but to his astonishment, the wave parted, moving around them to crash far behind the ship.

As Cormac sailed the ship into the Temple, Doraan caught a glimpse of Kamira beside him grinning from ear to ear, which made him frown before he caught sight of what had her so entranced. A city so vibrant he had to throw a hand to his forehead, shielding his eyes from its brightness, sprawled out before them.

The Temple was made of the same shimmering marble stone that glowed with an otherworldly light. The air hummed with an electric energy, the sea swirling around the base of the Temple as if drawn to its power. Doraan felt a shiver run down his spine as he realized the magnitude of the sorcery that must be contained within this place. Something foreign began to buzz beneath his skin as they sailed closer—a tingling spark that began in the center of his chest, spider webbing out into each corner of his being. A new and sudden sensation that felt as if he had just awoken from a long sleep.

He shook it off, ignoring the strange feeling, and surveyed his surroundings further, gawking at its immense structure. It was not an island with sandy beaches lining its borders, but instead, an entirely man—or rather *Sorcerer*—made-structure of checkered obsidian and white marble blocks floating like weightless logs upon the sea. Marble and glass buildings were scattered throughout the vast city, with turrets that shot up into the sky higher than he could see. Fields of flowing grass and towers of black obsidian with flames flickering from their peaks were evenly dispersed throughout.

How many Sorcerers lived in a place like this? Doraan had expected a few dozen, maybe even a hundred, to be alive, hidden within these walls, but what he saw before him was thousands.

A lump formed in his throat that he couldn't swallow down.

For the first time he realized that Kamira had spoken the truth—no matter how long and how ferociously they hunted down these Sorcerers, they could never truly be defeated. He had been a fool. His father was a fool. No matter how much they tracked down and strung up in their city, the Sorcerers would always be stronger and more cunning. There was a reason they ruled this realm for so long before his father gained control.

Doraan shuttered as he watched Sorcerers of every element wielding their power so expertly before him. This place was like a training ground for every elemental Sorcerer there was. It was as if he had stumbled into another world—one ruled by sorcery. Just a week ago, he had been so sure of his victory, so sure he could take over his father's rule and enact the genocide of the Sorcerers, eradicating them from Emmoria completely—something that his father never could accomplish—but seeing this, he understood how futile his efforts would be. The Sorcerers were too powerful, too many, and too well-trained. What the Ungifted had was brute strength and ferocity, but it wouldn't be enough for what he was seeing here. This place was a force that Emmoria was not prepared for—a force they could not survive. His father had been lucky all those years ago. His entire success was based on the element of surprise. He doubted the Sorcerers would be so easily tricked again.

Cormac brought the *Cursed Soul* along one of the many docks lining the perimeter of the city. The crew were all frozen in silence and wonder, leaning over the portside railing, staring open-mouthed at the immensity of this place, the impossibility of it. Doraan was prepared to yell out a command for them to throw the mooring lines when he realized that the ship had stopped on its own, now gently floating beside the dock. He looked up to see four men and women in different colored clothing. The one in dark blue was concentrating, his hands held out before him. The reason they didn't need their mooring lines, Doraan assessed. He was a water Sorcerer.

A middle-aged blonde woman dressed in burgundy stood next to him, one arm crossed over her chest, the other held out, a flame dancing in her palm. On her other side was a very tall woman with black hair slicked up into a perfectly coiled bun, not one hair out of place, her golden cape billowing behind her as if a constant breeze surrounded her. The fourth was a man as tall as the dark-haired woman next to him, clothed in a rich brown, a crooked smile on his face, but no show of his ability, which had to be earth. He just stared with an arched brow, as if interested in how this ship of the Ungifted came to be upon their shores.

"What's your business here?" the air Sorceress whispered. Her voice carried upon the wind, brushing by each of their ears . Doraan shivered, several of the crew jumping beside him, startled.

Kamira stood unmoving, a wide smile still stretched upon her face. "We've come to ask for your help," she said before Doraan had the chance.

He cast her an annoyed glare.

It was the earth Sorcerer who spoke next. "Come, I'm sure you have all had a long journey. Join us in our welcome hall."

Doraan nodded at the man, turning to two of the crew members. "Jorne, Lindor, you two stay with the ship until we come back."

They each responded with a quick, "Aye, Captain," as the rest of the crew walked timidly down the gangway.

The Fire Sorcerer led the way for them, never letting the flame in her palm falter—like a warning that if they tried anything, she wouldn't hesitate to burn them all to ash and bone.

Behind them walked the Earth Sorcerer. Doraan turned to glance at him, which only made the man's smirk widen. Doraan spun back around quickly and tried not to look at all the Sorcerers around them. The arrival of an Ungifted ship would attract attention, but it only revealed to him how many of them were here. Alive.

Hundreds of faces stared at them as they were led like a procession through the crowd toward the tallest building in the city's center. It was the most ornate of all the buildings, reaching at least twenty, if not more, stories high. As Doraan looked up, he noticed that each story was slightly smaller than the last and at the very top, on the smallest tier was a solid gold statue of a woman, face pointed up to the sky and hands held out on either side of her.

Windows and ornately carved marble pillars lined each story. As they walked closer, he realized the carvings seemed to tell a story, depicting a tale he didn't yet know.

Two black iron doors at the base of the building were etched with each of the elemental symbols. As they approached, the doors opened, welcoming them inside. Through them, they entered into a large room with a ring of chairs circling a large marble table in the very center and four larger, almost throne-like, chairs at the head, each of a matching color to the robes the Sorcerers wore.

"Please," the Fire Sorceress said. "Take a seat."

Fires sparked to life around them, illuminating the room in a dancing orange glow. The doors behind them closed on their own, sending an eerie feeling down Doraan's spine.

They each took a seat, a stillness settling over them, the only sound was the flickering flames on the wall sconces. Doraan opened his mouth to speak, but the Water Sorcerer spoke first.

"How did you come to find our Temple?" His face was stern. Doraan noticed the brown waves falling over the man's shoulders looked wet and he found himself wondering if it was on purpose.

"I was told how to find your sanctuary by the Brothers of the Spring," Kamira said, voice strong, echoing around them in the large room. "I led us here."

The Water Sorcerer's blue eyes moved to her. Doraan watched, looking from one to the other as the two of them locked eyes, unblinking, until suddenly the man nodded and Kamira seemed to relax in her seat. *What in the skies name was that?*

The Fire Sorceress spoke next. "What is it that you have come here for?"

Doraan stood before anyone else could speak, chair scraping against the stone floor as he pushed it out behind him. He brought a hand up to his mouth and cleared his throat before saying, "We have come to ask for help."

The woman's lips thinned. "Yes, you've said that."

Heat rose to his cheeks as a tingling of annoyance started in his belly, burning toward the surface.

The woman raised a brow, head tilting to the side, waiting.

Cormac coughed beside him and Doraan cleared his throat again, clasping his hands tightly behind him. "We need your help to break a curse put over us by a powerful Sorceress."

The woman frowned, her straight blonde hair fanning out as she turned her head sharply to the Earth Sorcerer to her right. The smirk was gone from the man's face, replaced by a frown that matched the woman beside him.

"What do you mean?" the man asked, leaning forward and placing his clasped hands on the table in front of him. "Cursed, how?"

"We have been cursed these past ten years to never walk on land. We are unable to sail our ship closer than ten miles to shore. No one can even come aboard our ship." Doraan's voice faltered, his eyes darting to Kamira for a split second. The Sorcerers missed nothing and he watched as all four of them turned their gaze to her.

She took that as an invitation and stood. "I have been with this crew for weeks and, although I don't understand it, I can vouch for them. Everything the Captain said is true. They cannot go on land."

The Air Sorceress had been very still throughout this entire exchange, her face set into a flat, disinterested look ever since they had arrived, but she suddenly said, "If no one could board their ship, how is it that you joined them only weeks ago?"

Shit, Doraan thought. "We don't know. We only know that many have tried over the years and none have succeeded except for Kamira."

A grunt was all they received in response.

The Fire Sorceress spoke again. "Who is this Sorceress you say cursed you?"

"Her name is Forcina, a powerful air Sorceress," Doraan answered.

All four of the Sorcerers gasped in unison.

The water Sorcerer shot to his feet, "Has she followed you here? Does she know where you are?"

Doraan frowned at their response. "No. We have not seen her in many days, but we never truly know what she knows or when she is following us."

"You must leave now," the man said.

It was the Earth Sorcerer who stood next, angling himself toward the Water Sorcerer. "Rogaan, you speak too soon. If Forcina had followed them or knew where they were, she would be here already."

"You know her, then?" Doraan asked, curious. He wanted to know why they feared her. Technically, he knew why, but he had assumed they were just as powerful as she was. Was she someone so powerful that even the strongest Sorcerers in the Empire feared her? Forcina's words came back to him. *I am something that you cannot even comprehend.*

"We do," he said, voice calm and even. "We will offer you a place to stay for the evening and a meal, but you must leave at daybreak."

Doraan furrowed his brow, but nodded. "Thank you for your hospitality."

The Earth Sorcerer smiled, "Come, I would like to speak with you privately. Lariin."—he motioned toward the Fire Sorceress—"will take the rest of your crew to have a hot meal."

Cormac rose beside him, but Doraan put a hand on his shoulder. "I'll be fine."

The quartermaster only frowned, but stayed and did not follow as Doraan walked toward the stone archway the man had disappeared through.

Doraan found himself in a winding hallway that sloped upward, following the brown flowing robes that spread out like a span of wings behind the Sorcerer. Doraan picked up his pace, coming to the door the man walked through only to find himself in a room filled with shelves of books and strange artifacts.

The man sat in an oversized chair, one of two angled toward a large hearth, where a single blue flame sputtered, producing more heat than he would have imagined for such a small fire.

He motioned to the chair opposite him. "Please, sit."

Doraan obliged, a sudden flutter of anxious unease moving through him in anticipation of what this man wanted to speak to him about. Did he know he was the son of the man who murdered his kind in droves?

"My name is Melik and I am the Earth Warden here at the Temple," he said in a soft but commanding tone. "Tell me, how did you come to find us?"

"The woman sailing with us got the information from the Brothers of the Spring."

Melik snorted, narrowing his eyes on him. "Will you tell me more of this curse? How exactly did it happen?"

"It was on my fourteenth birthday. Forcina appeared from nowhere. She was angry with my father over what…" Doraan stopped short, eyeing the Sorcerer in an attempt to gauge what his reaction to his next words might be. "Well, what he did to the Sorcerers. My father is Emperor Amir."

The man didn't react to his words—not even a flinch—so Doraan continued, "She said something about *'you took my son from me, so I'll take yours from you.'* I don't remember the exact words she said next. It was all a blur, but the next thing I knew, I was in the middle of the ocean on a ship with a group of men I didn't know, and each time we tried to sail to shore, we couldn't."

Melik frowned. "I'm afraid what Forcina did to you and your men is far beyond our abilities. She…" He paused, leaning forward in his chair, and rested his elbows on his knees as he clasped his hands in front of him. "She is something we don't fully understand. We have managed to stay hidden from her, but her gifts are not the same as ours. If what you say is true and you truly cannot go on land, then she has found a way to enact the impossible by bending your very soul to her whim."

It was Doraan's turn to frown. "So, you cannot help us?"

"I'm afraid not. She has accomplished something far greater than even a Legion can do. The only way to get out of your curse is through Forcina herself."

The witch has made it impossible for this curse to end. She had made sure that he would be left to roam the sea forever, or die. Her words from that fateful evening all those years ago grated at his mind, embedding into the forefront of his mind. *"The only way to enact your freedom is to perform a selfless act on my kin. Sacrifice yourself to reverse the crimes of your father, and you will be unbound from this curse."* Doraan's anger ignited and sweat began to bead on his brow.

"Are you alright?"

"Fine," Doraan said, between clenched teeth. They had come here for nothing. The last two weeks had been utterly useless. Doraan looked out the far window, watching as Sorcerers wielded their powers. "Are you planning to attack my father and Aksahri?"

"What?" The man scoffed. "Why would you ask such a thing?"

"Your Sorcerers are out there practicing combat skills. Plus, you've been forced to this place, forced to hide because of my father. I assumed you had been planning an attack all these years."

"We are completely self-sufficient here. We never want for anything, and we are free to use our gifts. We are *free*. We have no need to attack Aksahri."

"But it's your home. All of Emmoria was yours for thousands of years before my people forced you from your lands. Why aren't you angry?"

"We have no interest in war. We only want peace. We are a people who absorb change and welcome it. The uprising was a terrible, heartbreaking event, and if we could go back to save those we lost, we would, but Emmoria was just a place to live. War has been waged in Emmoria for thousands of years. The lands are muddled and rotted with the blood of our ancestors. We have created a new world here. A peaceful, untainted world away from war, bloodshed and resistance. The Temple of Gorria is our home now."

Doraan looked out at the Sorcerers training, noticing for the first time the smiles on their faces. The joy radiating from their movements was palpable. They did look happy and truly at peace here.

"You know, every civilization has to embrace change as it comes. Your people came from war to start a new life in Emmoria, shifting the Elementalists' lives. When your father started the rebellion, it was time for us to move on.

The sands of fate are always shifting and we must embrace whatever they bring."

Doraan thought about that for a long moment—thinking about all he knew of his people, his father, the rebellion. A part of him had seemed to shift this past week, and he found himself thinking that maybe, just *maybe,* these people didn't deserve to die. Maybe they weren't as evil as he thought. Maybe the true culprit in all this was Forcina. She was the true enemy, even to these people. Kamira's words came to him then *I want you to give sorcery a chance. I'm risking my life for you and your crew because I believe in you, Doraan. You are my Emperor, you are the peoples hope, both the Gifted and Ungifted alike. They need you. Emmoria needs you.*

"Tonight, we celebrate the origins of our Temple. You and your crew are invited to join us in the festivities. I will show you out so you can find your crew and tell them." The Sorcerer stood and headed toward the door.

Doraan followed suit, calling after him, "You want me to join you? My father is the entire reason you are at this Temple. Wouldn't my presence just ruin it for you all?"

"The sins of the father are not the sins of the son, Doraan. We welcome all who come to our doorstep. There is always a reason a person ends up at our Temple, and I think you have yet to discover your reason."

Doraan frowned as he followed him out the door and into the long corridor. "What do you mean?"

This Sorcerer already knew the reason they were there, to find a way out of the curse. Was there another way, something that Melik was keeping from him?

"The only way to find the Temple of Gorria is if a Sorcerer is on your ship."

Doraan stopped in the middle of the hallway, flames flickering beside him, sending dancing shadows to swirl around him. "Wait, what?!"

27

KAMIRA

Kamira watched as Doraan followed the Earth Sorcerer down a long corridor. Once he was hidden from view, she found herself looking around the room and up to the ceiling. The building was a large circle, and she was surprised to be able to see all the way up to the top of the tall structure. There was no ceiling—it was completely open all the way up. It was extraordinary, not like anything she had ever seen. Balconies lined the walls and spiraled upward. She spotted a few curious heads looking down at her, backing away as she made eye contact with them.

There was a strange pulsing sensation that had been with her ever since they arrived. A sort of itching that she couldn't get rid of, stirring the air, and it made her want to unleash her gifts for everyone to admire. She had been fighting against it and felt the fatigue setting in from holding it all back. Adonis had told her not to allow these people to know she was a Legion, and she would heed his word. He obviously knew something about these people that she didn't.

Cormac and the rest of the crew made their way back outside, and she quickly followed suit. She brought an arm up, shielding the sun from blinding her. It was the time of day when the sun had begun to set and was in your direct line of sight. At this time of day, there were less Sorcerers milling about, and she could better take in the sheer beauty of this magical place.

It was truly magnificent. She didn't know how to properly describe it, but the city felt like an entirely new world, as if she had jumped years into the future. The sun glinted off the glass buildings, reflecting onto the lush ground that was perfectly manicured, not one blade of grass out of place. Everything was just so perfect—even the atmosphere held the perfect temperature. You couldn't feel the heat of the sun's dying rays beating down, but there was also no cool breeze. It was spectacular.

Kamira bit back the urge to jump when a voice drifted from behind her. "Would you take a walk with me?"

She turned to find Rogaan, the Water Sorcerer, behind her, his deep blue eyes holding an intensity that sent an eerie chill down her spine. He was a broad-shouldered man of average height, and despite his intimidating presence, he offered her a soft smile.

"Okay," she said hesitantly.

"Come, we can walk by the water along the perimeter of the Temple. There is a path circling the grounds."

Kamira followed him, anxious anticipation of what he wanted to discuss with her crawling up her neck and along her shoulders, creating an uneasiness that faltered her steps.

"You are the one who brought your crew here, correct?"

She knew exactly where this was going. He knew what she was. "I did."

"You are a water Sorceress."

Kamira almost sighed in relief, thankful the word *Legion* didn't come from his lips. "Yes, I am."

"But you are more than that," he said, stopping their walk and turning to face her hands clutched behind his back as he narrowed his eyes on her.

The spindly, crawling feeling moved from her shoulders, shooting down her spine and through her arms and legs. "I...I.." she sputtered.

"You are a Legion," he finished for her.

Kamira felt herself taking a step backward, trying to distance herself.

"It's okay. I'm not going to do anything to you. You don't have to be scared." He offered her another gentle smile. "It's been a long time since I've been in the presence of a Legion. The others have never met one, but when a Legion is near, the air shifts around them in a way that feels like the currents of the sea. Something that the other Sorcerers wouldn't understand." He turned toward the path again and began walking, motioning for her to follow. "Do you know much about the Legions? I suspect you are probably only one of a few left in Emmoria. We had all thought they were eradicated long ago."

"I..." Kamira stretched her mind to find the words. "No. I only know the little my family has told me. That Legions control all the elements and the Emperor hunted them, destroying them long ago."

Rogaan nodded, bringing a hand up to stroke his chin before continuing, "Legions always were far and few inbetween, but they all descended from one being. The original Legion, Honoria the protector."

Kamira balked, stopping in her tracks. "The woman from the War of the Four Kings?"

Rogaan laughed. "Yes, the Legion who raised an army of the dead to end the Elemental War centuries ago. She is your ancestor."

"That story is real? All those things actually happened?"

He smiled. "As real as you and I."

Kamira noticed for the first time the true lines of age on his face and the subtle hints of gray hair mingled in with his dark tresses. It was known that Sorcerers hid their age much better than the Ungifted, living many decades beyond them. The average lifespan for an Ungifted was eighty years, whereas the average for a Sorcerer was thirty years beyond that. She wondered how old Rogaan really was. She imagined he was older than Cormac by at least a decade.

"Being a Legion is a special thing, even more so now. There aren't many left. You may be one of only a handful remaining."

One of three to be exact, Kamira thought. Her entire family, except for her father, were all Legions, but she was curious if there were more this man knew of. "Do you know of any other surviving Legions?"

"The only other one I know of is Forcina."

Kamira coughed, choking on her own saliva. "What?!"

Rogaan looked at her with an arched gray brow. "I thought you knew. Forcina is a very, very powerful Sorceress. We believe she is a Legion and, likely, closely related to you, but she is also something else. She has traveled for decades, roaming the seas, looking for more power in other lands. And she has succeeded in finding it. She is far more powerful and terrifying than a Legion now."

Kamira couldn't breathe. This was more than she had ever learned about herself, about Emmoria even. Forcina had traveled outside of Emmoria. She didn't even know any other lands existed beyond theirs.

"It is why I had my outburst earlier. I have taken great measures to hide this place from Forcina. She is unruly, and her power is too great for us to withstand. If she were to find our oasis," he paused, taking a deep breath, "there is no knowing what she would do. She can't stand the fact that the Ungifted were able to take over our Empire. We are now weak in her eyes. It is why you, another Legion, being here is dangerous for us. If she can sense you, as I can, then she may be on her way here as we speak."

Kamira frowned at that. If that were true, wouldn't Forcina have found her easily when she was in Neilmaar with Jaario? She had looked directly at her, but then simply just walked on. Maybe Rogaan was mistaken. "I've been on the ship with Doraan's crew for over a week, and she didn't know I was there until I made myself known to her. I don't think she can sense me as you can."

"Let's hope that is true, for all our sakes, but you understand why we must ask you to leave at first light?"

She offered him a small smile of acknowledgement. "I understand. Don't worry, we will honor your wishes."

He nodded his gratitude.

They continued to walk in silence for a time, watching as the sun began to set, casting a splash of fuchsia and lavender across the horizon. She was admiring the beauty of it, enjoying the change in color as the sun set further, the colors melding into one another, creating a darker magenta along the skyline.

That color had a thought suddenly popping into her head. "Do you think it is possible that Forcina somehow found a way to bend someone's fate during her journeys across the sea? That she learned a new skill, something that we are also capable of but just haven't had the tools to learn it?"

Rogaan furrowed his brow, thinking over her question. "It is possible. I'm still not sure I understand how she did what she did to your friends. If that is true, and she has really learned to change a person's fate, bending their lives to her will, then I'm afraid there is no hope for them. The only way to change it is to hope she reverses whatever strange magic she had wielded, or kill her and hope what she has done will be broken."

That wasn't the answer Kamira was looking for, but she knew it was the only one he could give. He was right. They didn't understand anything that Forcina had done. It was something that had never been done in Emmoria before, and so it was something so foreign that Kamira still could barely comprehend it.

But Kamira *was* a Legion, just like Forcina. If Forcina had been able to learn to bend fate, then maybe Kamira could, too. They needed to travel over the ocean, find the lands that Forcina had been to, and figure out what she had discovered. Their adventure didn't end here. There was more to their story, more to Doraan's and the crew's stories. She needed to find Doraan and tell him what she had learned.

"The festival will be starting soon. Tonight we celebrate the Legions who gave their lives to save us," Rogaan said. "Tonight we celebrate your ancestors and you."

Kamira smiled at the older man, nodding her gratitude to him for all he had told her—for the knowledge she had gained from him—all the while wondering why Adonis had told her to keep her gifts a secret from these people.

28

DORAAN

Night was closing in around them as the entire crew made their way to the island's center where the festival was to be held. Doraan's mouth dropped open as they turned a corner and beheld the spectacle before them.

Thousands of lights floated around them like little balls of fire, casting everything around them in a warm glow. The lights shifted as they walked through, floating around them like lantern flies. Long tables encircled a massive bonfire with blue flames. Tables and chairs rooted into the earth sprouted up to create their own unique shapes, decorated with snaking vines and floating lights that hovered above each table like fireflies. Hundreds of people milled about, some sitting at the tables already, while others talked among themselves, all dressed in elaborate robes with shimmering gold and silver thread. Each element could be picked out just based on what they were wearing, but their apparel was more elegant and beautiful than their day clothes. The mouthwatering smells of smoked meat and spices filled the air.

Everything was breathtaking, but the most magnificent view of the entire festival scene was the enormous tree behind it all. Doraan continued his way through the throng of people to its base. He didn't know how he hadn't spotted it earlier when they arrived because it stood taller than any of its surrounding structures. Shimmering green leaves shifted to blue and purple from different angles. The branches spread out far and wide—as if protecting them from the outside world—and the entire tree sparkled in the darkness from the beads of light hanging from each limb. An energy hummed around it, growing louder as he neared, almost as if the tree was the very power that kept this entire place afloat. But the most amazing part of the tree was its trunk. It was easily as thick as seven ship hulls.

Doraan felt like an ant beside it.

"Skies above," Kamira said as she walked up beside him. "It's colossal."

"Do you think that they could have made it any bigger?"

Kamira laughed, "I don't know. Maybe if all the Earth Sorcerers worked together. What kind of tree is it? It looks so strange."

"I'm not sure it's replicated after any tree we have at home in Emmoria. I think it's completely new—Sorcerer created." Even the trunk wasn't like the bark of the trees back home. It was a strange pinkish-red color, smooth and shiny like glass.

"They would have had to create it from some root or seed, possibly altering it somehow. It's so beautiful," Kamira said as she reached out a hand, placed it on the tree, and gasped. "It's so cold! It feels like ice. Here, touch it."

She grabbed his wrist and pulled him toward the base of the tree until his palm was flush against it. An electric spark shot into his hand at the contact, spreading through him like lightning. He didn't feel cold, but heat—so hot he yanked his hand back, inspecting it to make sure it wasn't burned. But only a smooth, unmarred flash stared back at him.

"What happened?" Kamira asked, taking his hand to look at his palm. "Are you okay?"

"It felt like my hand was on fire," he whispered, brows drawn together.

"Really?" Kamira brushed her palm against his. "Strange, your hand does feel hot."

"And yours is freezing, what..." He faltered. He suddenly turned to her, staring directly into her blue eyes, looking at her with a perceiving, curious eye. Melik had said someone on board the *Cursed Soul* was a Sorcerer. It was the only way to find this place and there was no way any of his crew were. There was only one person it could be. "Who are you?" he asked, taking a step closer to her.

Kamira frowned and took a step away from him. "What do you mean?"

He didn't have a chance to question her further as a voice came from the direction of the festival. "I see that you have discovered our Legion tree." It was Lariin, the Fire Sorceress they met when arriving. She came up to stand between them.

"This tree is a culmination of all four elemental powers. We all put a portion of our gifts into its creation, melding them together. It symbolizes unity between the Sorcerers, as well as a remembrance to the Legions who sacrifice themselves to save us during the rebellion."

Doraan didn't miss the quick glance she gave to him when talking about the rebellion. Melik hadn't wasted any time in telling these people who his father was then.

"It's what we're celebrating tonight. Today marks forty years we have been here—the beginning of the Temple and the creation of the Legion unity tree."

Doraan didn't know much about Legions, only that they were the most powerful Sorcerers ever to exist, able to control all the elements and perform horrific acts. It had been his father's ultimate goal to seek them out and destroy them ever since he took over Emmoria. It was a fixation. Ruling was an obsession to him, so much so that he practically ignored his family. Doraan snorted at the thought, wondering why he had ever tried to gain his father's love and approval. None of that even mattered anymore. He was never going home, and he was never going to see his father ever again.

Music began to play behind them. The festival was starting.

Doraan looked over to where Kamira had been standing only moments ago, but she was gone. His nostrils flared and he groaned. He wanted to ask her more questions. If she was a Sorceress, so many things would make sense. Number one being how she was able to get onto the *Cursed Soul* when no other had.

The music picked up, a chorus of strings and horns filtering through the air, sweeping around him and drawing his attention to them. Suddenly, the water from the neighboring fountains sprang forth, arching overhead, shaping into a great water serpent. It slithered through the air, raining droplets of cool water down on everyone before diving back into the fountains from which it came. Next, the earth rumbled beneath his feet, and he looked down to see shapes form in the grass. The elemental symbols were all molded into the ground in a checkered pattern all around them. Wind whistled in his ears, and he looked up to the sky once again, noticing a silken sheet dancing in the air, moving like a ballerina as it twirled above everyone in perfect rhythm to the music.

The Sorcerers were each using their gifts for the sheer beauty of what they could do. They weren't using it to harm—they were using it to bring joy and to entertain. The music picked up its tempo and many of the Sorcerers began to dance with one another. Laughter rose high over the festival, and Doraan expected to feel lighter. He expected to feel a happiness he hadn't felt in so long, but the music, the use of sorcery all around him, the strange tree behind him, and the incessant buzzing in the air around him...it made him feel as if he couldn't fully catch his breath.

Doraan stumbled back knocking into a couple dancing behind him. "S—sorry," he ground out, and they each furrowed their brows at him, asking if he was alright. "Fine," he bit out.

Sweat beaded on his forehead, dripping down his face and into his eyes as he blinked rapidly against the sting and his breathing became erratic.

What was happening? That same burning that had been coursing through him with every emotion he had felt these past weeks raged hotter, to the point of pain. He ripped at his clothing, desperate to feel the cool air around him, anything but this stifling heat, but his limbs felt weak, his fingers unable to work properly.

He fell back against something hard. The tree. But the instant he touched its smooth surface, that burning sensation inside of him turned feral. He was positive this would be his end. He was going to erupt like a volcano that had been building to explode for years and years.

Doraan pushed himself away from the tree, his vision beginning to blur from the agony, and tumbled forward, barrelling into one of the lantern poles. As soon as his hand grabbed onto the pole, glass shattered around him, the flames of the lantern exploding outward, shooting balls of fire across the festival. Doraan could just make out the screams in the crowd, but all he was focused on was his hand.

He stared wide-eyed at the flames licking his fingertips. He pulled his hand away, but the fire only followed, spreading out over his palm and stroking his hand like an owner would their dog. To his astonishment, he felt no singe, no burning pain, only coolness as it continued to roam up his arm and across his shoulders, down into his other palm.

That excruciating heat that had been coursing through him moments earlier now gone.

As he looked down to the flames whirling in his palms, the realization of what it meant hit him with the force of a thousand waves. He was controlling the fire—it was answering to him.

He was a Sorcerer.

"No!" he yelled, flicking his hands, trying to extinguish the flames, but with each jerk he shot sparks flying out toward the gathered crowd of Sorcerers. Small fires ignited in the grass and spread quickly, causing the Sorcerers to flee and disperse in all directions.

"I'm sorry!" Doraan yelled, eyes searching the crowd for a familiar face, but only strangers stared back at him, their faces set into varying looks of disgust and horror. "I'm so sorry!"

It was Lariin, the Fire Sorcerer who came up in front of him, taking his hands in hers and pulling the fire into her own palms. The Water Sorcerer behind her extinguished the fires he had started.

"I—I—" he stuttered. "I'm sorry," he said a final time before he fled into the night.

29

KAMIRA

Kamira was mesmerized by the display of sorcery around her. She had never been in the presence of so many at once. She felt transcended—like she was living out a vivid dream and at any moment she would wake up.

But she was torn from the beauty of the Sorcerer's show as movement caught her eye. She glanced to her left, stunned to see a man. Memories crawled forth from the recesses of her mind. It was the same man she had seen twice before, his pale hair like a beacon, begging her to venture closer.

She frowned, stepping away from the celebration and, against her better judgment, walked into the darkness to meet him.

He held the same smirk on his mouth she had seen when he was along the forested shoreline of Torheim.

"You," she breathed. "Have you been following me?"

"You could say that." His voice was low and captivating, but laced with a bitter tinge that made her skin crawl. She took a step back.

"Who are you?" she asked.

He stepped closer and the moonlight revealed the angles of his face. He was possibly the most beautiful man she had ever seen. His bright green eyes reminded her of fresh spring leaves and his square jaw was sharp like the edge of a blade.

He stepped closer and turned his head like a sand lion assessing his prey, causing gooseflesh to snake up her arms. "My, you look just like her, practically the spitting image."

She wrinkled her brow, backing away from him again. "Who?"

She didn't like how he ignored her question. This man had been at the top of the hill the night she fled. It had to be him—she recalled his white hair and how it flashed beneath the moonlight. She studied him, noticing how he wasn't wearing the ceremonial colors of the Sorcerers, nor the robes they all dressed in. He wore solid black—and odd looking clothing she had never seen before.

"The first of her name. The first Legion," he said with a crooked smile.

The night air suddenly seemed much colder and Kamira wrapped her arms around herself. "H—how do you know what the first Legion looked like?" There were never any depictions of the first Legion, which made it a very strange thing for him to say.

He ignored her question again and in a single blink he was mere inches from her face, glowering down at her. She jumped back, but he gripped her arm and held her in place. Any ounce of a smile that was on his face disappeared. "Your enemies are closer than you think, Kamira. Be careful who you put your trust in."

"How do you know my name?" she demanded, trying to dislodge his grip from her arm.

His hand burned like a brand against her skin, and at the same time felt cold as ice. She could feel the intensity of his power with that single touch. Every nerve ending tensed, her body on high alert, giving her the sudden urge to run. Something dark and sinister lurked beneath his surface, this was no ordinary Sorcerer. "They won't survive the fight that's coming. No one will, and I would truly hate to see this entire realm fall to ruin. I have so many fond memories here."

"Who are you?" she breathed. Everything around them grew deathly quiet, as if they were the only two people left in the Empire.

"Who I am isn't important. What is, is that you master the final element. You must learn to control your gift of fire, Kamira, and only then will you be able to unlock your full potential. Everything will click into place and you will be able to do more than you could even imagine." His mouth curved on one side and his piercing eyes grew dark, now almost black. "The blood of the first runs in your veins. The power of the Immortals is at the tip of your fingers. All you have to do is grasp it."

Kamira was too stunned to speak. Her heart was beating in her chest like the galloping hooves of a stallion. What was this man talking about? What were the Immortals? How did he know so much about her?

He stood over her, cocked his head to the side, and snapped his finger's beside her ear. A flame sparked to life between them. She balked and pushed her hands against his chest in an attempt to shove him away, but he didn't budge. How had he done that? He had commanded the flame with no source, created it from nothing.

"Take it from me," he said, the light of the flame dancing across his face, making him look far more menacing than he had before.

"H—how did you do that?" she stammered.

"You, Kamira, are special like me. Your gifts are not on the surface, but from within." He pointed a pale finger at her chest. "You know the word *Legion*, don't you?"

"Yes," she whispered.

"It is used to describe a Master Sorcerer of all the elements. But the truth of the Legion has been forgotten with time. A Legion of the true bloodline, a child of the first, is a conjurer of elements. You are something far more deadly than you know."

Kamira didn't understand. "What do you mean? What are you saying?"

"I think you know exactly what I'm saying, Kamira. I think you have known for a while now.."

"I—it's impossible. No Sorcerer can create without substance."

"Ah, but have you ever tried?"

Kamira narrowed her eyes. "Why would I attempt something that is impossible?"

The man snorted. "You never truly know what you are capable of unless you try."

He blew out the flame, and it sputtered into smoke before her. "Remember what I said. Those closest to you are not what they seem. Use your gut instincts." His eyes darted to the vial that hung around her neck. "Keep that close. You may need it sooner than you think."

Suddenly, the ground shook beneath her feet as a *boom* echoed around them. Kamira turned to see flames shooting near the base of the Legion tree. It was the Fire Sorceress' turn to perform. She turned back around to ask the man what he meant, but he was already gone.

30

DORAAN

D oraan stared down at his shaking hands. That didn't just happen. None of it was real. How could *he* be a Sorcerer?

But even as he tried to deny it, the memories of all the strange feelings he'd felt inside came bubbling to the surface. The burning in his veins, the tingling at his palms, and how every emotion had him feeling as if he might explode if he didn't let it all out.

He suddenly recalled all the times he had felt as if his insides were on fire over the past weeks, no, the past years. Any time his anger would rise, so would that scorching heat, traveling through his limbs as if trying to ignite him into a living flame. Had that been his sorcery trying to break free? It was the only explanation. He thought it was normal—that everyone felt that when their emotions began to rise to the surface, but maybe it wasn't. Maybe it was just him.

What did it mean? He wasn't sure he wanted to understand it fully just yet. If either of his parents were Sorcerers, wouldn't he have known? Wouldn't there have been some sign of it?

There was absolutely no way his father was a Sorcerer. His hatred for them was the only thing that kept him going. It was his entire life. It fueled him like dry wood does a flame. Was it his mother then? Had she hidden her powers for so long? How brazen of her to be with the very man who hated her kind the most.

If it was true, how could she live with a man like his father? How could she stand beside him while he massacred her people? It just didn't make sense.

Nothing made sense anymore. His entire existence had been a lie. Everything he knew and believed was now completely shattered.

Doraan walked out onto the balcony of the room he had been offered for the night. He stared down at the vast island, watching the flickering flames dancing throughout the landscape. The familiar prickling warmth built and urged him to reach out toward the fire to bend his will.

Doraan turned his back to it all, leaned his against the balcony railing and slid down it until he was sitting on the ground, knees against his chest, head in his hands.

This was a nightmare.

Suddenly, a knock came on the other side of his door. "Doraan?"

It was Cormac. Doraan groaned, curled his arms around his legs and pulled them close, wincing as his wooden foot scraped loudly across the ground, the sound echoing through the large room.

"Can I come in?" Cormac's voice came through the door again.

Doraan still didn't answer him. He just wanted to be alone, to wallow in his self-loathing by himself.

The door creaked open, and Doraan cursed. He hadn't locked it.

He looked away from Cormac as the older man walked toward him, taking a seat next to him on the balcony floor and leaning his back against the railing with a sigh. "Doraan..."

"I don't want to talk about it," he said, cutting off Cormac's words.

"I think you'll want to hear what I have to say."

"Doubtful," Doraan grumbled, refusing to look at Cormac.

"I knew your mother when she was young. My parents worked for her family."

Doraan whipped his head around, frowning at Cormac. "What? Why have you never told me that?"

"Because it never really mattered until now. I didn't think you had gained your mother's gifts and you hated sorcery so much that I thought talking to you about her would have made things worse for you. No one wants to think their parents lied to them."

"So...so all this time you knew? My mother is a Sorceress and I could be a Sorcerer? Does my father know, too?"

"Yes, and no, he doesn't know."

"Why? Why would you keep this from me?"

"You were too young, too angry, and it wouldn't have made any difference. We were still all cursed and couldn't have done anything about it. I just didn't think it would help the situation. I felt you knowing would have made it worse, and there was no one on board that could have helped you learn to control your powers. As the years went by and you showed no affinity for sorcery, I just assumed you had no gifts, taking after your father."

"Ever since I was a boy, I've felt an ember inside of me, brewing, growing with each year trying to spark into a flame." Doraan's voice was low, a subtle growl in his tone. "I've always felt something foreign inside of me and to think all this time you knew. You had ten years to tell me this Cormac! Ten fucking years!"

"I'm so sorry, Doraan. I thought I was doing the right thing. I didn't want you to hate yourself for what you are."

"Well it's too late for that Cormac!" he yelled, saliva spraying from his lips from his rage. "Get out."

"Doraan," Cormac attempted.

"I said get out!" he bellowed.

The fire in the balcony lanterns exploded and shot upward to the sky.

"No," Cormac said simply, unphased by the wayward flames. "You are acting like the child you were when Forcina first cursed us. It's time to grow up, Doraan. In the real world, people deal with their problems and face new challenges head on. They don't sulk, wallowing on balconies."

Slowly, Doraan's anger ebbed as Cormac's words settled in. He was right. He was acting like a child, not a prince, and definitely not like the possible leader of the Empire.

Doraan took a deep breath, the flames returning to their original small flicker.

"I'm sorry, Cormac. It's just that everything has been too much these past weeks. First, going back to Aksahri. Then Kamira came aboard, and now this. My mind is so overloaded and constantly anxious. And on top of all that, this whole trip has been for nothing." Doraan closed his eyes and let his head fall back against the marble posts of the balcony railing with a thunk. "I'm leaving here with more questions than answers. I give up, Cormac. We are never going home. Let this King in the North destroy Aksahri. My whole existence has been nothing but a lie, and I'm done with all of them. I'm done caring."

"You don't mean that. There is still time. We could still find a way."

"It's over," Doraan moaned. "Tomorrow, we leave at first light and we sail toward the coast to find a merchant ship to steal from just like normal."

Cormac opened and then closed his month before shaking his silver speckled head and getting up, leaving the room without another word.

For someone who was so against finding the Temple for so long, he would have assumed Cormac would be happy that he was giving up. The Sorcerers here had been fairly adamant. They could not help them. They didn't even understand the curse or how Forcina had done it.

So, tomorrow, just before sunrise, he would gather his crew, forget about this place, forget about his own manifestation of gifts, and go back to living a life of piracy until he drew his last breath.

31

KAMIRA

Dawn had come too soon. Kamira hadn't slept a wink. She had spent all night walking the Temple grounds after her encounter with that strange man. There had been something very different about him, an ominous feeling that she was in the presence of someone very powerful. It had caused a sense of dread to fill her, making her skin crawl.

She looked down at her hands resting in her lap, remembering how he had snapped his finger and a flame appeared, conjured from nothing. Kamira closed her eyes, searching down to her core for something, anything, that could help her create an element. There was a small swell of something deep inside. She poked and prodded it, testing its abilities, pulling on it. She opened her eyes and snapped her fingers, but nothing happened. She huffed a laugh, shaking her head, "So, stupid," she whispered and rubbed her tired eyes. She couldn't create elements. No one could. That man probably had something up his sleeve—it was all some trick.

As she lowered her hand, it knocked against the glass jar hanging around her neck. She gripped the vial, studying the swirling purple liquid with a curious eye. The man had known what it was and told her she might need it soon, but why? And how would he know when she would need it? He had also warned her about an enemy who was close to her. What did that even mean? Honestly, she was beginning to think it had all just been a dream—that the man wasn't real at all, just some figment of her imagination that came out to play. She had been running on little sleep these last few days, so she wouldn't put it past her mind to be playing tricks on her.

Kamira dropped the vial, sighing as it thudded against her chest. She had learned so much last night that it was all just a jumbled mess in her head. Supposedly, she was a descendant of the first Legion, Honoria the Protector. Did Adonis know? Did he realize the type of power they had? But the most shocking discovery was that Forcina was a Legion. And if Rogaan was to be believed, then they were closely related. But not only that, Forcina had somehow learned to bend fate, and if she could do that, then maybe

Kamira could learn, too. She could finish what they had set out to do and end the curse of the *Cursed Soul* for good.

She hadn't had the chance to tell Doraan what she had learned yet. He was locked away in his room and had supposedly had a very eventful evening himself. The entire crew was whispering about it and she couldn't quite believe it herself.

Doraan was a Fire Sorcerer and the explosion she had heard last night was from the manifestation of his gifts. She couldn't imagine how he was feeling right now. Well, she could to a certain extent, but she had been so young when her gifts manifested, and her family had been there to help her. But for someone who hated sorcery as much as Doraan, the shock would be debilitating.

Kamira sighed heavily, looking out at the shimmering ocean as the sun peeked over the horizon. She was in her usual spot on the ledge just outside the kitchen windows at the ship's rear. She watched as they left the floating Temple behind—watched as it was there one moment and, with a single blink, it was gone again, leaving nothing but miles of open sea in its wake.

Skies, it had been a long night. It was best she get some decent sleep so that she could really sit down and go over everything that had happened. She also wanted to speak with Doraan and make sure he was okay about last night. She wasn't sure if she should tell him yet that she was also a Sorcerer. It was still so fresh and chances were he was still battling with his hatred of the Sorcerers.

Kamira was so lost in thought, she almost missed the glint of something twinkling far out in the sea behind them. It winked in and out of the horizon like a diamond glinting in the sun, but it was too far away to make out what it was. She grabbed the spyglass Cormac had given her from her belt and extended it fully before closing one eye and peering through it with her other.

It was a ship—a large one with a brass roaring lion as its figurehead, shining like gold in the dying sunlight, and boasting three tall central main masts. Only someone with extreme wealth could afford such an extravagant vessel. That very thought had her moving the spyglass up to the flag flying atop the largest center mast where a roaring lion head on a checkered bed of red and white could be seen.

"Shit!" Kamira yelled. She should have realized it from the ship's figurehead alone. It was Tarkiin's sigil. Her mind reeled, heart racing uncontrollably in her chest. That couldn't be right. She looked at the banner whipping in the wind again, the lion head menacing, threatening to bite her. She angled the spyglass at the deck, and there, looking as if he were staring directly at her, was her husband, Tarkiin. She gasped, shutting the spyglass quickly. It *had* been him she saw in Neilmaar that day.

Her husband wasn't dead after all. And he was after her. Greedy for blood.

32

DORAAN

They were being followed. Both Doraan and Cormac had spotted the ship an hour ago, and it had been steadily gaining on them ever since.

"Doraan! Where's Doraan?" Kamira came sprinting up the steps to the helm, wheezing from the exertion. "There's a ship!" She pointed behind him.

"I know," he said looking down at his compass, one hand on the wheel. He had drastically changed course twice in the past hour to see if it was actually following them, and there was no doubt about it. It was. "It's been following us for some time now."

"It's Tarkiin," she whispered so the crew couldn't hear. His head whipped toward her. "What?!" he exclaimed. She handed him her spyglass. "Look at the sigil."

He grabbed it and turned around to look through it. Sure enough, the angry lion roared its head in their direction. Why hadn't he thought to look at the ship's flag? His mind was too preoccupied. "How is that possible?"

"He wasn't as dead as I thought he was. Obviously," She choked out, her face pale. She was scared. "I never told you because I thought I was seeing things, but when I was in Neilmaar, I caught a glimpse of him in one of the town squares. I thought my mind was playing tricks on me, but it must have actually been him. He had to have seen and recognized me. He's probably been following us ever since."

Doraan's chest grew tight and he breathed out a shaky breath. That was a big ship. The *Cursed Soul* didn't hold a chance against it.

Kamira must have noticed him grow anxious because she said, "He's come for me. He won't stop until he has me, Doraan. I'll go to him. There is no need for any of you to get hurt on my behalf."

"I won't send you off for execution, Kamira. He'd have your head on a spike the instant you boarded his ship. You know his secret. A secret that would see his own head severed from his body."

"I know, but..."

"No buts," Doraan growled. "You will stay here. We'll figure it out. We always do."

"Drop sails!" Cormac yelled out beside them.

They would face him head on.

The crew did as commanded and the *Cursed Soul* slowed. They all went silent as they watched the other ship come up alongside theirs.

The Lord's ship was a hulk and a clumsy excuse for a vessel. It was a massive ship of obvious simple construction—made for its looks rather than its seaworthiness. Doraan wanted to set it ablaze and watch it burn with Tarkiin strapped to its main mast. A smile tugged at the corner of his mouth at the image.

The very man himself, as if summoned by the tempting thought, walked to the portside railing that was lined up with their starboard one. His sniveling face caused the now familiar burning to travel up his spine. He bit back against it.

"My, my, I didn't expect to find a ghost on this ship. So, this is what happened to you, Doraan? Did you flee from home, from your responsibilities?" Tarkiin's smile turned into a malicious leer.

Doraan growled, the fury bringing that fire closer and closer to the surface, threatening to boil over. He now knew what that feeling was. It had always been there—a foreign thing he didn't understand. He wasn't sure he even understood it now that he knew what it was. He wished he could rage at Tarkiin, that he could yell back some insult, but the blasted curse wouldn't allow it.

"Tarkiin," Kamira smirked, intercepting the Lord's jibe and bringing Doraan's thoughts back to the present. "You're looking fatter than usual."

Tarkiin turned, focusing his gaze on Kamira. The leer fell away from his face, and his nostrils flared as he narrowed his small eyes on her. "It seems I fell ill a few weeks ago and was taken to bed for some time. You wouldn't know anything about that, would you?"

She smiled at him, throwing all the sweet innocence she could into that smirk. "What a pity. You seem quite recovered."

"Yes, quite." He brought a hand up and rubbed the back of his oily head, wincing slightly before bringing it back down to rest on the pistol at his hip.

"What can we do for you, Tarkiin?" she asked, innocently.

Doraan bit back a laugh as he watched Tarkiin's face contort, turning a fiery shade of red.

"You will call me Lord Tarkiin, wife!" he spat. "You know exactly what you can do for me. It seems the Prince here has stolen my property and whisked it away on this—" He looked around at the *Cursed Soul*, nose scrunching in obvious abhorrence, "—unique vessel."

Kamira took a step forward, fists balled at her sides. "You are mistaken, sir. There is no property of yours on this ship, only what belongs here."

Tarkiin bared his teeth, leaving any and all pleasantries aside. "Come here, wife!"

"I am not your wife," she said, crossing her arms over her chest.

"Funny, but I remember standing in the courthouse with your parents present, exchanging vows and even signing our documentation of marriage." He narrowed his eyes, a sly grin spreading on thin lips. "That makes you mine."

"I will never be yours. I'm staying right here. If you want me, you'll have to come and get me."

Doraan whipped his head to her, noticing the mischievous glint in her eye. She knew exactly what she was doing. She was baiting him.

Tarkiin's fury shone bright on his face, but quickly changed into something far more terrifying as an amused smirk spread across his lips. "Pity your parents aren't here. They've been absolutely wracked with worry these past weeks."

Kamira's smile fell. "W—what have you done with them?"

"They are perfectly fine residing in my manor house." His eyes turned feral. "For now."

Kamira surged forward with a growl and Doraan placed an arm in front of her stopping her movements. "You can't go onto his ship, Kamira. If you do, there is nothing we can do to stop whatever he might do to you."

"What are you saying, Prince?" Tarkiin called out. "We can't seem to hear you."

A chorus of laughter rose up around him.

Doraan glared at the man and his eyes flicked quickly to one of the lanterns dangling to his left. Could he send the flame across to their ship? He wanted Tarkiin to burn for what he had done to his father. His nostrils flared.

"Well? Are you going to give me back my property or do I have to take it back by force?" Tarkiin tapped a finger on his pistol, wrapping his hand around the grip.

"I'm not going anywhere with you," Kamira spat.

"So be it," Tarkiin snarled and in a flash, faster than Doraan could have ever imagined from him, the pistol was in the bastard's hand and a shot rang out.

Smoke billowed and Doraan's eyes went wide. Everything around him slowed. His heart pounded loud like a drum in his ears and he didn't even need a second to think about what he was doing before he jumped in front of Kamira.

Pain exploded in his chest as blood sprayed. Someone screamed out his name. He fell to the deck and chaos erupted around him, but he heard nothing. He could feel the blood leaving his body, he tried to pull air into his lungs, but could only cough, red spraying from his lips. He was dying. This was it—his last moments—and strangely, he felt not fear or anger, but peace.

His entire body felt numb, and his eyes grew heavy. He was so tired, and all he could think as he took his final choking breath was that he was glad he could save one person if he couldn't save all of Aksahri.

33

KAMIRA

"Doraan!" Kamira screamed. He had saved her life and now he lay dying, collapsed on the deck in front of her, and all she could see was red.

She looked up at Tarkiin and the sneer on his face. "Oops, I missed," he said, his crew chuckling around him.

That was all Kamira needed to hear for her to snap.

She no longer cared about hiding her sorcery, she no longer cared about anything but seeing Tarkiin dead. For weeks she had dealt with the guilt, the self-loathing of thinking she had killed him, but now that he was here and she could truly see that Emmoria would be a better place without him, all she wanted was to see him dead again and make sure it was for good this time.

Kamira brought her hands out in front of her, glaring at the man who her parents forced her to marry, and pulled against the ocean. The entirety of Tarkiin's crew stared at her and she could hear them asking, *"What is she doing?" "Is she daft?"* while others simply pointed and laughed. All the while, she unleashed her power on the waves beneath them, watching as a massive wave rose behind their ship, glinting in the sunlight. It churned, spraying droplets on them as it grew like a massive sea dragon preparing for an attack.

The crew of the *Cursed Soul* gasped beside her, watching the wave build around Tarkiin's hulking vessel. Her former husband's crew frowned, turning in unison to see what was behind them, and Kamira took that as her time to strike.

She sent tendrils of swirling ocean shooting toward them, wrapping around Tarkiin and each of his crew. They thrashed, kicking and trying to swim through the water, but she only replaced any displacement with more of the sea. Her hands were tingling from the sheer multitude of power at her fingertips. She coaxed the waves, watching as the shimmering water climbed up their backs and over their shoulders. The men roared, yelling for help, but nothing could be done. No Ungifted could fight against her sorcery.

She moved the water farther until each man was completely engulfed, joining them all into one raging, whirling ball of sea. The sorcery coursed through her as if a dam had been opened, and she could do anything. She reveled in it—the pure power rushing through her.

Her breathing was heavy, her power beginning to take a small toll as she held the ball of drowning men there, hovering above their extravagant ship. She watched as, one by one, the men stopped convulsing and their bodies went limp, until only Tarkiin was left. Kamira drew the sphere of water closer and stared at Tarkiin, watching his eyes as the fear etched there winked out like an extinguished flame, his life now truly taken from him at her hands.

She released her power, drawing it all back into herself, and the men scattered on the deck like fish thrown from a net, wet and unmoving.

She loosened a sigh of relief, turning and expecting to see horrified faces at what she had just done, but everyone was huddled in a circle behind her, staring down at Doraan. It was Lindor who turned to her, the sun catching on the tears glistening down his dark skin. "Can you help him?"

Her chest caved at the plea in his voice, at the thought of the ship surgeon knowing there was nothing he could do to help. Doraan was dying.

She moved past the men to see Doraan lying in a puddle of blood. He was so pale. She knelt beside him, blood seeping into her pants, and brought two fingers to feel the pulse at his neck. There was the smallest flutter. He wasn't dead yet, but he was mere breaths away from his last.

Tears welled in her eyes, dripping down her cheeks to join Doraan's life-blood beneath her. A large hand came to rest on her shoulder. "He's gone, lass," Cormac's words were heavy with emotion.

"No." She wiped at the tears staining her cheeks and shook him off. "No, I can fix this. I can save him."

Cormac shook his head, eyes sparkling with unshed tears. "It's too late."

"No, I can do this. I *will* save him."

For years, she watched as her mother used her sorcery to heal those who were sick or wounded in secret, but she had never seen her mother heal someone from a wound this severe. She wasn't even sure it was possible, but she knew he wasn't yet completely gone. Doraan was teetering between life and death, his essence still shown through and she could feel the low flicker of his energy. But he was fading fast.

Kamira closed her eyes, feeling the energy that sang around her. Everything was thrumming with life, with its own energy. It was something she had only recently discovered. The more she used her gifts, the more she felt connected to it, to everything. Energy connected every-thing—the crew members who looked on with heavy hearts and bated breath, the sea that ebbed and flowed around them, the wind that whisked through the sails urging them onward, and the sun that shone down upon them, warming their skin. And herself. She pulled on all of it, coaxing it to bend to her will. Channeling it all onto one task.

First, she needed to remove the blood from Doraan's lungs. She could feel the liquid pooled there and she willed it to ease from his chest, flow back into his veins, and pull the blood puddled beneath him with it. From there, she pushed air into the collapsed lung, returning it to its full splendor, and then she twisted the elements together, using them to knit the punctures back together until there was no sign of injury besides the blood soaked in his clothing.

Now came the part she was unsure of—the bending of life itself. She had no idea if it would work, but she pulled forth each of the elements, melding them together into one. First water, then air and earth, and with a calming breath, she drew on fire. She extracted the living energy from each elemental source and pushed it down into Doraan's heart where she could feel it swirling and coaxing, until a single beat pounded in his chest. Her breathing hitched as she waited for a second beat.

When it came, a gasp sounded behind her and then another, until a chorus of awe rose up around her. She looked into Doraan's once still and lifeless eyes. "Please," she whispered. "Come back."

She placed a gentle hand on his chest where the bullet hole had been only moments ago. The rhythm of his heart was slow, but it was there, steadily growing faster until suddenly, an invisible force lifted him from the blood soaked deck. Kamira fell backward as he rose higher above all of their heads.

"What are you doing?" Jorne yelped beside her. "Bring him back down!"

"I'm not doing anything. This isn't me." Her eyes were wide, fear falling to the pit of her stomach and making her nauseous. Had she done this? She never used her sorcery the way she just had, there was no knowing what the side effects might be.

Kamira stood on shaking legs, joining the crew as they all watched Doraan's limp body begin to spin in the air above them.

Cariin climbed the netting beside him, reaching out for him, but it was no use. Doraan's body spun and a scream rang out, not from any of the crew, but from him. The crew yelled, more of them climbing the rigging in an attempt to grab him.

Kamira choked out a sob. What had she done? But then as suddenly as he had begun to spin, his body stopped. Everything stopped as if time itself was at a standstill. Kamira's breathing quickened as she looked at each of the crew, all of them frozen in whatever pose they had just been in.

"What in the blazing stars?" Kamira whispered.

She looked back up to Doraan. His face was locked in a scream, each of his limbs stretched out to his sides. A heavy wind picked up, swirling around her as her clothes and hair whipped harshly against her skin. She looked at each of the crew members and they all stayed perfectly still, the wind appearing as if it wasn't even touching them.

Kamira could barely keep her eyes open from the strength of the wind, so she brought an arm up to shield them. She had to do something, anything, to help them.

Reaching back into herself, she used her gifts to push against the raging whirlwind around them, gritting her teeth from the force of it. But her sorcery did nothing against it. It felt the same as when she had tried to use her gifts to push the *Cursed Soul* to shore. There was a barrier, something she couldn't push against.

And then it stopped. An eerie hush fell over the ship. Not even the sounds of the water could be heard. She looked up to Doraan once more and, suddenly, something powerful exploded from him, pushed out in a wave of energy, and knocked her to the ground. A high pitched squeal screamed in her ears, coming from nowhere and everywhere at the same time. She covered them with her hands, yelling out in pain until with one final pulse, each of the crew jerked, looking as if a string had pulled them all forward in unison. And then it all stopped, and they fell to the deck, the world around them back as it was.

Kamira cowered on the deck, hands still held over her ears as she watched the crew slowly push themselves up. She turned sharply as she heard Cormac yell, "Doraan!"

The Captain was sitting up, a hand held over his heart as his chest heaved with deep gasping breaths. "It's gone," he whispered. "The curse. I—It's gone."

Several of the crew cheered while others wept with joy. Kamira was too shocked to understand. She looked down at her hands, at Doraan's blood stained there. What had just happened? How could the curse be broken? How did they know?

She looked back up to see Doraan's eyes on her. "It was you."

She blinked, unsure what he meant by that, and pushed herself up on wobbling legs.

Doraan did the same, holding onto the main mast beside him as he slowly limped toward her. "You're a Sorceress."

She only nodded, looking up at him as he stared down at her, brows creased.

"You saved me, brought me back from death. You broke the curse, Kamira. It was you all along."

"I—I—," she stuttered, not understanding. Everything that just happened was too overwhelming and she burst into tears.

"Kamira," Doraan breathed and grabbed her, pulling her against him and wrapping her in a tight embrace.

Suddenly, more arms were wrapping around her as the entire crew encased them both in one giant embrace, squeezing tight. "Thank you." Cormac whispered in her ear.

She looked back at him, seeing the relief in his features, and a knowing look in his blue eyes. He knew, she realized. He knew all this time that she was the one that could help them. She had come aboard their ship for a reason, and that reason being that she was the one person who could break their curse.

"Thank you," the crew echoed after him.

Her tears turned into laughs. She still wasn't sure she fully understood how she had broken their curse, but she had. They were cursed no more. They could finally go home.

34

DORAAN

The nightmare was finally over and Doraan felt reborn. The air smelled fresher, the sky looked brighter, the sound of the waves seemed louder—everything felt real. He could do anything, go anywhere, and it was so incredibly freeing.

He had felt the very moment the curse was lifted. It was as if he had spent the last few years only seeing the world through black and white and could finally see in color. The strange veil that had hung over him like a curtain was now lifted.

Yet no matter how much lighter he felt, how happy he was, one dark shadow lingered along the horizon. Forcina. Did she know the curse was broken? Was she on her way to them now? It was enough to have him on edge.

She had to know that the curse was broken, but if that were true then where was she?

Doraan sighed, pushing away from the starboard railing that he had been resting his elbows on and headed down to the galley, knowing he would find Kamira there. It was the morning after she saved him and broke the curse. The reality that she was a Sorceress hadn't fully set in—not just a Sorceress, a Legion. It had come as a shock, but at the same time, it made sense. She had been able to come aboard their ship because of it, possibly only because she shared blood with Forcina. Did she even know?

Sure enough, she was sitting on the ledge in her usual spot, looking out at the calm, sparkling sea. He climbed through the long window and joined her.

"I love this time of day," he said, breaking the ice, "when the sun hovers just above the water, showing its full glory before retreating for the night."

Kamira huffed a laugh. "It's quite blinding in my opinion. It's right at eye-level and almost impossible to look out over the ocean without your eyes stinging from the brightness."

Doraan gave her a half smile. "How are you doing?"

She turned to him with an eyebrow raised. "Me? I'm not the one who almost died yesterday. I should be asking you how you are doing."

"Well, I'm not dead, so I'm doing great. And the curse is gone, so I'm living the good life at the moment."

She frowned at that. "I still don't understand how I did it. Was it because I saved your life? Were you dead and the curse broke in death?"

"It's because you are related to Forcina."

Her brows shot up and her mouth fell open slightly as she stuttered, "H—how do you know that? I only just learned it at the Temple."

Doraan shrugged. "It was a part of the curse. It's why I never really put much thought into breaking the curse before then. To break it, I had to die saving the life of one of Forcina's kin. I was just lucky enough to find one of her only relatives that also possessed the ability to save my life. A Legion."

Kamira looked away from him, rubbing her palms along her thighs anxiously.

"It's okay, Kamira." He placed a hand over hers. "Your secret's safe with us. We know how dangerous it is for a Legion in the realm." He paused, looking away from her. "Especially with my father at the helm."

"So, you've changed your mind about Sorcerers? You don't want us all to die?"

He winced at how cruel he had been before, a string in his heart pulling at her question. They hadn't spoken about everything that had happened over the past few days. He hadn't even gotten the chance to fully comprehend it all himself. He was a Sorcerer, too. To think that he had spent most of his life feeling the same kind of anger as his father did toward the Sorcerers. How so much of him had changed in just these past few weeks. The corruption of his father that had taken root in him so long ago had finally relinquished its hold over him.

"No," he said simply. "I don't want any of my people to die."

Her face softened and she squeezed his hand. "I knew you would come around."

He laughed. "It only took me finding out I'm a Sorcerer myself, going to an entire Temple full of them, and a Legion saving me from the brink of death to realize it."

She snorted, shaking her head.

They eased into a comfortable silence and stayed that way for a long time, simply content to be in one another's company and watch the subtle swells of the sea.

Kamira broke the companionable silence. "Doraan, I think we are almost to Aksahri. We should head up to the main deck." She stood and lowered her hand to help him up.

He looked up at her shimmering blue eyes full of light and took her offered hand.

Ever since Kamira had come aboard the ship, she had done nothing short of helping them. She hadn't even known any of them, and yet everything she did was solely for the crew. She had fallen into their lives and changed it forever. They might be headed home to Aksahri, but he knew that even once they got there, they would still all be a family. Even if they were spread apart, living new lives as they reconnected with the families that they had left behind, nothing could change what they had.

They were bound–all of them–their souls forever connected.

As they ascended the final step to the main deck, Doraan headed for the helm. Kamira gave him a parting grin before walking toward the bow of the ship.

Doraan stepped beside Cormac at the helm, his second in command, his ally in all things, and ultimately, his friend. There was a stillness, a sort of contented calm that had settled over his quartermaster since the curse was broken, something he could sense with all the crew. They were headed home. All of them would finally be able to not only step foot on solid ground, but see their families, interact with people beyond their small crew of eighteen.

Doraan looked out at the bow where Kamira stood leaning over the edge, her short curly locks whipping in the wind, arms stretched out in front of her as she helped the *Cursed Soul* move faster through the water—something he had only recently realized she had done for most of their trip.

He smiled, watching as she looked out at the glistening ocean, surveying the movement of the water as they sailed. The sun was beginning to set, bathing everything in a golden glow as he felt the prickle of heat on his skin, the sea breeze quickly chasing away its warmth.

Cormac sailed the *Cursed Soul* through the calm waters of the Estdar Sea beside him. "Look, Doraan." He pointed, his voice holding a tinge of emotion. "Aksahri."

Through the fog and haze of the early morning that hovered like a blanket above the ocean, the twinkling of lights upon the shoreline could be seen.

His home.

They had made it. They had actually done it. The curse was broken. They could go home, and not just as ghosts upon the sand, but as solid, living beings.

With each breath, the closer they got, the more anxious he grew. It had been over a month since he visited—a month of not knowing whether his father recovered from Takriin's poison and a month of fearing for his people and the rising force, not knowing whether the city was still standing. Had those ships they passed gotten to Aksahri already?

Were they about to come home to a massacre upon the beach?

But as the fog cleared and the sunrays illuminated the full splendor of the harbor, there was not one of those Samaarian war ships in sight. No indication of war at all.

"The ships aren't here," he whispered to Cormac. "Why are the ships not here? Do you think they passed Aksahri? But why would they do that?" The questions didn't stop coming. He was so sure that they would be sailing into a war zone, into some kind of catastrophe, and that they hadn't broken the curse in time, but Aksahri glimmered like a diamond along the sand just as it always had. No billow of smoke above it, no crumbling city buildings. It looked perfect, just as he had left it.

Cormac's entire demeanor changed. He grew very quiet as his entire body went rigid, as if preparing for a surprise attack. He was on high alert. He didn't understand it either. "I don't know," he finally answered.

The entire crew grew eerily still as they got closer to the docks. A hush fell over them so that the only sound was the waves lapping against the ship as it cut through the still water.

Ships dipped and bobbed in the harbor, but none bore the Emerald King's sigil. Townspeople could be seen milling along the streets. Everything looked completely normal, as if nothing had changed but had picked up exactly where they had left it on that cursed day ten years ago. But even still, Doraan held his breath as Cormac yelled out, "Prepare for docking!"

It took the crew a moment to respond—still in shock over how close they were to shore. He knew they were in disbelief, still expecting something to happen, something to stop them from getting closer to land as it always had. That invisible force never came.

A man stood at the end of one of the open docks, waving them in.

Doraan's heartbeat quickened. His gaze collided with Kamira's as she sprinted across the deck and up the helm steps to stand beside him.

"Are you ready?" she asked.

Doraan could hardly hear her through the pounding in his ears, but he nodded numbly. He wasn't sure he would ever be ready. He wasn't even sure what he would say to his parents when he saw them. Would they even recognize him? Would the palace guards even let him in? Probably not, seeing as he had been declared dead for ten years.

"I'm not," Kamira said.

He looked down at her with a frown. "Why not?"

"I feel like so much is up in the air still. I don't know if Tarkiin told anyone what I did. Do my parents know? Will I be arrested as soon as I set foot on the streets?"

"Hey." He turned her head, tilting it up to look her in the eyes. "I won't let that happen. It will be okay. You will be okay. I promise."

She sighed, pulling her chin from his grasp and looking back down to the wooden planks of the ship. "Nothing is guaranteed, Doraan. It's best not to make promises you can't keep. The Emperor is the ultimate ruler. Not even you can go against his rule."

"If he's even still alive," he added.

"Don't you think the black banners would be lining the streets and docks if that were true? Look around; everything is just as it always had been."

Doraan took a deep breath. For some reason, her words only added to the uneasiness that had continuously grown the closer they sailed to the dock. Everything seemed *too* perfect. He should be happy that there were no signs of attack on Aksahri, no signs of Forcina, and no sign of his father's death, but he wasn't, because the first two didn't make any sense.

Where had that fleet gone? And where was Forcina? A lifetime of expecting the worst in life obviously had him paranoid.

"We are docked, Cap," Cormac said, placing a hand on his shoulder. "It's time to disembark."

Adrenaline coursed through Doraan's body. This was it.

He took a deep, calming breath, trying desperately to settle his nerves, but his entire being felt jittery, like all of this was just a dream still.

He watched as they lowered the gangway, flinching as it clanked onto the dock below. A small hand slid into his, holding on tight. Kamira looked up at him and nodded. Doraan squeezed her hand back just as tight as the entire crew walked down onto the Aksahrian dock. Each creak of the wood and clatter of his footsteps grated in his ears. Why did he feel like he was walking to his doom? Like the moment he set foot onto Aksahri land, something catastrophic would happen?

Doraan froze at the bottom of the gangway and stared down at the wooden dock beneath.

"It's okay, Doraan," Kamira whispered beside him. "It will be okay."

He closed his eyes, extended a leg out in front of him, cringed as he lowered it, and stayed that way until his foot landed on solid ground. He opened his eyes again to see and gasped. He was on the dock. Doraan brought his hand up and inspected it. He was fully intact, not translucent like a ghost.

He was home.

The rest of the crew followed suit, and they all headed quickly toward the city streets. Doraan, Kamira, and Cormac all stood at the very end of the dock, just before wood switched to cobbled streets. Each of the crew nodded to them as they passed by, their eyes showing what they couldn't voice. They were thankful to Kamira for breaking the curse, to Cormac for being their quartermaster and their voice of reason, and to Doraan, their Captain and companion over the years.

Once they had all gone, Cormac turned to Doraan wrapping him in a hug.

"You will always be a son to me, Doraan."

Doraan felt the sting of emotion behind his eyes and swallowed it back down. "You will always be the father I wish I had. Thank you, Cormac, for everything."

The older man grunted, released the embrace, and cleared his throat before turning to Kamira. "Kamira," he began, but sputtered, catching her as she jumped into his arms to wrap him in a giant hug.

"Don't be a stranger, Cormac," she said.

Cormac laughed, setting her back down and said, "We'll see each other often, lass. I'm sure of it." And with a final nod to each of them, he headed off to his family, to hold his daughter in his arms after so long apart.

"Well," Kamira breathed, wiping a wayward tear from her eye. "It's just us now."

Doraan smiled, holding out his arm. "Come on. I want to show you my home."

She hooked her arm through his and they made their way through the darkened streets of Aksahri to the palace.

Doraan drank in the views of the city as if he had been dying of thirst, reveling in the scent and feel of being home again. Cinnamon filled the air, mingled with baking bread and spiced, smoked meats as they passed by inns and taverns. He was still amazed by how little had changed over the past ten years. The same sandy cobbled streets were beneath his foot, the same domed copper roofs glimmered in the evening light. The columned open air rooms could still be seen at the tops of the brown sandstone tower homes with colorful silken curtains blowing in the desert breeze.

Palms lined the main road leading to the palace, although he could admit they were significantly taller than he remembered. The closer they got to his home the more his heart raced. The scent of lilies drifted toward them just before the entire palace revealed itself to them.

Doraan stopped, gazing at its columned turrets and massive golden domed roofs. It was strange to remember his time there, running through the enormous arched hallways and roaming around the extensive network of gardens.

"Do you think they'll let us in?"

Doraan blinked several times before looking down at Kamira with a frown, "You know, I hadn't even thought of that." He chuckled, shaking his head as he brought a hand up to rub at the back of his neck.

It had been too long, and he was supposed to be dead, so of course they wouldn't let him in.

Suddenly, a hidden memory sparked to life, "Actually, there's a way we can get inside without anyone knowing. Come on!" He grabbed her hand, pulling her down a side street until they stood before one of the public gardens just beside the palace.

Doraan grinned, "You're going to love this. Follow my lead."

He expected there to be a guard or two patrolling the grounds, but there were only a few townspeople admiring the blooms.

He cocked his head, furrowing his brow, but headed for the long row of hedges that lined the base of the palace. He was fairly certain there was a hidden grate just below one of them. A vague memory of his mother sneaking out with him in tow to tour the city played out in his mind. Doraan smiled at the memory.

Glancing around to make sure no one was watching, Doraan pushed his way inside the hedge. It was as if he was standing in a tunnel, the thick leaves completely hiding this beautiful arched walkway within it.

"Doraan?" he heard Kamira whisper. "Doraan!" She said more frantically.

He peered through the brush and she squealed as he wrapped his arms around her and yanked her inside.

"Shh," he brought a finger to his lips. "This way, there is a hatch somewhere nearby."

"Skies, this is beautiful," she breathed. "I could walk in here for hours. It's so quiet and peaceful."

"Aha!" Doraan said, bending down to brush away the leaves and sediment that had covered the handle of a small hidden door.

"What is with places having hidden entrances? I swear the people who built these cities were daft."

"Well their stupidity is our gain, I suppose." Doraan smirked, grabbing the brass ring and lifting the wooden hatch. It screeched as it opened like a bat hunting its nightly meal. Doraan winced, flinging it the rest of the way as it thudded to the ground leaving a large gaping hole in its wake.

"Alright, who's first?"

"What do you mean who's first?" Kamira scoffed, "You of course. This is *your* home."

"Alright, alright," he put his hands up. "I'll go first. Too bad we don't have any…"

"Fire?" Kamira finished for him. "I'm pretty sure I know someone who can fix that."

Doraan snorted, feeling his pockets. Even since he discovered he was a Sorcerer, he had carried a small matchbox with him just in case, not that he had any time to practice over the last two days since the discovery.

"I'm not the only one," he raised a brow at her, pulling the box from his pocket. "Do you want to do the honors or shall I?"

She looked away from him, "You do it."

He frowned, striking the match against the side as a flame lit at the top of the wooden stick. Doraan took a deep breath. He hadn't tried to actually control his ability yet.

"Just breathe and pull its energy to you," Kamira said, blue eyes illuminated by the flicker of light. "Command it, bend it to your will."

Doraan breathed out slowly, letting the life of the flame seep into him where he grasped it and pulled it down the fire stick to engulf his hand.

Kamira gasped, "You did it. You commanded the flame."

Doraan stared at his hand, now a ball of fire, but he didn't feel the burn of the flame. It was as if his skin repelled the heat. He smiled an exhilaration traveling through him at the pure astonishment of what he had done. He was literally controlling fire.

"Alright," he said. "Let's go."

He climbed down the rickety old ladder almost falling the rest of the way when one of the rungs split in half under his boot. No one had used this entrance in a long time. Kamira climbed down after him and they headed down a small hallway, coming to a door that looked as if it was for only a small child to fit through.

"What's on the other side? What if we walk right into the throne room?"

Doraan narrowed his eyes at the door. "I can't remember exactly."

He leaned down and pushed, the door scraped loud against the floor.

"Stop!" Kamira said. "It's too loud. What if there are guards on the other side?"

"Well what do you suggest? We just stay here and live in this cave?"

Kamira rolled her eyes at him. "Move, let me try. I might be able to move it more quietly with my earth sorcery."

He raised his brows and stepped aside, holding his flaming hand over her for light. He kept forgetting she was a Legion.

Kamira closed her eyes and Doraan watched her intently as she raised her hands out before her. The dust and dirt around the doorframe began to move, creating gaps on all sides until light spilled through the small cracks around it.

"Ok it should be good now." She said, gently pushing it open.

It opened to the main hallway that led to the throne room. They quietly climbed out, Doraan extinguishing his fireball before standing up and closing the small door behind them. It faded into the molding of the wall as if it didn't even exist.

"Where are we?" Kamira asked, beside him.

Doraan drew his brows together, "We're in the long hallway; it's the only corridor leading to the throne room, but it's different." A cold sweat washed over him. "Something's wrong."

Kamira looked at him, eyes suddenly widening just before she gasped and pointed to something behind him ."Doraan, look!"

He turned and was greeted with a large green satin banner hanging on the wall, still and unmoving as if it had been there for ages. Embroidered in its center was the rising sun over a mountain peak—the Emerald King's sigil.

"No," he breathed, not even thinking as he sprinted for the throne room.

"Doraan!" Kamira called after him. "Wait!"

But he drowned her fading pleas out—drowned everything out—all but the pounding rage filing his ears.

He stopped, soles of his shoes screeching as he slid in front of the large golden doors of the throne room. He took a moment to look left and right, noticing he was completely alone in the long hallway. Normally the corridor would be lined with guards along the walls every ten feet, but it was empty. An eerie feeling settled over him, hair raising at his nape. Where had Kamira gone?

He frowned before looking back at the imposing floor to ceiling doors, engraved with the four elemental signs, something his father had never removed from the palace even though he hated the Sorcerers. Doraan took a deep breath ignoring his inner self telling him to run, and pushed open the doors.

Doraan's nostrils flared. Nothing was as he remembered. Green banners surrounded him, engulfing the space and casting a sickly hue of olive across the white marble floors. Gone was his father's ruby studded throne, replaced by a golden dais, and atop it was a golden throne, emeralds glinting in the sunlight that streamed in through the high windows along the perimeter of the room.

Doraan let his gaze travel to the man sitting on it, fingers drumming in a rhythmic pattern on the armrest, legs crossed over one another, until he let his eyes travel all the way up to the man's face.

He stumbled backward, breath hitching as he opened and closed his mouth several times, sputtering incoherently. Light hazel eyes stared back at him, eyes that he had memorized, eyes that he knew well. His hands trembled as he moved them to the pistols strapped at his hips.

"I wouldn't if I were you," the man on the throne said, his voice so familiar, honeyed and brisk, and yet it couldn't be. He shook his head in disbelief as a pounding began at his temples and his heart began to beat at a breakneck speed. A tingling started in his fingertips and a burning in his center.

He blinked, hoping, wishing his eyes were playing tricks on him, because seated on the throne, with an amused expression twisting his features, was himself.

"H—H—How?" Doraan finally squeaked out the word.

He watched as his own head cocked to the side, brow raising in interest before the man—himself—rose from the throne and yelled out, "Guards! Seize this man!"

Soldiers stormed into the room, grabbing Doraan on either side. Where had they even come from?

"No!" he yelled, pulling against their grip. "Stop! I'm Doraan! I'm the Prince, not him!" But his pleas fell on deaf ears as they dragged him from the throne room, and the last thing Doraan saw before the heavy throne room doors closed was the imposter smiling at him.

Acknowledgements

As I do in all my books, the first person I want to thank is you, the reader. Thank you for picking up this book and reading. I appreciate you taking a chance on my books.

Troy – I love you, always. You are my biggest supporter, my moon and stars. Thank you for all you do. Life is better with you in it.

Cass – Bestie! I am so happy we found one another. Being your friend is the most fun and your constant kindness and support mean everything. Having a friend who cares as much as you do is a wonderful thing. I love you.

Whitney – Your friendship has been a breathe of fresh air, a necessity for the sake of my sanity. Thank you for everything you did to help me get this book out into the world. I appreciate you more than you know. You are my ride or die. I love you.

Tiff – This is the most emotion you will get from me so don't expect it again. You were brought into my life for a purpose. I think the universe knew I needed your energy and light. I love you. Stay fierce.

Katelyn – Your constant support and excitement for my writing means everything to me. Thank you for reading the early drafts of my books and for being such loving friends.

Alexis – Literally this book wouldn't have been published without you. Thank you for always being there to answer my texts and tell me what I needed to hear when I would start spiraling.

Michelle – Thank you for reading the early copy of this novel and doing the grammatical edits! Your friendship is so special to me and I appreciate you more than you know. I love you.

Tank – My trusty companion and sweetest munchkin. Thank you for sitting by my side every night until the early hours of the morning as I wrote this book!

My Street Team – All of your support, enthusiasm, and encouragement keep me going. Thank you for reading and helping me spread the word of this book! I adore you all.

About the Author

Katelyn is an author of fantasy adventure novels. Working as an Accountant by day, writing has give Katelyn a creative escape from the corporate world. Her only goal in writing is to create adventurous stories full of magical worlds that allow the reader an escape from the real world for a while. She wants you to have fun when reading one of her books! Katelyn lives in Maryland with her husband and their chihuahua, Tank.

Visit her on the web:
https://www.kcsmithbooks.com/
https://www.instagram.com/balancingbooksandcoffee/
https://www.facebook.com/kcsmithbooks
https://www.threads.net/@balancingbooksandcoffee
https://www.goodreads.com/kcsmithbooks

See all of Katelyn's titles on her amazon page:
https://www.amazon.com/author/kcsmithbooks

www.ingramcontent.com/pod-product-compliance
Lightning Source LLC
Chambersburg PA
CBHW030109310726
48970CB00004B/1214